PRAISE FOR

COUNTLESS

'A heartbreaking, hopeful and highly unusual debut'
Metro

'*Countless* is written with empathy and deep compassion and we could all do with more of that'
Bookbag

'Moving and thought-provoking'
Irish Times

'Insightful, authentic and profoundly moving ... This is an important, impactful, mightily impressive debut about love, reaching out and taking one step at a time'
Lovereading4kids

'*Countless* is a bold and brilliant piece of debut fiction'
Books-a-Go-Go

'Gregory writes with a realism worthy of Ken Loach'
Inis Reading Guide

'I inhaled this book. I was emotionally involved from the very start and couldn't bear to put it down ... Though *Countless* is heartbreaking it is also full of heart and it celebrates the power of finding your people and your self and the resilience to keep going'
Rhino Reads

'An emotive stor ... y one of
the s

Skylarks

Also by Karen Gregory

Countless

KAREN GREGORY

BLOOMSBURY
LONDON OXFORD NEW YORK NEW DELHI SYDNEY

BLOOMSBURY YA
Bloomsbury Publishing Plc
50 Bedford Square, London WC1B 3DP, UK

BLOOMSBURY, BLOOMSBURY YA and the Diana logo
are trademarks of Bloomsbury Publishing Plc

First published in Great Britain in 2018 by Bloomsbury Publishing Plc

A catalogue record for this book is available from the British Library

ISBN: PB: 978-1-4088-8361-7; eBook: 978-1-4088-8360-0

2 4 6 8 10 9 7 5 3 1

Typeset by RefineCatch Limited, Bungay, Suffolk

Printed and bound in Great Britain by CPI group (UK) Ltd, Croydon CRO 4YY

For Mum, with love

Part One

CHAPTER ONE

We did this school trip to a castle once, where they got us dressing up as either knights, princesses or servants. No prizes for guessing which one I got. Right now, I feel like I'm still wearing that servant costume. Dad senses it too; he keeps putting down his pint to pull at his shirt collar. We're on one of our three-times-a-year meals out, on account of Jack turning twelve, but the place is packed with people who look like being here's as normal as going up the chippie.

'So,' Dad says, 'twelve eh? That means next year you're going to be …' he does a drum roll with his two forefingers on the table, then says in a voice of fake doom, 'a Teenager.'

Dad did this routine with Jamie, then me, when we both turned thirteen. Mum smiles around the table, while Jamie leans over to ruffle Jack's hair. Jack ducks, and when he comes up runs his fingers over the gelled bit he's got going on at the top. The rest of it's shaved; it's what all the lads are wearing and Lorraine next door's pretty good with the clippers, so we treated Jack this morning. I catch Mum giving me a don't-take-the-mick look and a faint wink.

'Yep, it'll be all slamming doors and "I never asked to be born" and *girls*,' Dad goes on, trying to make Jack go red. He made pretty much the same speech to me, substituting the 'girls' for 'boys', back before everyone cottoned on that there wasn't exactly going to be boys on the cards for me. As if sensing my thoughts, Dad says, 'You'll be giving your sister a run for her money before long, I'll bet.'

Everyone groans, and I say, '*Urgh*, Daaaad,' in a way that lets him know I'm partly exasperated, but mainly OK with how he's not fussed who I like. Then he seems to have the same thought, because he says in an even louder voice, 'Or you might decide you like boys, son, and that's fine with your mother and me, isn't it, Marian?'

Mum nods, but I spot her glancing around as Dad downs the rest of his pint. She's always the one who's more worried about what people will think. I follow Mum's gaze and meet the eyes of a woman at a table across from us, with perfect make up and smart-casual clothes you can tell cost a bomb. She sniffs and looks away.

I can't help the faint flush that works its way over my cheeks. Dad's trying to get the attention of a waiter, but it seems my six-foot thirteen-stone father has somehow become invisible. I stare around the restaurant. It's the third nicest one in our little market town; we wouldn't go for Molray's which has two Michelin stars and is definitely too pricey, even if it wasn't for Jamie getting the sack from there, or the local gastropub, but none of us wanted to go up The Olde Inne, where Jamie's got his latest job as a sous-chef. So we've ended up here, where the floors are wood and there's hunting prints and a massive stone fireplace with a real fire blazing away, though spring is definitely here and it's pretty nice out. I guess it's a tradition of sorts, even if none of us are totally ourselves in a place like this.

There's a gust of laughter from the next table down. They came in after us; two boys and two girls about my age, all slouched walks and those accents all the kids have at the local posh school. No parents in sight. When one of them, a girl with super shiny dark hair, swears, Mum frowns in their direction.

'I'm full,' I announce to no one in particular, mainly to distract Mum. Jamie doesn't bother to ask before he spears the last of my veg with his fork. I had the veggie option – I'm not massively down with eating animals – and I probably could've managed that last piece of purple broccoli, but it's worth it because Mum pulls her attention back to the table and says for the hundredth time, 'How about you, Jack? You want anything else? You can have a dessert if you want.'

The word 'dessert' instead of 'afters' sounds wrong, especially the way Mum says it, and Jack gives her a bemused look. 'Nah, you're all right, thanks.'

'Go on, it's your birthday.'

Dad has finally got the waiter's attention. He clears our plates, ignoring our thank yous as he piles them up. Maybe you're not supposed to say thanks, just pretend the waiter doesn't exist, like that twitchy-nosed woman sitting there like something got rammed up her behind. I realise, looking around, how upright everyone else is. My family all tend to lean down to meet our food, but it isn't the way other people sit in here. I feel my own spine lengthen, then I purposely slouch back down.

'*Who cares, Joni?*' That's what Kelly would say. I'll go over to hers later, tell her all about this, and even though her family could afford to eat at Molray's any time they wanted, she'll have a laugh with me and tell me I'm being ridiculous. She'd probably have a point.

The waiter brings back some menus.

'Can we have some more water, please?' Dad says.

'Still or sparkling?' the waiter says.

'Just tap again, son,' Dad says.

I catch a smirk on the waiter's face when he turns away. Fish and chips at home followed by one of Mum's cakes sounds just right round about now, especially as the group next to us are still laughing like only they exist. When one of them drops another f-bomb, Mum turns round and says, 'Do you mind not swearing? My son here's only twelve.'

They apologise, but when she turns back, the dark-haired girl and the two boys pull faces and whisper together. There's another girl with them, her hair arranged on top of her head in that expensively messy way you see on the posh girls round here. She's not smiling.

Mum's persuaded Jack to have the biggest pudding on the menu, some sort of sundae which comes with sparklers, although the rest of us all pretend we're too full. You're not allowed to bring your own cake in here but we'll all sing 'Happy Birthday' anyway, stuff what anyone else thinks.

We wait for the sundae to arrive, chatting about nothing

stuff like what's been on telly. Mum doesn't watch much, but she loves *Call the Midwife*, even though she's guaranteed to bawl at pretty much every episode. Jamie's quiet compared to usual; he'd normally be joking around with Dad, but I can see he's not happy about having to yell over the top of the brayers, who've got even louder, if that's possible. They have wine and everything on their table, even though they only look my age. Maybe the management turns a blind eye for people like them. But where it makes me a wee bit irritated and a lot uncomfy, like I've done something wrong except I don't know what it is, the expression on Jamie's face is pure lava. It's one I've seen too many times the last few months, since whatever it was that got him the chop from his last job. His rants at the tea table are getting way too regular, and with a sinking feeling I can see he's winding up to start one now.

He leans forward. 'So Dealo reckons this thing with the estate's going to go through. We could all be out on our ears by –'

'Jamie.' Dad doesn't use that voice often and it stops Jamie in his tracks, but only for a second.

'But how is it f–'

'Jamie.' This time there's a real warning in Dad's voice. 'Not tonight.'

Fair. We can see the shape of the word Jamie was about to say. Things being fair, or not fair, is becoming a right theme with him. Far as I'm concerned, I'm with Mum and Dad: don't borrow trouble, and concentrate on what you do have is their motto. What's the point in spending all that energy hating random people because they've got more than you? Even if there's a few at the next table I could work myself up to disliking.

But Jack's birthday is definitely not the time for one of Jamie's lectures. He knows it too and shuts his mouth as the waiter shows back up and plonks down a new jug of water.

Maybe to diffuse the tension, or because he's seen it on telly or something, Jack picks up a spoon and taps at the side of his Coke. 'I'd like to make a speech,' he announces.

We look at him, amused, and I smile as he gives a cough, goes red, then says, 'Just to say thanks very much for my birthday and for the PlayStation,' – me and Jamie managed to find an old PS2 and some vintage games on eBay – 'and for my tea.' He gives us a Jack-special – this innocently cheeky grin that always makes you want to hug him, even when he's done something annoying like scoffing the last of the biscuits and not telling anyone.

Then I notice the restaurant has gone quiet. The lads on the next table are sniggering, both the girls trying to shush them, although the dark-haired one is laughing as she does.

Before I have the chance to get irritated, I spot the sparklers approaching. I nudge Jamie and we start to sing 'Happy Birthday'. Jack's eyes get wide, and Mum and Dad exchange smiles as they begin to sing too and suddenly everything is perfect, because we're a unit, us Coopers, never mind about Jamie being weird these days. He's got over himself anyway and is singing loudest of all, and Jack's face is all happy and pink. He's already reaching for his spoon.

Then one of the boys at the next table, the arrogantly good-looking one, shoves back his chair without looking, because he's busy still braying, just as the waiter goes past.

The waiter trips, does a comedy run for a couple of paces before finally losing his balance and crashing to the ground, propelling the sundae, sparklers and all, up into the air. We all watch in horror as it comes down.

Right into my lap.

CHAPTER TWO

'*Aargh!*' The combination of cold sundae spreading over my legs and hot sparklers in the vicinity of my boobs is not the best feeling in the world.

Mum lunges across the table and throws a glass of water over me. Two waitresses rush over. One helps the waiter up, the other starts saying sorry to me. Mum grabs two napkins, hesitates for a second because they're these thick cloth ones, then chucks them to me. I use them to scoop the worst of the ice cream off and dump it on the table. Dad's saying, 'Are you burnt, Joni?'

Jamie says, 'Je-sus,' and Mum says, 'Watch your mouth.'

Jack's gone quiet, his round face shocked.

The boy who tripped the waiter is saying, 'So sorry,' in a lazy voice, but behind him the black-haired girl and the other boy are killing themselves laughing, and not trying to hide it. I can't see the face of the blonde one.

I stand, lumps of sundae still dripping off my top. Arrogant-face boy spots my expression and his apologies turn slightly more sincere. He says to one of the hovering waitresses, 'I'll pay,' without directly looking at her, then looks me up and down and says, 'I'll get one for all of them.'

And maybe it's something about the way he says 'them', but even my hackles go up.

Jamie shoves his chair back too. 'No thanks, *mate*,' he spits out and I know his 'mate' is standing in for a totally different four-letter word. Jamie's white with anger.

The atmosphere sharpens. Arrogant-face boy stares at Jamie in the worst possible way and I suck in a breath and step closer to my big brother, but Dad puts his hand on Jamie's arm and propels him outside to cool down before anything else can happen. The waiter is already bringing in another sundae, but even though Jack smiles, I can feel the moment's ruined. Once Jack's started eating, Mum chatting at him in a too-bright voice, I get up.

'Going to sort this out,' I say.

Mum nods.

In the toilet I take off my shirt and rinse it under the tap. There's a singe mark on the front and I wince; that was my favourite shirt. At least I was wearing a vest top underneath. My jeans are spattered with ice cream as well. I bundle the shirt into a ball and leave it on the side of the sink while I go into one of the cubicles.

I'm finishing up when I hear the door open and a loud, posh voice drawl, 'Oh, come on, Annabel, it was hilarious. I wish I'd been filming.'

If the other person makes a reply, I don't hear, because I've already pushed my way out of the cubicle in time to see the blonde girl picking up my shirt. Next to her, the other girl's laughing.

I can't help channelling Jamie. I glare at them.

The first girl looks like she couldn't care less, but the blonde girl's pale face flushes, as she holds out my shirt to me. I can see she's about to say sorry, but I take it from her before she gets the chance and walk out, conscious my greying bra straps are showing under my vest top.

Dad's come back in to sort out the bill. 'I told Jamie to wait outside,' he says in a low voice to Mum. We get the sundae for free and on the walk home, we try and keep the mood up for Jack, but Jamie walks a couple of paces apart from the rest of us.

When we get home he turns on Dad, his jaw jutting. 'You should've let me lump him. Bunch of –' he glances at Mum, 'idiots.'

Dad sighs. 'And what good would that've done, son? Eh?'

Jamie mumbles something about, 'Teach him a lesson,' but I can see the anger's draining out of him now. Jack's looking from one face to another and I chew at the side of a nail. This isn't how his birthday was supposed to be. In fact, nothing seems like it's supposed to be these days, and it's all since Jamie landed that swishy job and then got fired. Since then he's stopped being my usual laid-back big brother and turned into some rant-machine.

But it's Jack's birthday and I can't stand to see him looking so worried. I nudge him on the shoulder. 'Didn't you say your PlayStation's got Tetris Worlds on it?'

Jack's face lights up.

'Come on. I'll show you how the master does it,' I say.

The next day, I manage to sleep right through my alarm, so by the time Mum comes to investigate why I'm not up yet

I've got about twenty minutes to get ready and bike it down to the library. I take the world's speediest shower, cursing myself for being such a heavy sleeper. Kelly insists I snore like mad, which is clearly a total lie, but all I know is sleep is like this great comforting blanket to look forward to at the end of a long day. And I always seem to have exciting dreams.

Mum's already on her way out – she's on a double today – and Jamie will have left hours ago; but Jack's there at the table, hunched over a bowl piled with Weetabix. He never sleeps in on a Saturday.

'Morning,' I say, stretching out my Wiltshire accent to make it all Farmer Giles-like.

He replies through a mouthful, so it comes out a muffled *muuhh-ihh*. I go to the bread bin and it's empty. So's the milk, apart from a dribble I'd better leave for Dad.

Jack gives me a guilty look over his spoon, then treats me to a Jack-special, cheeks chubbed up as he grins. How does that work every single time?

I smile back. 'I'll go to the shop on the way home. What you up to today? Going round Dylan's?'

He nods. Jack and Dylan next door have been mates about as long as me and Kelly. Dylan's all right, even if Lorraine can be a bit much sometimes. She knows everything about everyone and if she doesn't, she makes it her business to find out.

I check my phone; I am seriously late. 'Got to go. Take a cup of tea up to Dad before you go out,' I say. I give him a quick kiss on the top of his head, getting a waft of warm Weetabix and sleep. It reminds me of when he was a baby. He'd sit for hours on my lap in front of the telly. Mum reckons he was born happy. Apparently, I was 'a tornado'. I wonder where that energy all went, because this morning I'm hanging.

I stop at the back door. 'Make sure you take your phone and tell him when you're back. And don't be late for tea.'

Jack waves his milky spoon goodbye and I'm off out into the morning air.

The sky is white as I pull out of our little cul-de-sac on Jamie's knackered old bike. I've lived here my whole life, know every pothole and grass verge. I like being up high with the wind pushing across my cheeks as I whizz past tall hedges and trees that are just beginning to show signs of spring blossom, reaching towards each other to form a tunnel over the road.

I settle into a rhythm, pushing away worries about the essay I didn't quite finish last night, about money for food, and the thing Jamie keeps bringing up – that our houses are all getting sold to some private company. They're owned by a charity now, but from what Mum and Dad say, the charity's 'gone downhill' over the last few years, so I figure it might be a good thing for someone else to take over. Could mean there's more cash for stuff like fixing the damp, or the shower, which comes closer to packing up altogether every year. Maybe we'll even get proper double-glazed windows and central heating, so it's nice and toasty instead of the usual hop-about-freezing-your-butt-off nightmare on winter mornings. Last time I tried saying all that to Jamie though, he just laughed like I don't know anything, but I'm with Dad on it: why borrow trouble? Better not to think about it at all, and especially not about the homework I've got piling up at home. An image of my French teacher, Miss Armstrong, comes to my mind. She stopped me again after lessons the other day, going on about uni open days.

'I don't know, Miss,' I said, when she showed me a pile of prospectuses. I didn't want to ask how Mum would get time off work to drive me, or where we'd get money from for petrol or train fares if I went on my own. Or what I'd even do at uni anyway.

'Have a think about it. Perhaps we could chat again next week?' she said. Her hopeful look, and thoughts of the prospectuses shoved at the bottom of the recycling box go on to my mental list of things to stop worrying about.

I stand on the pedals again, pushing, pushing. The future is like that great white sky above me – I don't have a clue what I'm supposed to write on it. What I'm allowed to. And then for some reason, the restaurant pops into my head. Jack's face, the shock of that sundae going into my lap. It would've been funny if it had just been us lot. And that girl in the toilet …

I'm coming up fast on a sharp bend when a car suddenly appears on my side of the road. I slam on the rusty brakes and swerve on to a patch of gravelly stones, the bike going out from under me. I hit the ground, pain jolting up my leg like a firework and wind up half in the hedge.

I lie still as the car roars off behind me. Then I untangle myself from the bike, wincing at the hot throbbing in my shoulder and knee. I bend my leg a couple of times, decide it's probably fine, although I'm going to have one hell of a bruise, and take a look at the bike.

It seems OK – if there's a new scratch it's merged with the existing ones. The chain's popped off, and I kneel on my good knee to push it back on, getting my hands covered with grease. I wobble the rest of the way to the library.

Mrs Hendry's car is already in the car park when I creak in, red in the face and puffing hard, leg still on fire and shoulder not much better. Next to her car is Dave's blue transit, one back door open to reveal a stack of boxed donations. Someone's scratched a pair of boobs into the dirt on the back. A couple of spaces down from it is a really posh Audi parked all wonky, paintwork gleaming like the shiny new *Huntington Library* sign with that weird little crest thing they put up a couple of weeks ago. I liked it better when it was just plain old *LIBRARY* in black letters. Above it, the clock reads ten past nine. I chain my bike to the railing and run up the steps.

I bang through the double doors and nearly barrel right into Mrs H, who's standing next to the desk.

I jump back, still panting. 'Sorry I'm late. I fell off my bike.'

Mrs H's irritated expression changes to one of concern. 'Have you hurt yourself?'

'Bashed my knee, but it's OK, I think.'

'Well, good. I've been waiting for you to get here.' Mrs H's face takes on this satisfied shine. 'I have some news. We've got a new helper starting today. She's going to be with us for the next few months.'

I frown; we can't afford to pay anyone else. I've been doing this library job ever since I got the chop from the vets after Jazzy, our cat, got run down and we couldn't afford to pay the bill. They fixed her for free and once the Huntingtons gave the library a load of cash, I managed to get my Saturday job here, at sub-minimum wage, obvs. But still, it's a job and anyway I like it in the library.

'She's volunteering. To help with her university application,' Mrs H says.

'Oh right. Fair enough.' I wonder who from school Mrs H has got in. No one mentioned it to me. I go over to the desk and turn on the second PC.

'I want you to help her settle in,' Mrs H says. She has this nervous smile on her face, like the time when the local MP came for a visit and it was in the *Evening Gazette*. I follow her gaze to where a tall girl is walking towards us holding two cups. The adrenalin that's just started settling after my bike crash dials straight back up to ten as I take in her messy-yet-stylish ponytail, sunglasses pushed up on top of her head, her pristine clothes. The look of surprise on her face as she clocks me.

'Ah, here she is!' Mrs H says in an overly bright voice. 'Annabel insisted on making the coffee.' She turns to me. 'Annabel, this is Joni. Joni ...' There's the tiniest of pauses, as though Mrs H is about to make some important announcement. 'Meet Annabel Huntington.'

I bite back an exclamation that was probably going to end in a swear word.

It's only the girl from the restaurant.

CHAPTER THREE

Annabel Huntington. Blimey. And she's going to be volunteering here? What for? Is it to keep an eye on us all for her dad? Then I remember Mrs H said about her UCAS or something. Surely any uni would let her in if her dad had a word in the ear of someone important – that's how it works for people like her, isn't it? Then I flash back to the restaurant, and her handing me my wrecked shirt, and I feel a flush pushing up my neck.

I reckon Annabel's having similar thoughts, but she recovers fast, puts the coffees down and holds out a long, pale hand, which she's clearly expecting me to shake.

I give it a stiff up-and-down, wondering how hard you're supposed to hold on. Her fingers are cool, but it seems like mine heat up as she says, 'Lovely to meet you again,' and looks right into my eyes.

Something weird happens in the vicinity of my stomach.

'Er, yeah, me too. I mean, you too … likewise.' I look down, which is enough to see she has amazing legs, ending in what even I can tell are designer sandals. I snap my eyes back up to her face, feeling my own go redder, if that's even possible.

Likewise?! For God's sake, Joni.

She smiles. The sort of self-assured smile that makes me feel like I'm about twelve again, with a crush on Miss Narayan, my old Geography teacher.

My face forgets to smile back.

I drop her hand suddenly, see her eyes go to my fingers, which are still coated in grease and for bonus points there's a whacking great grass stain and a smear of mud up my jeans leg, so that makes twice I've met this girl while covered in muck. Brilliant.

'Uh … I'll just go and sort myself out,' I say, and make a dash for the toilets.

I give my jeans a quick rub down with some toilet roll, which gets the worst of the mud off, but does nothing for the grass stain. I wash my hands and tell myself to get a grip. So she's working here, it's not a massive deal. I bet she lasts a couple of weeks, tops, before she gets bored. Can't imagine someone like her sticking about for too long. I'm still red in the face when I come out and see Annabel and Mrs H relaxing with their coffees in the two chairs by the desk. I hover, scanning my brain for something to say and ignoring the too-rich smell of the coffee. Mrs H clearly cracked out the posh stuff you have to make in one of those pots with a plunger, but I've never liked the smell – it's too loud somehow.

I realise Mrs H is waiting for me to reply to something she's just said, but I don't have a clue what it was. Annabel arches her perfect eyebrows.

Luckily, Dave barrels through the doors at that moment with a massive box in his hands and plonks it on the floor.

'Where do you want all these?' he asks the room in general. I notice he's avoiding looking at Annabel, like he's shy of her. Dave lives on our estate and does painting, decorating and various odd jobs.

'I'll give you a hand,' I say and follow him out. Anything to get away from the two of them in there. Dave's admiring the Audi, which must belong to Annabel. As I come up beside him he gives a low whistle.

'That's top of the range, that,' he says.

'Yeah?' I say and I'm surprised to hear a hard Jamie-like edge creeping into my voice. As I heft up the first box, I realise the prickling feeling in my stomach has intensified into something approaching anger. I'd just got settled in the library, liked it, as far as a job goes, and now I'm going to be stuck with Annabel Huntington. What am I going to say to her? The library, with its threadbare carpets and ancient PCs, isn't exactly her sort of place, is it?

Or maybe it's way more her sort of place than mine.

I remember when I first used to go in the library. Mrs H would give me wary looks from behind her desk, assuming I was with the kids from school who used to hang around. They never did anything much, maybe smoked a few fags outside, left a couple of crisp packets lying about, but the main thing they were guilty of was just being there. It got so that people only had to sit in a circle at the edge of the car park after school before the woman who lives in the old Victorian house at the end of the road was calling up the school or the local council to complain. Eventually, everyone moved on and it was only me left. I'd sit in the corner of the library, next to the radiator doing my homework, or reading. Still took weeks before Mrs H properly chatted to me and a good while later until she asked me if I was interested in a job. And someone like Annabel gets that straight away, because of who she is, or at least who her dad is. Suddenly it strikes me as totally unfair.

Just like Jamie always says.

The thought makes me plonk the box down extra hard when I've heaved it inside, like I'm having a go at squashing it flat. I don't want to be angry all the time like my brother. I give a sigh. Mrs H is watching me from behind the computer. Annabel seems to have disappeared already.

'You will be nice, won't you?' Mrs H says, her voice aiming for jokey but coming out with a warning bite to it.

I give her an I-don't-know-what-you-mean look, eyes wide. Then, to wind her up, I say, 'Where's Madame got to anyway? She hasn't gone home already, has she?'

I don't mean my voice to sound so hopeful.

'Not quite.' I turn around to see Annabel lugging in a gigantic box. We've done all right with donations this month.

I stare and then she says, 'Would you take the other end, thank you.' It doesn't come out as a question, more of a command. I feel like Jazzy when he spots next-door-but-one's huge scraggy ginger cat in our garden. If I had a tail it'd be puffed out like a bog brush right about now, getting ready to fight if I'm cornered.

I grab the other end and almost pull the box out of her hands, so that she staggers a step, then lets go as I swing it down on top of my own box. We straighten and I catch her eye, my eyebrows raised in a 'yeah?' expression as if she's about to start on me. Annabel's face takes on a flush which probably mirrors my own; apparently neither of us wants to be the one who looks away first.

Mrs H's voice breaks into the stand-off. 'That was the last one, wasn't it? Well then, you girls can take these to the storeroom to sort through them together, yes?' She doesn't wait for a response. 'Wonderful.'

Annabel's face seems to be saying the same thing that's going through my mind, which is something along the lines of *oh yeah, wonderful.*

Completely, totally, *wonderful.*

CHAPTER FOUR

'So then she opens up a box and lets out this little shriek, seriously, like a proper girly shriek, and looks at her nail to see if she's chipped her manicure,' I say in the pub later on that night. The whole gang is here: tall, skinny Pete, looking at Kelly with hopeful eyes, me, and Ed and Stacey who've been a thing for a few months now. Stace is sat on Ed's lap in the corner, while Pete's kicking my arse in a game of pool. Kelly's leaning against the pool table, a drink in her hand. The Crown always lets us in, as long as we stick to soft drinks. My knee's still hurting and my arms feel like I was doing press-ups for the last four hours, courtesy of lugging boxes about half the day. And I'm knackered from the effort of trying to be polite to Annabel and find things to say to her; one day has already shown me we have literally nothing in common.

I think about Mrs H giving Annabel the 'grand tour' of the library, and the community hall which is through a linking door, and the way Annabel looked at everything with this totally inscrutable face so you couldn't tell what she was thinking. I could probably join a few of those dots up, seeing the place through her eyes; the windows with their flaking paint and the scuffed-up floor in the hall, the worn patches on the carpet and our motley donations lining the shelves.

Kelly's got one eyebrow up like she knows I'm enjoying my rant a teensy bit too much, but I'm on a roll. 'Honestly, she's so annoying. I don't 'spect she'll last too long though.' I lean over and crack the pink into the top left-hand pocket with a satisfying – and to be truthful, fairly rare – *thwack*.

When I look up, Kelly's pinching her chin between her finger and thumb, her eyes narrowing in the way they do when her brain's on overdrive. There's a small smile on her face, which I pretend not to notice, conscious I may have neglected to mention Annabel actually looked at her nail because she'd broken it down to the quick. I felt pretty bad when I saw that as it happens. I even said, 'That looks nasty – do you want me to get you a plaster?' but she drew herself up and said, 'No, thank you, I can manage,' like me offering to help her was an affront or something. The version I told fits better anyway. And don't ask me with whose idea of her. It just does.

'Come on, maybe you should give her a chance,' Pete says.

'I would, but she's –' I break off. What is Annabel like? She has this thing about her, like some sort of invisible protective bubble – you can see it in the way she moves, how she looks at things. I don't know exactly what it takes to get that sort of shine, but I'm guessing it's easier when your family aren't exactly short of a fortune or two. '... annoying,' I finish up, my voice sounding lame even to me.

‘I can’t believe her dad’s *the* Mr Huntington. They’re minted,’ Stace says from Ed’s lap.

‘Do you remember that thing in the paper, with the ball?’ Pete says. He’s talking about this massive charity ball the Huntingtons put on last Christmas at the Town Hall. They even got the High Street shut off. Mum got caught in the resulting traffic jam.

‘Yep, minted,’ Ed says.

‘So what?’ I take another shot and miss.

Pete takes the cue and starts cleaning up the table.

‘Wouldn’t mind her money though,’ Stace says. She’s still on Ed’s lap, one leg hooked behind his. ‘They’ve got a massive mansion out by the Downs, don’t they?’

I shrug, as if I don’t already know this.

‘If I was rich,’ Stace says on a sigh, ‘I’d do some serious shopping. And get extensions.’

‘You don’t need them, you’re gorgeous already,’ Ed says, to a general chorus of sick noises. Stace winds one arm around his neck.

I watch them for a moment, how natural they are. How they seem to be really happy together. A tiny part of me wants that; to have someone sitting on my lap, my arms around them.

I spot Pete giving Kelly a swift look, all open and longing, and her pretending she hasn’t noticed. Most of the time Pete’s crush on her isn’t awkward; she’ll laugh it off or say, ‘Stop trying to get into my pants,’ if Pete says something nice to her, but it’s never in a mean way.

He gives his head a little shake and then looks at me. ‘If I was rich I’d travel, go to China. See the Great Wall,’ he says. ‘What about you?’

I pause, listening to the jukebox blaring, and the babble of voices. What would I do if I had a shedload of money? Get Mum and Dad a house, for starters, so Mum stops worrying about her evil boss and getting shifts, and Dad stops having to mainline painkillers for his back. But that's a bit sad, so I take a deep breath of beery air through my nose and say, 'I don't know. Get some driving lessons?'

'Boring,' Stace says. I know she's just joking, but I feel a flicker of annoyance; Stace's parents got her driving lessons for her seventeenth a couple of months ago.

Pete cracks in the last ball and turns to me with a smirk. 'I'll have another Coke, please.'

Loser always gets the winner a drink. I go to the bar and wave at Nic. She was a couple of years above me at school and has a younger brother who Kelly dated for a bit a while ago. Everyone knows everyone else, or at least us townies do. The posh kids have their own places to hang out, I guess.

Nic's got stunning skin. It has this warm glow about it, unlike mine which seems to break out on a monthly basis. Bloody periods, excuse the pun. Her skin reminds me of Annabel's; she's not got a spot in sight either. Then I shake my head, annoyed I'm still thinking about her.

Kelly appears. She leans over the bar to grab a straw, then twirls it between her fingers before looking up through her long fringe at me. 'So Annabel. I take it she's a hottie?' She taps the straw against her mouth and grins.

'I haven't really thought about it,' I say, aiming for breezy and totally missing, which makes Kelly grin even more and say, '*Mm-huh*?' with a waggle of her eyebrows.

'*No,* Kelly. There will be no *mms* or *huhs*,' I say in my sternest voice.

'OK, OK. Was just saying.' Kelly laughs, then turns to Nic and says, 'Can I have half a cider, please?'

Nic rolls her eyes. 'You've turned eighteen since last week, have you?'

Kelly shrugs. 'Worth a try. Lemonade then. And one for Joni too.'

I open my mouth to protest, but Kelly says, 'Don't bother.'

I get this warm rush of affection for her; trust Kelly to know I'll stand my loser's round, but I've only got enough cash left for one drink.

'Thanks,' I say.

While Nic pours our drinks, Kelly stretches her arms up to the ceiling, showing off a dark stomach where her top's ridden up, and yawns. 'God, I'm knackered. I think I've been to every shop on the High Street. I've probably got blisters.' She pulls off a shoe to look at her heel, then wafts her leg in my face. 'I have as well, look.'

I push it away, laughing. 'You get no sympathy from me.' I think about Kelly's room – with its heaps of clothes on the floor, piled on her chair and spewing out over the top of her tall chest of drawers – and shake my head.

Kelly takes a sip of her drink, then says, 'So … back to this Annabel girl.'

'Oh my God, stop, for the love of …' I cast around for inspiration, 'shoes.' I'm grinning, but for once Kelly has a straight face.

'It's just, I reckon this is the first time I've seen you get worked up over a girl since you were going out with Lara.'

I shake my head. 'I swear, it's really not like that,' I say.

'Oh yeah?'

'Seriously yeah. It's about as far from that as it's possible to be.'

'*Uh-huh.*'

'Way-*huh.*'

'OK.' She pauses for a moment. 'But she is fit though?'

I think about this a bit too long before I say, 'Not really.'

'Ah-ha!'

'Shut up, Kells.'

I take a long drink because, to my extreme annoyance, I'm blushing.

CHAPTER FIVE

Lie ins are my favourite things about Sundays. If I had the choice, I'd stay in bed till ten all the days. I'm still pretty stiff from the bike crash/box lugging when I wake up. I stretch, then lie back for a moment, listening.

The birds are back from wherever they go in the winter. They start up again somewhere in that weird time just before early spring, when the days could be anything from freeze-your-nuts-off to let's-take-a-chance-and-not-wear-a-coat. That point when you think the dark and cold are going to exist forever. Then just when your legs are screaming to be out and running somewhere where there's clear air that isn't going to numb your face half to death, you realise you can hear the birds again. Only one or two at first, but as the days get lighter, more arrive, making their nest in the chimney, flitting from the hedge that lines one edge of our garden up to the old horse chestnut tree and back to the roof.

Jamie hates it when the birds are at their loudest, even though they're definitely noisier in my room, not his and Jack's, owing to the fact that the tree's on my side, but I love them.

Today it's only a couple of birds, but they sound happy, and busy. Jazzy (everyone except Mum and Dad has a name starting with a J in this house, it's a whole thing), will be on the hunt. Luckily, he's too fat and lazy to actually catch anything, at least most of the time. I can see his outline on the window sill, gazing at the bird, with the tip of his tail flicking from side to side.

I bung on my dressing gown and pad downstairs to find Mum already dressed and humming along to the radio as she peels potatoes for later. She likes to do a roast on Sundays when she's not on shift.

Mum looks tired but relaxed, like the song she's nodding along to has taken her back to some place in the past.

She spots me and smiles. 'Morning, chicken.'

I loop my arms around her. She smells faintly of apples, from her shampoo. Of Almat washing powder and clothes dried indoors, and then just her – warm somehow, like home. 'Morning. Do you want me to do that?'

'No, it's all right. You can make me a cup of tea and take one up to your dad though,' she says, her fingers moving fast over a potato. Her hands are red and dry from the antibac gel she uses for work. The washing machine's already going with the first of several washes; there'll be clothes hanging off all the doorways for the rest of the day. A sudden flash of guilt goes through me. Mum does so much for us all, especially at the moment with Dad's back being bad. He would usually be in here prepping the veg with her.

'How was work yesterday?' Mum asks, as I wait for the kettle to boil.

'All right.'

'And your schoolwork?'

'Under control.' Sort of. I don't add this though. As ever, Mum picks up on the unspoken bit of my sentence and frowns at me.

'I don't want you going out until you get it all done, lovey.'

'It's fine. I'll do it in a bit.'

'Joni …'

I stiffen, but here it comes anyway.

'You know, it's important to do well at school, not waste your chances.'

If I was really mean, I could ask, 'What, like you?' Mum did all right at school, but then she met Dad, and Jamie kind of happened and well … she'd be gutted if she thought we believed she had any regrets. And she doesn't. She loves us all. But still. I see how the years of getting by, the endless bills and everything going up a bit more while wages stick where they are, sit on her, making her hair greyer than other mums' who've got ten years on her easy.

But I'm not about to say any of that. Still, maybe Mum picks up on what I'm thinking in some way because she says, 'There's a whole world out there. You don't want to be stuck on the minimum wage, living at home.'

She doesn't say *like Jamie*, but it's suddenly in the air. Mum adds, 'Not that your dad and me would let you get away with that.'

I smile, but I can't help feeling the weight of all those dreams she has for me. Of something bigger than she's got, better.

I don't say any of this, just crack on with making the tea, and after a pause that feels way longer than it actually is, she turns back to the potatoes. I take a cup up to Dad, who's fighting himself awake through a haze of painkillers. His face is on the grey side.

'Thanks, love,' he says as I plonk the cup of tea down on the rickety cabinet by the side of his bed, which is piled with George R.R. Martin books and old copies of the *Daily Mail.*

I give him a careful hug, and he squeezes me back with one arm; even though he's in pain, Dad still gives the best hugs, squishy and safe.

'You be OK for work tomorrow?' I say.

'I'd best be, hadn't I? No work, no pay,' he says and then he smiles just like Mum did downstairs, as though he's trying to take away the sting of it. 'Could be worse, least I've still got work, even after the stunt they pulled.'

He means when everyone got laid off from his building company, then told they could still work there if they agreed to be self-employed as subbies. And pay for their own materials. Oh, and forget about holiday or sick pay.

I hate how deep the lines on his face look, and the white strands speckling through his hair. I can't help wondering how much longer Dad can keep on working, with his back so bad.

Later on, when Dad's managed to get himself up and Jamie's come home between shifts, we all sit at the table for Mum's roast. She does officially the best roasties – crisp and golden on the outside, fluffy on the inside. I take five and scoff the lot.

Jamie looks about as knackered as Dad as he munches through his stuffing.

'You're quiet,' Mum says. 'Work going all right?' She can't help the hint of anxiety in her voice; we still don't really know why Jamie got the boot from Molray's when it had all been going so well.

Seems like a long time ago when my brother talked constantly about Anton, the famous chef he worked under, and how he'd get a Michelin star too one day and open a restaurant by the sea. I can still summon up echoes of his voice and that look in his eyes, like Jack's shiny look, as he'd bang on about the ingredients they used.

'They bring the fish straight from the sea, caught that morning. You should see them, Joni,' and he'd get this look and I'd know what the next word out of his mouth would be. Sure enough, he'd say, 'Anton says, you can always tell by how firm they are. You've got to check they're real shiny, no dull eyes. And if it's hard to get the skin off and backbone out you know it's a good one …'

I'd be making puke noises by then, especially if it got to him going on about how loads of blood was a good thing. I used to shudder at the thought of those fish eyes. I sort of miss them now.

Today, Jamie simply gives a short nod and shovels in a mouthful, then puts down his fork as he chews in a way I've started to recognise. I open my mouth, ready to make some chat about the library or whatever, but he's already started.

'Me and Dealo have been looking into this White Light buyout thing and I'm telling you now, it's bad news if it goes through.'

I stop myself from rolling my eyes. Mason Deal has been working at The Olde Inne for a couple of years and since Jamie started there, his name is about the only thing that gives Jamie the look he used to get talking about Anton. I've only met Deal once or twice, and there's something about him I really don't like, which is weird for me because I usually get on OK with most people. If – ahem – we ignore Annabel the other day. He's just a bit too sure of himself.

Dad helps himself to another Yorkshire pudding as Mum frowns. 'Do we need to talk about this at the table?' She gives a meaningful glance at Jack, which Jamie chooses to ignore.

Instead he bangs his knife down. 'Well, when are we going to talk about it? We should be getting ready, not pretending like it's not going to happen.'

'We don't know if it will,' Mum says, using her extra patient voice.

Jamie laughs, but not in a nice way. 'Course it will. Those companies always get what they want. And then we're all going to be screwed. You really think they'll let us carry on renting this place once they've bought all the houses up? Not likely. First thing they'll do is kick us all out and then flog them on to the highest bidder. The one per cent never care about anything except getting richer.'

This last sentence has a ring to it that tells me Jamie's got it on loan from someone else.

I look round the table, wondering. Mum and Dad exchange a glance and I suddenly realise they are worried, maybe have been for a bit now. And that makes the last potato I'm eating wedge itself in my chest, hot and heavy.

For a moment, no one speaks and then Dad says in a really firm voice, 'We'll worry about it if it happens and not before. And that's a big if, in my opinion.'

I can see Jamie wants to say more, but even he's not going to argue when Dad uses that voice. But later that day as I'm going through my homework in between the usual Snapchats from the gang, I can't stop myself thinking about the look in Dad's eyes and I wonder whether that 'if' is really very big after all.

CHAPTER SIX

Monday rolls around way too fast. I walk the same route to school I've done since I was five – my old primary school is literally across the road from St Francis – picking up Kelly on the way. I have a free period first, which I use to finish a History essay. Usually, I'd have stayed late at the library to get it done. Mrs H gave me a set of keys a few weeks back, which felt like a pretty big milestone. But with Annabel there I pretty much forgot. Of course, Annabel got her own keys straight away, because obviously a different set of rules apply to her ...

'Oi, daydreamer.' Kelly's waving a hand in front of my face.

That makes three times a girl I've barely met for a couple of hours is taking up my brain space. I focus on Kelly. 'What?'

'I said you're off the hook – Mr Weston's off sick again.'

I glance down at where I've only written an extra two sentences. 'Thank God for that.' I fold up the pages. 'That's the third time this term. What do you reckon's wrong with him?' I say.

Kelly pokes her tongue out of the side of her mouth. 'Man flu probably. Or the plague. Or something super embarrassing like ... syphilis.'

'Eww.'

Kelly wiggles her eyebrows. 'What? Alvin probably has a very healthy sex life, he –'

'Kells!' I put my hands over my ears. Mr Weston – or Alvin as we're now allowed to call him in sixth form, but no one does because it's just too weird – is about two years short of retirement.

Kelly's trying to pull my hands away from my ears, and we end up laughing so hard she's in danger of falling off her chair.

Eventually, I straighten my face and look at the clock. 'We've got to go. English.'

'Have they said anything about a tutor to replace Denise yet?'

'Nope.'

'Ah well, skiving all round then.'

I grin, but then it fades as I think about the revolving door of supply teachers we've had over the last two months. No one wants to work here. 'Yeah, I guess.'

The rest of the week doesn't really improve. Mr Weston's off the whole week – hopefully not with syphilis – so History ends up being a write-off. Don't suppose it really matters anyway; it's not like I'm planning to do a lot with my A Levels. For the millionth time since starting in the sixth form, I wonder what I'm doing here and whether I should've taken the Business and Administration apprenticeship I got offered. It would've meant a pretty long bus journey every day though and the fares were so expensive, although I'd have been earning more than in the library, to put towards the bus. But then there's smart clothes to think about and I'd probably need to get a sensible haircut and take out my nose ring … plus Mum really wanted me to do the A Levels she never did. And I did do pretty OK in my GCSEs. Recently though, it's seeming like a bigger and bigger waste of time.

The bust of a week means I'm not in the best of moods as I bike it to the library on Saturday morning. I manage to make it without falling off, and on time, which is an improvement on last week. What's not an improvement is the way I feel when Annabel comes in ten minutes after me, and five minutes late by the old plastic clock. Mrs H doesn't say anything to *her* though. Instead she jumps up and says, 'Good morning! Lovely to see you. Why don't you help Joni get ready for toddler group while I make us both a nice coffee?'

I watch Mrs H's retreating back with my mouth hanging for a second. Can't remember her ever offering to make *me* a coffee – even if we're ignoring the fact I only drink tea. I turn to Annabel, trying not to let the annoyance show on my face, but I think she picks some of it up because she says in that startling, clear voice of hers, 'I'm sure Genevieve would make one for you too.'

Genevieve? Bloody hell. That's worse than Alvin.

I feel my eyebrows climb, but I get my face under control. 'Nah. Hate the stuff.' I search for something else to say. 'So you ever refereed a toddler group?'

'Well, I don't have much experience with children, but,' she flicks back her hair and gives this big, confident smile, 'I'm sure it can't be too difficult.'

I open my mouth, ready to tell her, but then shut it again. She can find out the total carnage that's toddler group the hard way. Mind you, it probably won't be for someone like her. She'll probably scare them into their best behaviour.

'Come on then,' I say.

We set off towards the hall, Annabel's heels clipping on the parquet floor. I unlock the storage cupboard and haul out mats, dropping them in a pile so they make a booming noise, then give Annabel's clothes a swift look.

'Some of this stuff's a bit dusty,' I say, and there's a small challenge in my voice.

Her eyes give me a quick once-over. 'I'll find something a little ... ah ...' I see her searching for the word. She finally settles on, 'Older, for next time.'

I stiffen, realising what I must look like in my jeans that are fraying at the knee and my hoodie with the lettering peeling off and the sleeves rolled up. I guess it must seem like I'm in my worst clothes to her, but actually I wear this all the time because one: it's comfy, two: I hate clothes shopping with a fiery passion and three: I can't afford to keep buying new stuff anyway. But now, with her looking at me like that, I feel wrong suddenly.

I turn away to hide my expression and wrench the first mat from the pile, sending it spinning harder than I meant to towards the middle of the hall, then repeat the process with the next two before dropping to my knees to push them together. I'm breathing fast, wondering where this sudden burst of anger has come from. Then I hear Annabel's footsteps.

‘I didn’t mean to offend you.’ Her voice is about as stiff as I feel.

‘I’m not offended.’ We stare at each other. Her eyes are super blue. I won’t compare them to anything, because that’s too cheesy even for me, except maybe they’re a bit like the sky on the Downs in summer … I shake my head.

What is wrong with me today?

‘I can do the toys if you like – why don’t you get out the chairs?’ I say.

Annabel seems like she’s about to say something else, but I’m looking past her ear, my face set. Then she turns away and starts lifting chairs down from the stacks at the edge of the hall. I grab some toys and scatter them around. We’ve got a little slide, a couple of scrappy old rockers and some balls which I leave where they are. I learned my lesson the hard way with those.

I’m dragging the slide out when I feel the other end lift. I peer around the ladder to see Annabel holding the other end. Her cheeks are flushed from the lifting and one or two strands have come down from her piled-on-top-but-stuck-in-place-with-two-zillion-pins hairdo, so they tickle the sides of her face. It makes her look … I give a quick cough and concentrate on positioning the slide.

‘Thanks,’ I say.

Our eyes meet again and for a crazy moment, this strange, familiar feeling grabs me in the gut.

You see, there’s this look. I’m not saying it’s gaydar exactly, but very occasionally I meet some girl’s eyes and this thing happens, like a low bell sounding somewhere inside me and I … well, I wonder, I suppose. Nine times out of ten, I tell myself it's nothing, and I can never be sure if someone's interested in that way, but I can't stop thinking how startling Annabel's eyes are and that bell is definitely there, this gentle, deep chime.

What is going on?

I'm telling myself not to be a dumb-ass, yet neither of us is looking away, and the look is turning from a simple eye-meet to what feels like another kind of meeting altogether, even though maybe only two or three seconds have gone by. Then Mrs H clatters down the hall holding a cup.

'Here we are!' She hands the coffee to Annabel and I swallow, knowing I've gone red. I busy myself inching the slide to the left. When I risk another glance at Annabel she's totally relaxed, like nothing unusual happened at all. I immediately get this sinking feeling I've got it wrong again, that she's probably got some posh brayer of a boyfriend anyway. Maybe the arrogant one from the restaurant the other evening. My imagination has gone and let me down yet again, not that I was really imagining anything, obviously.

'Nearly ten o'clock,' Mrs H says and goes off to greet the parents.

My face is calming down now. There's a shout from the library as the first few kids arrive. I look at Annabel. If it'd been Kells standing there I would've been laughing and saying, 'Brace for impact,' but I can't imagine saying anything like that to Annabel.

The first of the toddlers charges down the hall and goes straight for the slide while the parents follow. They quickly separate out into little groups. There's people like Linds who lives around the corner from me, has four kids and needs some kind of medal if you ask me. Then you get the occasional posher one, who's trying to get the kids out of her husband's hair after his long week in the City or wherever (I listen in a fair amount). One or two dads as well, giving their other halves a break. I guess it must feel like a pretty long week when you've only got a two-year-old for company.

I like most of the kids fine and spend some time with Teddy, Linds' toddler, putting a big floor puzzle together. It's got the Teletubbies on, which he totally loves. His big brother, Alfie, is busy scoffing all the biscuits while Linds sorts out her twin girls, who are six months old. She parks their double buggy, kneels in front of them and plugs a bottle into each mouth. I'm about to see if she needs a hand; I'm all right with giving a baby a cuddle and a bottle as long as it doesn't puke on me or anything. It's not like I need to worry about it, because I'm about ninety-five per cent certain I never want kids. No way do I want the same worries Mum's got.

Annabel gets there first. Linds unclips Poppy – I can tell because she has more hair than her sister – and settles her in Annabel's arms. Annabel suddenly looks nervous, fumbling with the baby like she's worried she might drop her, but she gets the bottle plugged in and Poppy starts glugging and I see a small smile come over Annabel's face.

Just as suddenly, it falters. I glance in the direction Annabel's looking and there's a really posh woman approaching with an actual Versace buggy. I know the Medusa logo courtesy of Kelly, who likes her designer brands – or knock-offs anyway – yet another thing I simply don't get. It's not like a logo makes you a better person, right?

The woman strides right up to Annabel and even though I'm still talking to Teddy, I can't help hearing what's she's saying, given that her voice is the carrying sort posh people seem to have.

'Annabel, darling!' A loud air-kiss. 'Your father told me you were helping out here and I was absolutely tickled. I had to come and see you.'

Annabel's reply is unfortunately lost in a wail as a little girl topples off the slide. Her mum scoops her up and I go over with a biscuit and some juice and by the time I turn around I can see Poppy has finished her bottle and Annabel has given her back to Linds, who's looking on the stressed-out side. I'm pretty sure Annabel is too, if her smile as she answers the buggy woman's questions is anything to go by; it's kind of tight and doesn't get anywhere near her eyes. I don't have much time to consider this though as the buggy woman's let her spawn out and he's made a beeline for Teddy's jigsaw. Next thing I know, he's only gone and broken it all up. Teddy lets out a wail as I say, 'Oi, don't do that.' The little boy has really long blonde curls, like a painting of an angel, but the look on his face is definitely not angelic.

His mum's next to me in a flash. She gives me an icy look, then scoops up her son. 'You were just looking at the lovely picture, weren't you, Hugo?' she says. In response Hugo kicks her.

Linds is red in the face as she tries to sort out Teddy with Poppy balanced in one arm. Daisy, still in the buggy, starts to scrunch up her face.

Alfie starts tugging on Linds' sleeve. 'I want more biscuit,' he says.

'In a minute, Alfie!' Linds says in a near-shout. I see the posh woman by Annabel looking over, her top lip curled.

'You OK?' I say to Linds.

'I think she's filled her nappy,' Linds says, her voice with an edge of despair. That is definitely a duty way too far for me, so I grab Teddy and take him over to the biscuits while Linds disappears to the toilet with Poppy. Obviously, at this point Daisy starts to cry.

Like I said, carnage.

The group winds up eventually, only one or two stragglers left. Annabel is still busy chatting to Hugo's mum, or being talked at by the looks of it. I hear Hugo's mum say, 'You must send my love to your father. It's wonderful what he's done here.' There's a shine on her face like he's some sort of hero.

I start picking up toys on my own. Linds is struggling to get her lot rounded up.

'Need a hand?' I say.

'Would you walk Teddy out?' Teddy never wants to leave.

I take his sticky little hand and we go out through the library. At the top of the steps, I slip him an extra biscuit and Linds gives me a grateful look. 'See you next time!' she says. I smile, but I'm secretly wondering whether I can't persuade Mrs H to reduce toddler group down to once a month.

I go back into the library and hear rather than see Annabel and Hugo's mum, mainly because Hugo's mum can definitely project.

'You do have to wonder why people have so many children when they clearly aren't able to cope.' She gives a little *huh* of a laugh. 'For the welfare of course.'

They've almost reached me now.

'This two-child cap on welfare can only be a good thing. Stop them breeding,' Hugo's mum says.

'I suppose …' Annabel begins, but she breaks off because I've reached them now and she's spotted the expression on my face.

Hers changes too, but I'm already swivelling on my heel. I storm out, slamming the door behind me as I go.

CHAPTER SEVEN

I'm still stomping all the way round Lidl as I pick up some stuff for tea. We're out of toilet roll, so I sling some of that into the trolley with a satisfying *thunk*.

Who the hell does Annabel Huntington think she is? I keep replaying what Hugo's mum said, and how Annabel stood there agreeing. *Must be nice*, I think as I whack in some economy beans, *to be sitting up on high without any clue how real people live.*

I whip round the aisles, my thoughts piling one on top of the other. How could Annabel go along with that crap? Is it what she thinks too? And I was just starting to reckon she might be OK. I wrench the trolley around a corner, hating that I'm bothered by it. Why should I care about her opinion? I'm so busy ranting in my head as I lob everything down on the conveyor belt I don't even realise for a few minutes that it's Theresa Wójcik behind the till. I used to go to school with her. She was all right, really sporty – she could run the fifteen hundred metres in about half the time everyone else could, not including those of us who skulked at the back not bothering running at all.

Theresa has on a crap ton of make-up: HD Brows, winged eyeliner, the lot, and she's dyed her hair really red. She looks amazing.

'Hiya!' she says as she recognises me.

I grin, feeling some of my annoyance melt away. 'All right? How's you?'

'Yeah, you know,' she says, whizzing all my stuff through at lightning speed. I fling it all in the trolley higgledy-piggledy just as fast.

I'm suddenly taken back to Science class with Miss Lilless, whose name was way too close to a major tampon brand to get away with. There was one incident involving a tampon and a Bunsen burner I won't forget in a hurry. I sort of wish we hadn't arsed about quite so much in Science now; I only scraped a C at GCSE so any thoughts of going on to do Science A Levels, like I'd planned to when I was younger and had the idea I wanted to be a vet, went out of the window. It was a dumb dream anyway. Vet degrees cost tens of thousands of pounds.

Theresa looks so much older now.

'What you up to these days?' I say. Theresa never stayed on at the sixth form.

'Still doing my NVQ, but I might quit when I'm eighteen. I'm failing it anyway, and there's more shifts going here,' she says.

I want to ask if it won't be boring stuck in Lidl all day, but she grins. 'I was always thick as hell anyway, me.'

I open my mouth to say that's not true, because it's totally not, but she speaks before I can. 'At least here I'm earning my own money. I can move out, get a room somewhere,' she says.

I remember Theresa complaining at school about how strict her parents were, so this is not the biggest surprise. I look at her face, suddenly drawn under the strip lights, imagine her still sitting on the same stool in ten years' time and get a flash of sadness, but she gives a grin and says, 'Remember Miss Lil-lets?'

I laugh. 'Oh yeah.'

'Good times,' she says, her voice suddenly soft.

On the way home – the carrier bags dangling from the handlebars, whacking me in the shins – I wonder why I felt sad. Does it matter if Theresa wants to work in Lidl? It's a job, isn't it? Better than none at all, and the pay's pretty good. Then I imagine Annabel in a blue polo shirt. I'm guessing Lidl would never feature in her future plans. Why would it?

Why is she still taking up my brain space? For God's sake.

I bang into the house and dump all the shopping on the side. Jamie's in the kitchen. He watches me. 'Something on your mind?' he says.

'You can give me a hand with this,' I say, my voice coming out grumpy.

He helps me put the shopping away, except for a couple of pizzas which he leaves on the side, and puts the oven on to warm up.

'Come on then, what's up with you?' he says and I think it's because he looks genuinely concerned, like the version of him I'm more used to; the older brother who'd make sure we all had tea after school when Mum and Dad were still at work, that I say, 'I don't know.'

Jamie flicks on the kettle, then sits down at the table. I sit next to him. 'There's this new girl working at the library … Annabel Huntington.'

He gives a low whistle. Everyone round here knows who the Huntingtons are. 'What's she working there for?'

'That's exactly what I thought! Mrs Hendry said something about UCAS, but who knows? I thought she might be all right, but today, well, I guess not.'

I tell him about toddler group and the conversation I overheard. 'I just feel weird around her … like I'm not good enough or something and it feels … I dunno …'

'Pretty crappy?' Jamie's looking at me like he really understands and then I get another flash of how he was last year, when he landed that job at Molray's. He talked about Anton so much, Mum had to tell me to stop taking the piss, so I did. He never talks about it now. I hold his eyes. For a second I think he's going to open up, it's there in the hurt twist of his mouth, but the next minute he jumps up and grabs an orange from the fridge.

He sits back down and starts peeling it. 'Right. This is the world,' he says and there's something in his tone that makes me think he's rehashing a speech he heard from someone else. Again. Mason Deal's face with its stubble and flashy cheekbones pops into my mind.

'O-K, what's that got to do with Anna–'

'You'll see. So this,' he pulls the orange apart and pushes half to one side then points to the other half, 'is what the top one per cent of the world's population owns. The other ninety-nine per cent scrabble for a share in the rest. Which means this,' he pulls out a tiny sliver of orange from the remaining half, sharp-smelling juice spraying across the table, 'is what people like us get. And I'm not even counting people in really poor countries. We all have less because they always have to keep grabbing at more. The eight richest people in the world own the same amount as the bottom half of everyone else. Like, over three billion people or something. More, I think. Eight people, Joni.'

I make a disbelieving face, but he says, 'It's true. Oxfam did this study.'

'Bloody hell. Really?'

'Yep. And the main thing you've got to remember about people like her is they've got one priority,' he says, 'and that's to keep hold of as much of this' – he points to the orange – 'as they can, and stuff the rest of us struggling to get by on the scraps. Once you understand that, you can protect yourself. And the best way to do that is to steer clear of people like her,' he adds.

'That's gonna be a bit hard, seeing as I've got to work with her,' I say.

'Well, yeah. But just keep your distance as much as you can.'

I fall silent while I think about this. Jamie suddenly stirs himself and pops one of the segments into his mouth, then gets up. 'Best get these pizzas in the oven or Mum'll be steaming when she gets in,' he says.

I stare at the glistening segments still on the table, the little shred of flesh sitting to one side next to its juice trail. I put one into my own mouth. It tastes sour.

I decide to get to the library extra early the following week. I want to get on with some homework and the fan is knackered on the old laptop school gave me. Wouldn't mind looking up that stat Jamie told me either; it's been going round my head for days.

I'm expecting an hour of early morning peace: me, a cup of tea and the work PC, but when I ride into the car park I spot Annabel's Audi out front. I can't help frowning as I lean my bike against the wall and go up the steps. I unlock the door and lock it up again behind me, then stand for a moment, listening.

A really bizarre noise is floating out into the lobby. It sounds like two cats fighting to the death. It takes me a second to realise it's Annabel singing.

Oh. My. God.

I can't help it; my face is smiling whether I want it to or not, stuff being annoyed she's here. I have never heard anything quite that out of tune. I think it might be a Rihanna song, but it's kind of hard to tell. I walk in to the library and then stop again. There's books and toys everywhere, all of it brand new by the looks of it. Annabel's got earbuds in and she has her back to me, singing her heart out. Yep, it's definitely Rihanna. She takes a few dance steps, hips going, then does a pose with one arm up in the air as she belts out the chorus. She's so bad I'm half thinking it's on purpose. There are dogs at least three streets away that are covering their ears and whimpering right now. I think about tiptoeing out and making a louder re-entry, but before I get the chance, she's done a wobbly swivel-turn thing, her loose hair whipping round, so that she's facing me.

She screams, 'Fahking hell!' and I'm gone. My shoulders are shaking with the effort of trying to keep the laughter in.

This is all made worse by the small detail that Annabel is also clutching a teddy bear in one hand. She yanks her earbuds out of her ears. I'm still desperately trying not to laugh, but two tears roll down my cheeks.

'You scared me,' she says, the teddy now pressed up against her chest. Her face is rapidly going past pink and into the deep mortification zone. Sort of nice in a weird way, to know it's not just me that happens to. It makes her seem more … normal.

I open my mouth to say sorry, and this gigantic snort comes out of nowhere and now I'm properly laughing, trying to apologise, but all that comes out is something like, 'You … teddy … oh God … posh swearing … sor-sorry … gonna pee myself.' Actually, I'm laughing so hard wetting myself might be a real possibility.

Annabel stiffens and starts to glare. I swallow, trying to get myself under control, but all of a sudden, her face relaxes and she says, 'You'd better go to the loo then,' and there's a tiny smile on her face too.

I'm still sniggering as I pee, but I sort myself out and go back into the library with my face now straight. Annabel's bending over some books, sorting through them. This time, I say in as sincere a voice as I can manage, 'I'm really sorry. I didn't mean to sneak up on you.'

She puts down the book she was holding and looks at me, and the tiny smile is back, then it gets wider as she seems to think about it. 'I suppose I did look a little strange?'

'Look? I was more worried about how you sounded, mate.' I say it without thinking, just like I would to Kelly, then stop abruptly, not sure how she's going to take this, but she rolls her eyes as if to say 'fair enough'.

'Well, yes. That's why I tend to do my singing in private. In fact, you may be the first person who's heard me sing since I was eleven.' She shudders and I can tell there's definitely a story there. I'm going to leave it, but my nosey side wins out and I say, 'Oh yeah? What happened when you were eleven then?'

For a moment she doesn't reply, just stands up even straighter, like she's reminding herself to. I realise she does that quite a bit.

Then she turns this big smile on me, and says, 'Oh, Mummy made me do a recital in front of the whole school. She wanted me to read a poem, but I completely insisted it had to be a song, which needless to say didn't go quite as planned.' For a split second I think she looks pained, but then she laughs again. 'I really did think I could sing until then, despite what Mummy said, but she was right as always. Totally ridiculous.' She shakes her head at herself, smiling again.

This is possibly the most she's ever said to me all in one go, and for a moment I'm not sure how to react. Then I blurt, 'My mate Kelly's got an amazing voice.'

She doesn't answer except with a cool smile. There's a silence while I think of something else to say and realise I've got nothing. Eventually, I gesture at the piles of stuff. 'Where did this lot come from?'

'Oh. Well, after the group last week I had Mary – she's our housekeeper – look in the attic to see if there were any of my old things. Mummy does tend to hoard, but there wasn't much so …' She does the sort of shrug Kelly would do when she was definitely bothered but trying not to let on.

I gape at her, trying to get my head round the words 'housekeeper' and 'Mummy' and then remembering that the last time I saw her I flounced off in a strop. Then I say, 'What, like you went to Toys R Us or something?'

'Well …' She spreads her arms wide.

'Bloody hell. This lot must have cost a mint.' My voice comes out with an accidental edge to it.

'Some of it was in the sale.' Her tone's defensive now.

There's a small pause.

Then I kneel down near her and say, 'OK. Well, it was nice of you. We'd best sort it all out before Mrs H gets here though. She hates mess.'

'That was the general idea, until –'

'You got sidetracked with your Grammy winning performance?' It sort of slips out again and I wonder for a sec if I've gone too far, but she gives me that unreadable smile.

'Something like that.'

It doesn't take too long to sort everything out. We stack the books on a shelf in the store cupboard, ready to be catalogued and shelved. I leave a few in a pile on the desk to do today; some Enid Blytons and ballet stories, plus a few Jacqueline Wilsons. Annabel puts the kettle on. I let her make me a cup of tea and we sit behind the desk with our cups.

I wonder what to say to her, and settle on, 'So … er, it was nice of you to buy all this stuff.'

'It's nothing,' she says.

I nearly say, 'Well, yeah, to you,' but that seems too rude. I wonder whether to bring up last week, but perhaps it's better if I steer clear, given we're getting on. I pick up an Enid Blyton book – one of the *Malory Towers* ones, but with new covers, not like the ones I used to take home from primary school.

'I had these when I was little, totally loved them. I kept asking my mum if I could go to a boarding school. I think it was the swimming pool in the rocks that did it for me,' I say.

Annabel takes a careful sip of her coffee, staring off into the middle distance. 'Boarding school's not really like in books,' she says.

I put my head on one side.

'I was a boarder from the age of eight until I was thirteen, then I became a day girl at Edrington.'

Edrington is the local posh school.

'No midnight feasts or anything?' I say.

She laughs. 'Sadly no.'

'Well, that bursts my bubble then,' I say. Then I risk asking, 'So what was it like?'

'Very cold. I always seemed to be cold.' She looks at me. 'The buildings were beautiful but very old and there was a constant draught in the dorms. Everything's timetabled so you're busy all the time, but I still missed home, and Puzzle –' She gives me another look, swift and slightly embarrassed. 'My pony.'

'Oh.' I can't think what else to say. 'Eight's pretty young to be going away from home, I guess? I'm not surprised you got homesick.'

Annabel nods.

'Did you tell your parents you didn't want to go?'

She gets brisk suddenly. 'Oh well, that's not going to make much difference. It's what's expected when you move in the circles my parents do. You just have to push on and make the most of it.' She's drawn into herself, sitting up taller, chin tipped up. It's almost like she's trained herself or something. Then she asks, 'Why were you here so early?'

I blink at the abrupt change of subject. 'Needed to use the computer. Mine's busted.'

'Oh.' For a second she's lost for words, as though this has never crossed her mind as a possibility. Then she says, 'I could do that while you use the computer?' She gestures to the book in my hand.

'It's OK, I'll stay for a bit after.'

I show her how to catalogue the books and we work together until Mrs H comes bustling in. She gives a satisfied nod when she sees us. 'You're both here already! How lovely.' She's so overeager it's almost painful, but a funny thing happens: I catch Annabel's eye and notice her mouth's twitching slightly. I get that pulse through me again; of something being exchanged between us, and then I raise one eyebrow. Annabel turns away so that Mrs H doesn't see her smiling, but I catch the side of it, and it makes that bell start up again inside.

There's no toddler group to deal with today, which is probably for the best, although Linds comes in. I watch Annabel closely, but she's polite and friendly, helping Linds find some jigsaws to borrow from the toy library. I think about her pony called Puzzle and the loving look that flitted over her face when she said its name, like me with Jazzy, or maybe even Jack when he's not being a pain in the backside. I wonder what happened to it, along with an avalanche of other things, but I hold back the millions of questions I suddenly want to ask her. I'm still not sure what I can get away with.

By lunchtime, I'm definitely starting to wonder if maybe I was a bit quick the other week. Annabel works hard, no slacking off, and at one point when she drops a book, she looks at me and says, 'Insert posh swearing here,' with this funny little smile, before she bends to pick it up. I laugh and it suddenly strikes me she'd probably be decent company if she unwound a bit.

It helps the sun's out too. We've got all the windows open and there's a crisp wind floating through them, chasing all the dust and winter smells away. At lunchtime, Mrs H, who seems to be delighted me and Annabel are getting on, says, 'Why don't you both go and eat outside on the wall, in the sun? I can manage in here.'

I sneak a quick look at Annabel, and she seems pleased with the idea.

We sit on the low stone wall ringing the car park. I've got my lunch in a carrier; marmite sandwich and some cheese puffs. Annabel opens up her lunch bag thing and makes a face. 'Olives. Mary never remembers I hate them.' She puts the pot to one side and pulls out a salad with the M&S logo on the front.

I've already finished my sarnie and most of my crisps by the time she's put away a few mouthfuls; she is one slow eater. I guess I inhaled mine a bit, but what can I say? I get hungry and I like my food.

At first the silence as we eat feels OK. I can hear my own jaw crunching down the crisps, birds tweeting overhead, the odd car going by. The wind's fresh, but not too cold. After a while though, the lack of conversation starts to feel awkward, at least to me. I'm so used to everyone chatting away at home. And it's pretty hard to tell what she's thinking. I look at Annabel and immediately look away again.

Annabel puts her salad down. 'How long have you worked here?'

'Few months now.'

'Do you enjoy it?'

'Yeah, it's all right. It's a job anyway.'

'And when you're not here, you are … ?'

I frown, trying to work out her drift. 'School. I'm at St Francis.'

'Of course.' She pauses. 'Daddy says they have a good vocational programme there.'

I feel like a shadow's gone over my head, but make myself answer in a neutral voice. 'I'm doing A Levels same as you. English, French and History.'

Her eyebrows go up before she can stop them. I narrow my eyes, feeling that same anger as when I heard her agreeing with Hugo's mum about Linds. Why is this apparently a shocker?

'You didn't think someone like me would be doing A Levels?' I say.

She blinks. The pause is only for half a second, but it's enough to tell me I'm right. 'No, of course not. I –'

'Oh, come on.' I jump down from the wall. 'Course you did. You had me written right off, didn't you? I guess you thought, I'm what, some chav?'

Her voice is almost as angry as mine. 'I would never use that word.'

We scowl at each other. I'm having to tip my head back to look up at her and this makes me even angrier.

'Should've known you'd be –'

'Be what?'

'A judgemental cow!' It bursts out of me before I can stop it. I want to take it back just as fast, and not only because her face gets this really hurt expression on it.

Annabel straightens her shoulders and levels her chin. 'I don't think I'm the person doing the judging here.' Then she pushes off from the wall and walks inside, and it's me who's left behind this time.

CHAPTER EIGHT

The wind pushes my hair back and up from my scalp, clattering in my ears as I stand on a ridge right towards the top of the Downs, letting its full force pummel me. This used to be one of my favourite places to go; we'd come up and have picnics and stuff, before Dad's back got too bad for much walking and Mum got so tired from her extra shifts. It's still a place I think of as mine; somewhere I can come to when things aren't going right. My legs are tingling from the walk up – I ran part of the way, my feet thudding on the turf, following a bridleway. Below me, the Downs are littered with boulders, like a giant was playing a game of marbles. To my left I can see the ridged remains of a hill fort, and splashes of yellow rapeseed. The sky is a wide purple-blue, rain clouds gathering in the distance.

Up here there's space to think, to breathe. I can let all my worries go on the wind. I think again about the argument with Annabel at the library, and the awkward afternoon that followed, neither of us wanting to speak, but being polite for the sake of Mrs H, who kept looking between us; clearly neither of us were doing the best job at faking everything being OK.

Mrs H stopped me after Annabel left and put one hand on my arm. 'Is everything all right between you girls? You both seemed rather … strained this afternoon,' she said.

I tried to shrug it off, but my, 'Oh yeah, I think we're both a bit tired, you know,' wasn't cutting it because Mrs H said, 'Listen, Joni, I want you to make an effort to be friendly to Annabel. You have to work together and besides, I get the sense that she's – well, it's probably not my place to say.'

I'd been about to ask why I had to be the one making an effort, but I have to admit my curiosity button was pushed. 'She's what?' I said.

'Well. Not entirely *happy*.' Mrs H mouthed the last word, like it was a swear word or something.

Pause.

'Oh yeah?' I said casually, like I wasn't dying to find out more.

'Yes, well, between you and me, I believe there was some trouble at school. Her father certainly wasn't pleased. I don't think his plans for her include –' She broke off, and pursed her lips. 'But I don't mean to gossip. Forget I said anything.'

'All right then. I'm off,' I said, when it was apparent she wasn't going to say any more.

'But if you could just … be nice,' Mrs H said, and I promised I would.

Now up here, I think again about what Mrs H said. I mean, you've got to wonder what Annabel's really got to be unhappy about. That it was a bit chilly for her at her posh boarding school? Or maybe her Audi isn't the latest model. If my family was as rich as hers, we'd be laughing.

I open my mouth and let the wind rush in, so it feels like it's doing my breathing for me, and I imagine all my worries – Annabel, schoolwork, cash, this house-buying thing Jamie keeps going on about – floating out like they're feathers whirling away on the breeze. A couple of birds, too small to identify from here, arc over my head.

After another ten minutes, I feel lighter, my shoulders less up round my ears and more where they should be.

I walk back to my bike at the bottom of the bridleway. It's getting dusky and I don't have lights on my bike and I know Mum worries. Sure enough, my phone goes as I'm about to set off and I grab it, ready to text Mum back.

But the text isn't from Mum; it's from a number I don't recognise. It reads: *I'm sorry about today. Truce? A.* – with an emoji of a white flag.

She must've got my number from the contacts list on the PC. I think for a minute. I'm still angry about earlier, but she is saying she's sorry, which I suppose is something. The look on her face as I said she was a judgemental cow plays back in my mind and that decides me. I tap back an emoji of a white dove and add, *Have a good week, J.*

Then I pedal home with only half my thoughts on the road.

When I get back, I recognise Mason Deal's banger parked next to our clapped-out old car on the driveway, which is both good and bad: good, because it means Mum's home, bad that Deal gave Jamie a lift, because he might be staying for tea. I prefer it when it's just us Coopers, and apart from that, Deal's hard to work out.

When I go into the kitchen, Dad's hunched over a pan on the cooker, while Jack sets the table. There's an extra space laid. I get a whiff of garlic bread and what smells like lentil spag bol.

'You want me to do that?' I kiss his bristly cheek and hang my arms over his shoulders.

'No, love, you've just got in. Take a seat and watch the master at work,' he says. 'Jack, grate some cheese would you?'

Jack grins at me and gets the grater out. I love that grater. It used to be Nana's before she passed, and it's about a zillion years old, with a misshapen handle and a bent-in bit at the top, but it always reminds me of her fast hands as she grated nutmeg for traditional mincemeat at Christmas time. It's been five years since she went, and I know Mum still misses her every day.

Jack puts some water in front of me. 'Thanks. What you been up to today?' I say.

'Been round Dylan's.' He grins. 'He's got his Xbox One X Project Scorpio already!' I can't help laughing at the way he gabbles out the full title, his eyes huge.

'Thought his birthday was next week?'

'I know, his mum let him have it early.'

I fake an enthusiastic face; Lorraine's forever coming round ours because her washing machine's packed up, or to borrow tea bags or whatever, but she's always got cash to spare for Dylan.

Jack's going on about the 4K gameplay and I nod. I wouldn't mind trying that out myself. Then he stops for a moment and looks all wistful.

'It's going to be another ten minutes on the garlic bread. You got any homework to do?' Dad says.

Jack grabs his bag out of the cupboard under the stairs and flops at the table, chewing his tongue as he concentrates. I pick up a piece of paper that fell on to the floor when he pulled out his worksheet. It's a letter from school. I'm about to hand it over to Dad when I see the words *Year Eight Residential* and *Instalment Plan.*

Jack meets my eyes, and we come to an understanding in a fraction of a second, but I'm too slow; Dad's already reaching out, saying, 'Another letter from school? What they after now? Book night? Comic Relief? Children in Need? We should get them to give you a quid, we're People in Need!' Dad's joking, but as he scans the letter his face falls, and he repeats quietly to himself, 'In need. I'm in need of a drink.'

I'm looking at Jack's face as Dad mutters this, and I see the way his eyes go from a teensy spark of hope to resigned. I feel a sharp twist in my chest. I remember everyone going off to that residential at the beginning of Year Eight. Having to hear the whole gang talking about what they'd pack, who was going to stay up all night, all that. They didn't mean to leave me out, but for weeks after it felt like every other conversation began, 'In Pengelly ...' while I tried not to let on I was bothered.

I swallow, then say in as bright a voice as I can: 'Tea smells lush, Dad. Shall I shout up for Mum?'

Dad folds the letter and puts it in the kitchen drawer. 'You can go and ask her, not yell at her. You'd best get the lads down too.'

He says something in a low, apologetic voice to Jack as I leave the room.

Jamie and Deal come down a moment later. Deal gives Dad a clap on the back with one hand and shakes his hand with the other. 'All right, Derek?' he says in this 'guys together' sort of way. I don't know what it is about the way Deal says it, but it feels weird, like if you've got a handful of popcorn you think is sweet but when you shove it in your mouth it turns out to be salty.

'Holding up,' Dad says and only someone who knows him as well as I do would catch the edge of pain in his voice. For a second I hate Mason Deal for not noticing Dad's bad back. Then Deal goes over to Jack.

'Here you go, thought you might like this.'

Jack gives a yell of delight and I look over to see he's holding a pile of PS2 games. 'Thanks,' he says.

'No problem.' Deal gives him such a warm smile I almost forgive him for Dad's back, but then he sits himself at the end of the table, where Dad usually goes because it has the most space, and kicks back with his legs stretched out. Jamie sits down too without offering to help. I'm about to say something when Mum comes in, her wet hair twisted into a loopy ponytail at the back of her head. Mum's really pretty, although there are more lines between her eyebrows and on her forehead than there used to be, and a few wiry grey hairs springing loose as they dry. Jack's inherited Mum's big eyes and narrow face, while I take after Dad; I'm stocky, with a biggish nose. Jamie seems to be more of a cross between the two of them, although he got the nose too. I don't mind it; I reckon it gives us character. I do kind of wish I wasn't the only one who got the short-arse gene from Nana though.

Me and Jack help Mum and Dad bring the spag bol over to the table, then Mum looks at Deal and says, 'Budge round, Mason. Derek needs to stretch his legs.' She says it lightly, but I know she means it.

Deal was mid-flow about something to do with politics – I've already caught the words 'globalisation' and 'capitalism' and a load of other 'isms' – Jamie listening intently and nodding away like he's taking mental notes, but he moves over. I lever my legs into the rickety garden chair we've squeezed in on the other side, elbow to elbow with Jack.

I'm so hungry I concentrate on shovelling in my food and I'm already halfway through my spaghetti and on my third slice of garlic bread when I realise Jamie and Deal are talking about this buyout thing again.

'They bought up another estate near Newcastle a few months ago. Tripled the rents overnight. A few months down the line, everyone was out,' Deal says. He's got a piece of garlic bread in his hand, which he waves in the air.

'That'll be us, if it goes through,' Jamie says, nodding a few times.

'Jamie.' Mum flicks her eyes to Jack and then back to Jamie, but he doesn't back down this time. Instead he's clenching his fork, his face getting flushed. I stop reaching for another slice of bread; my appetite's evaporated.

'You think you're doing the right thing by pretending none of this is going to happen? He's better off knowing what's coming,' Jamie says. Deal gives a nod of approval.

Dad bangs the flat of his hand down on the table, which makes everyone jump, and now I definitely don't feel hungry any more.

'Will you stop bloody well going on about this bloody company, Jamie,' Dad roars.

Jack is giving Mum an anxious glance, but for once she doesn't say anything about the swearing; she just sits there, her lips pressed together the way they get when she's extra worried about money or something.

Then Jamie stands up. When he speaks, I'm surprised at how rough his voice is. 'You carry on then, pretending everything's fine, spouting all that crap about being "rich in love",' – he does this horrible high-pitched voice as he says it – 'when we all know it's a load of bollocks.'

'Jamie!' Mum's voice is shocked.

'You're out of order,' Dad says.

'Whatever.' Jamie stalks out of the room.

No one says anything for a minute, then Deal says, 'He's a bit stressed out. I can see you guys need to think about it though.' His voice is soothing, sympathetic. Then he adds, 'Thanks for dinner.' He disappears from the room.

Yeah, and who's got Jamie this stressed out? I think, watching the silent looks being exchanged between my parents. Jack has a million questions in his eyes and his mouth firmly shut, like me. I never chimed in like I usually would because I don't have the first clue who's in the right any more.

There's yoghurt for pudding, but I don't bother; I'm too busy thinking. I offer to wash up with Mum while Dad goes to watch telly and Jack knocks for Dylan. Jamie and Deal have already gone out. Mum runs some water into the washing-up liquid bottle to get the dregs out, then boils the kettle because we're out of hot water.

I think about how angry Jamie is, how he says things aren't fair. About the letter for Jack's school trip we can't afford, even with seven months' notice, and how I bet someone like Annabel doesn't need to know the price of bog roll and milk down to the last penny. In fact, if I had any cash, I'd be putting it on her never having to go down the supermarket anyway, what with the fact her parents seem to have *staff*.

But I can also see Mum and Dad's perspective. I mean, what's the point in always looking at what everyone else wants and wishing you had it? That never stops, does it? Someone's always going to have a bigger house or a better car or whatever. And I always used to like the 'rich in love' thing. Nope, best not 'make waves' or 'stick your head above the parapet' or any of the other million sayings my parents have.

Except … love gets hard when you're skint and worried all the time. It gets to be that you're too tired, like how Mum and Dad don't seem to hold hands so much these days, or bump hips as they're cooking together in the kitchen. I think about how we don't go up on the Downs any more, or play board games on a rainy Saturday afternoon all together, because someone's always working.

As I start to dry the plates, I think again about how that little light went out in Jack's eyes earlier, and at what point he won't even have the light there in the first place.

I put the plate down and get the letter out of the kitchen drawer.

'Jack got this from school,' I say, waving it under Mum's nose. She squints at it, suds dripping from her fingers, and sighs, but before she can speak I say in a rush, 'I could help out with Jack's trip. I've got some cash saved from the library. The first instalment's only sixty quid, look.'

Mum rinses another plate and puts it with a measured movement on to the draining board. Then she turns eyes that are red rimmed with tiredness to me. 'I know, love, but what about the one after and the one after that? I can't let you use your money for this, I'm sorry. It's kind of you to offer.'

'But I don't mind –'

'No, Joni.'

The way she says it, I know the topic's closed, but in bed that night, I make up my mind to see if I can find a way to send Jack anyway. He's always so good-natured, he never complains. And I know how much he'd love it.

No, I don't care what Mum says, Jack's going.

I'll make it happen.

All week at school, I'm thinking up ways to raise money. The obvious one would be to get more work in, but I know there's no more hours going in the library and even if there were, a job pretty much anywhere else would pay more. Maybe I can take on some waitressing in the evenings. I say this to Kelly, sitting in the refectory with a plate of chips in front of me one lunchtime.

She looks doubtful. 'Mate, you've got all that catching up to do in History. Plus you already work at the library. You've got to have some time to chill.'

'Yeah, well, I'll manage. I'm more worried about whether there's any jobs going anywhere.'

Kelly opens her mouth to say more, then seems to think better of it. Instead she swipes a chip from my plate and says, 'I've got a gig booked in a couple of weeks. They're paying me too. Fifty quid.'

Mum reckons Kelly's voice is like a young Joni Mitchell. She should know, seeing as Joni Mitchell is one of her all-time favourites and the reason I've got my name. But despite all her usual confidence, Kelly always needs a hand hold at gigs, at least until she gets going.

'Awesome. I'll be there.' I say.

A moment later, Pete comes over. Kelly immediately turns to him. 'You coming to my gig?'

'Definitely!' Pete's voice is so eager, it hurts. Then he adds in this casual tone, 'Do you mind if I bring Ananya?'

I blink. Ananya Pillai is in Pete's Drama class. She's the polar opposite of Pete: loud, self-confident, beautiful. Kelly jumps up. 'Better get going. Psychology.' She rolls her eyes, but I know she loves it really.

It's just me and Pete left at the table now. 'So … Ananya, *huh*?' I say.

Pete shrugs. 'No point hanging around waiting for something that's never going to happen,' he says.

I wonder if he really does like Ananya or if he'll be hung up on Kelly forever. Ananya doesn't strike me as the type who's going to put up with any crap though, so I just say, 'Well, good for you. Chip?'

He takes one off me and as he does I can't help wondering when life got so complicated. Sometimes it feels like yesterday we were all in juniors together, playing games of Bulldog on the field when the teachers weren't looking. Now everyone's in couples, or aiming to be, thinking about uni and moving away. Worrying about cash if you're me. It all seems to be going so fast.

I guess sometimes I wish the most important part of the day was still those playtimes, running and shouting, the playground hot under our feet and our futures not even thought of yet.

CHAPTER NINE

'You're here, marvellous. Annabel was telling me about a wonderful idea she's had.' Mrs H is practically wetting herself the second I come through the library doors. I meet Annabel's eyes and give a faint smile. I haven't forgotten our argument, but at the same time she did text and I guess we need to draw a line, as Mum would say.

'What's that then?' I say.

Annabel pushes back her hair, which she's wearing down today in stacks of blonde waves, and says, 'Well, it's nearly Easter so I thought, we could do an Easter egg hunt for the toddler group. And anyone else who would like to join in.'

'Sounds good.'

The expression on her face tells me she wasn't expecting me to think it was anything other than a good idea, but it seems that was only the warm-up. 'Perfect. We'll get a costume so the children can have a visit from the Easter bunny. And make Easter bonnets Then we'll play some games – I thought musical chairs – and hand out Easter eggs as prizes.'

'You've got it all planned out,' I say, trying to keep my voice light. Mrs H beams at Annabel. Then a thought strikes me. 'Hang on,' I give them both a suspicious look. 'Who's wearing the costume?'

Mrs H looks at me. 'Well, I thought you might like –'

'I will!' Annabel says brightly.

'Too bloody right.' Mrs H's mouth falls open, but Annabel smiles at me, a proper full smile with a hint of something else underneath it.

'Well, I do think you'd look lovely in bunny ears, but as it was my idea …'

Something goes wrong with my face; it's like I'm frozen on the outside while inside everything seems to shift. I pull my eyes away from hers, not even listening properly to what Mrs H is now saying, while my brain goes into overdrive.

Do I fancy Annabel?

No.

No way.

Definitely not.

That would be totally stupid.

'… Well, if Joni doesn't mind?'

They're both looking at me.

'Uh, yeah, OK,' I say.

'Really?' Annabel asks.

'Course!' I try and make my face upbeat.

Mrs H brings her hands together in a short clap. 'You really think you can manage to get two costumes at this short notice, Annabel?' she says.

Hang on, what?

'Yes, it won't be any trouble at all.' Annabel gives me a look, suddenly full of mischief, and I realise she knows I wasn't listening.

'Two Easter bunnies! The children will love it,' Mrs H says.

Annabel's smile is conspiratorial.

Oh bollocks.

A week later, I'm in the toilets pulling on a giant bunny costume over my jeans and swearing as I get the tail caught. This is officially the dumbest thing I've ever done. I shove the ears on my head and trudge out, not bothering to look at myself in the mirror first.

'Would you like me to do you up?' How does Annabel look good in a fricking bunny costume? I guess it helps she's knocking on five foot ten or eleven, while I'm about as round in this costume as I am tall.

She goes around the back of me before I answer and I feel the pressure of her hand on my lower back, then moving up with the zip. Her fingers are cool for a second on the nape of my neck and then they're gone. As I turn around I tell myself that my red face is because it's already hot in the suit.

'I was right.' Annabel grins at me.

'What's that?'

'You do look cute in bunny ears.'

My mind circles the word 'cute' several times and I go redder. So as not to let on, I make my face grumpy and say, 'How long till the bratlings arrive? I'm boiling in this.'

Annabel laughs. 'Not very long, Thumper.'

I look down at myself and wonder if she ordered a costume for me in pink on purpose. I generally stay away from the girly end of the spectrum – not that I have anything against pink, mind, it's just not really me.

Annabel rearranges her bunny ears on top of her head and gestures to some brushes and boxes of stuff on the desk. 'Would you help me with the face paint?'

'Uh, yeah … I'm not that good.'

'I'm sure you'll be fine,' she says, handing me a brush. I sit in front of her and attempt to colour in her nose and give her some whiskers. At first, I try and keep an arm's length away, but I have to lean in closer to do the whiskers, trying to keep my focus on the brush and not on her eyes, or her mouth …

I cough and sit back. 'There you go. Told you I wasn't exactly a dab hand at the face paints.'

Annabel examines herself in a little mirror and smiles. 'Perfect. Now it's your turn.'

'Nah, you're all right.'

'I insist! At least have some whiskers.' She loads the brush with black and uses one hand to push my shoulder so I'm sitting back in the chair, then leans in so close I can feel her breath tickling my cheek. Then there's the cold shock of the face paint sweeping my cheek three times one side and again on the other, and finally some dots around my nose. I notice with a sudden sense of something softening inside, that Annabel sticks her tongue in her cheek when she's concentrating, like Jack.

'There,' she says, and she smiles at me again.

I swallow, pushing down the feelings that are definitely swirling as she holds my eyes, and say, 'Yep. We both look like muppets now.'

I regret it as soon as it's out of my mouth, but Annabel chooses to ignore this and carries on smiling.

A moment later there's a screech and I realise the first of the hordes are here.

Annabel has already stood up and I wonder how come she's so confident – where does she get it all from? Then I spot her straighten her shoulders, before turning to me with a smile that's gone both wider and more fake. 'Well then. Shall we go?'

I realise suddenly that's she's doing that 'fake it till you make it' thing Kelly's always banging on about, that she's doing it so well perhaps no one ever sees it.

But I do.

I see.

'Well!' Annabel lets out a long sigh and takes her bunny ears off as the last kid goes through the double doors clutching a basket of eggs and the Easter card he's made. 'That went well, don't you think?'

'It was super!' Mrs H comes bustling down the hall, having seen the kids off the premises. 'Well done, Annabel! You put together a fantastic event at short notice and everyone had such a lovely time. I knew you would be an asset to the library. I must drop your father a line to let him know ...'

'No need for that,' Annabel smiles, but her voice sounds strained. 'And Joni did a wonderful job too.'

'*Hmm*? Oh yes, well done, Joni,' Mrs H adds, then wanders off to start clearing away the debris scattered about the place.

I'm too hot and knackered to be that bothered, but Annabel's biting her lip, and for the first time, I feel a wave of something come over me, like I want to make things OK for her.

'Don't worry about Mrs H, she's just excited. And you do organise a killer game of Duck, Duck, Goose,' I say. I lift one hand up, thinking I might pat her shoulder or something, then chicken out and use it to lift my bunny ears off instead. 'Uh … I'm gonna go get out of this.'

She unzips me before I get the chance to say anything, and I scarper to the toilet to take the suit off. I could've changed out there; I've got jeans and a vest top on, but I didn't fancy the idea of wriggling in and out of a bunny costume with Annabel looking on. It seems … undignified or something.

I check my hair in the mirror and push at a bit that's sticking out from the bunny ears. I like it short; less hassle and most days I shove some wax in it and leave it at that, but now I spend a few minutes fussing, trying to make it do what I want, before I give up and go back out, the bunny costume folded up in my arms.

Mrs H says from behind the desk, 'Annabel's putting her costume in her car,' so I take mine outside.

'Here you go.' As I hand her my costume, I get a waft of perfume, sweet but with something underneath that's almost like aftershave. It smells exotic, whatever it is.

Annabel closes the car boot and takes a deep breath; the sun's out but the air is clear and sharp and I realise she's breathing it in like I do. She gazes at the dark edge where the tip of the Downs meets the sky, then turns her head to me. 'It's so beautiful. I used to take Puzzle on to the Downs all the time, before –' She breaks off.

'I know, it's like you're at the top of the world, with the sky right there at your fingertips,' I say.

I'm embarrassed as soon as I say it, but Annabel replies, her eyes bright, 'Yes! That's exactly it.' So I let myself carry on talking to her, like I would to anyone else, no checking what I'm saying first. 'You ever read *The Lord of the Rings*? There's this clump of trees that always reminds me of the first bit where they're travelling out of the Shire. When I was little I used to imagine I was one of the hobbits hiding from the black riders.' Her eyes brighten like she recognises something and is pleased. Then they seem to darken again.

'I don't go any more.'

'Why not?'

'Well, when Puzzle … went … there didn't seem much point, I suppose. But I do miss it.'

I don't know what possesses me to say the next thing. Perhaps it's because I've never really seen her look all sad and faraway like that. But I find myself saying, 'We could go together sometime, if you like?'

'Really?' A big smile comes over her face. 'That would be perfect!'

I smile at how she says 'perfect', but not in a horrible way. I've started to get used to the way she talks. A little bit anyway.

She hesitates for a second, then says, 'We could go today after we finish here?'

I feel my eyebrows go up and she says in a rush, 'It's only … it's a lovely day isn't it? Perfect for April. But I imagine you have things to do so …' She gives another one of those laughs like she's not bothered and I get the same sense I did before the kids arrived, like she's putting on an act when there's a whole other Annabel underneath that no one knows about. She's already starting to move away, when I find myself saying, 'Why not?'

She stops and this time the smile on her face is wide and genuine, like something's lit up inside her. 'Super! Why don't we finish early and dash to Waitrose first? We could have a picnic.'

I'm about to say it's not likely Mrs H is going to let us go early, when I realise if Annabel asks she probably will. Annabel looks so eager it's hard to feel annoyed about this, so instead I shut up the part of me that's wondering whether I'm mad, and Jamie's warning to keep my distance, and smile back. 'OK. That'll be … super.'

CHAPTER TEN

Annabel parks over the line again at the Waitrose car park, but doesn't seem to notice. I know it's right on the edge of my town, but I've never actually been in here, not that I'm about to let on to Annabel. Still, I can't help my gaze darting about as we go in, past a row of trees and picnic benches. Inside, everything feels bright and fresh, people ambling down the wide aisles. It's a different world from Lidl's bright yellow tills, cramped shelves and handwritten fluorescent offer stickers. And it's huge. There's about ten different types of cat food for God's sake, unlike Lidl where your choice is basically Coshida or Coshida, and what seems like an entire aisle of bagged salads. I tail Annabel as she lobs stuff into a basket without checking the price. She wanders over to the bakery section, which smells so good it's making my stomach rumble, and picks up a fresh loaf.

'Shall we have some cheese with this?' she says.

'Sure,' I say.

In the cheese aisle, Annabel says, 'What do you like?' I glance at the shelves. There's a whole section just for Cheddar, plus other packets I recognise like Dairylea and mini Babybels. Jack loves those so I sometimes pick some up if they're on offer, though I reckon he likes unwrapping the red bit more than eating the actual cheese. But I bet Annabel doesn't mean for us to get plain old Cheddar. I see with a sinking feeling that she's looking at a row of cheeses I don't recognise. I hesitate, then grab a wedge of something speckled with blue – posh people like all those weird mouldy type cheeses, don't they? I hand it to her and her eyebrows raise a fraction, then she says, 'Perfect.' As she turns towards the drinks aisle – if the size of the wine section is anything to go by, Waitrose shoppers are serious boozers – I start inwardly cursing myself, because now I'm going to have to eat the stuff.

Annabel insists on this pink lemonade that's £2.79 for a tiny bottle, as well as smoked salmon and a stack of other stuff.

We join a queue behind a woman who's taking her time packing everything just so into her bags. The girl at the checkout scans super slow and helps her to pack. There is no way this would happen in my world; there'd be a line of people glaring and tutting, and a massive pile-up as the checkout person whizzed it all through. You don't even pack at the till anyway in Lidl, you sweep it all in your trolley and use the bench to shove it in bags, which I guess is faster but kind of more work when you think about it.

The conveyor belt inches forward. Eventually, there's enough room for our stuff and I help Annabel unload the basket.

It seems like a lot. I say in a jokey voice, 'How much do you think I eat?'

'Oh!' she looks horrified. 'I thought … well, it's only a few bits and pieces.'

The total says otherwise; she spends over thirty quid, but when I offer to pay half she pretends she hasn't heard me, and shoves it on a card. I insist on grabbing the heaviest carrier off her though. She stops to pick up a free newspaper – oh yeah, you get a free paper – and slides that into her bag.

If I came here every week, I reckon I'd probably actually enjoy doing the food shopping.

On the way out, Annabel clocks a girl and woman coming towards us. She immediately does this weird flip thing into Confident Annabel. I could swear she gets taller.

'Annabel!' the woman exclaims and they do this air-kiss thing on both cheeks. 'Wonderful to see you. I was only saying to Charlotte the other day, we hardly hear from you now.' She wanders off towards the wine.

Charlotte's staring at me and Annabel. I'm pretty sure there's some sort of calculation going on in her brain, and whatever it is it's not good. Annabel says, 'This is Joni. From the library.'

'Oh. The library. Lovely,' Charlotte says.

Annabel flushes slightly, and her smile gets wider.

It's amazing how much meaning you can pack into one word.

Annabel's quiet as we drive. It's not until we've walked up a sloping track and found a big boulder to sit on that I ask the obvious question.

'I take it she's not your friend? That Charlotte girl?'

Annabel pauses from unwrapping the bread, and looks at me. 'I suppose … no, not especially.' She gazes out to where the sun is starting to get lower in the sky. 'We used to be. We were both boarders at prep school, we went through it all together. You know – homesickness.' She gives a light laugh. 'That sort of thing. Silly, really.'

'So when did she stop being your mate?'

'When we started at Edrington's, I suppose.'

I stare at her, a question in my eyes, and she shrugs and smiles. 'Edrington's not the same as prep school. Larger, you know. And boys of course, which always seems to be the main topic of conversation. You know, who fancies who? Charlotte's been crazy about Ollie since we started and I've never really been as interested in –' She breaks off.

I wait to see if she says anything else, brain whirring, but when she doesn't I ask, 'So she ditched you then?'

'Something like that. I try to keep up, but sometimes it's like everyone but me is talking in Russian, so a while ago I decided I needed to try to be more … well, to fit in. You see …' She glances at me and I see her decide against something and her posture changes. 'Then we got caught – smoking – by Miss Schiel, the headmistress. She wrote to our parents.' Annabel shudders.

I wait, confused, then say, 'Is that it? Not exactly hard drugs, is it?'

'That's not how Daddy saw it.' Annabel rolls her eyes and laughs like she's expecting me to join in, but I don't because her eyes are not matching her smiling mouth.

Instead, I take a punt. 'That why he's making you work in the library?'

'Yes, in part, although there were other reasons. He hasn't been happy since my GCSE results. I got a B in French – I still don't think he's over it. That's why I was surprised at your A Levels. I can't imagine taking French.'

Oh. I flash back to the argument on the wall. Then I say, 'So you got caught smoking and you got a B in French. Not really the crimes of a century. Bet you got A stars in everything else, didn't you?'

'Some As.' She smiles.

'And that's it?'

'Well, volunteering will be good for university applications, I suppose. And I got the sense Daddy wants me there for another reason, but I don't really ... well. Who knows?' She's trying to keep it light-hearted, but there's something desolate about her voice.

So I say in a teasing way, 'The library's not that bad, is it?'

She blinks, then says, 'No, it's not.' Her eyes seem soft as she looks at me.

I go red. Then a gust of wind makes her shiver. 'You want my jumper?' I say.

Annabel smiles. 'I'm not sure it would fit.'

'I don't know, it would definitely go around you – might be a bit short though,' I say.

The way we're sitting, her knee is almost but not quite touching mine. She passes me some bread and then opens the dreaded blue cheese. Oh Christ. I cut a tiny lump and take a bite.

It's not good. I chew as fast as I can, the taste of it bitter and overpowering, then take a long swig of lemonade to wash it down, hoping she hasn't noticed.

'You want some?' I say.

'*Urgh* no, can't stand the stuff. I've never understood eating mould,' she says and pulls a face.

'Oh. I thought you liked it,' I say.

She gives me a look like I'm crazy, then with something approaching understanding, she shakes her head.

For a second I'm teetering on the edge of humiliation, then I decide there's nothing for it but to style it out. 'Thank God for that – it's rank,' I say.

We both burst out laughing, then Annabel stands up, pulls the cheese from its wrapper and lobs it really hard down the hill. We watch it bounce a couple of times, then come to a rest next to a boulder.

'There. The sheep can have it,' she says. 'Or do you think it's poisonous?' She goes to stand up. 'Perhaps I ought to get it back?'

I put my hand on her arm to pull her back down. 'Relax. They probably won't eat it anyway, if they've got any sense.'

Annabel looks at my hand still on her arm. I pull away, but not before I see her go pink, then she grabs the nearest thing to her. 'Smoked salmon?' Annabel holds the packet out to me. It doesn't look massively appealing, sitting there all wet and shining in the sun, and maybe it's the cheese, but I feel OK saying, 'I've never actually had it. I'm a veggie anyway.'

'Really?' Annabel chucks the opened packet back into the bag and I frown. The price on the front said £4.99.

'You can have some though, I don't mind.'

Annabel shrugs and crumbles off a little piece of bread.

It's right at the edge of my tongue, to tell her what a waste of cash that is, but then I take in a great breath of fresh air and try to let it go. After a moment, Annabel says, 'Do you come up here often?'

Kelly's voice roars in my head, '*Mate, that's a total line, oh my* GOD*!*'

For a minute nothing comes out of my mouth. I can't read the expression on Annabel's face. In the end I swallow hard and then make my voice as casual as I can. 'Used to. My dad liked watching the birds. We'd come up here for picnics and stuff and he'd teach us all their calls. Before his back got all knackered.'

Before he got too tired, too stressed out. Stopped trying to find the beautiful bits to life. I realise suddenly that these days, Dad's more likely to say 'you can't eat the scenery' than point out a rare bird, and it makes me sad.

'It's been such a long time since I came here. It's lovely, isn't it, Joni?' Annabel says.

Her accent makes the 'o' in my name long. It sounds all right actually. And there's something about the way she's looking at me …

I shove a massive chunk of bread into my mouth. I'm imagining things. Definitely. When I look up, Annabel's staring at me. 'What?' I say, my mouth still full.

'Nothing … It's only … you really enjoy your food,' she says.

For a second I think she's saying I'm fat, and it's kind of true. Well, a bit cuddly. I'm not a size ten, let's say that, but Annabel can't be more than an eight at a push.

She looks like she's thinking the same thing. 'I didn't mean … I like it. I wish I was more … I find it hard to relax when I eat sometimes. Everyone at Edrington's on a diet. The other day a group of boys made Simran in my year cry, because they said she had chunky thighs. She doesn't, not that it would matter – she's gorgeous. But everyone's always watching everyone else.'

'Stuff that,' I say and hand her a pastry. 'Way I see it, food's there to enjoy, right? We're only here for that long,' I hold up two fingers close together.

'The girls at school don't see it that way.'

'What, like that Charlotte girl? Screw 'em.'

'Easy to say, harder to do when it's always been like that,' Annabel points out. Her eyes tighten at the edges. 'You know, school's not always … I mean, I know what a privilege it is, I do. Daddy tells me all the time they're spending a fortune on my education …'

I feel a sudden flare of jealousy. I've walked past the gates to her posh school so many times. Pete's even been in once or twice when they do outreach type stuff. They have their own proper theatre, a swimming pool, state of the art design studios. Everything is red brick and old and beautiful. Then I think about my school, the mobile buildings they put on the field because there was nowhere else for them to go, and the tiny hall where we used to squeeze in for assembly.

But Annabel's still talking as if the wind up here's freed something in her, like it does for me. 'There's all these expectations, that you will do something incredible, but it doesn't actually matter if you do, because someone else is always more extraordinary than you. Prize-giving is a nightmare. I suppose it can make you feel … trapped.' She pulls her knees up to her chest and shoots me a look like she thinks I might laugh, or argue with her. I could do. I think about saying, 'You try being skint all the time and see what being trapped really feels like.' But I can't summon it.

Annabel tips her chin up, so she's speaking to the clouds. 'And it's so tiring. The days go on forever with activities and prep.'

I tip my head to one side. 'Yeah?' I say, trying not to let her see I'm annoyed.

'Well, I suppose it's not as bad now I'm a day girl, but sometimes I feel like I've been exhausted since I was eight.' She glances quickly at me, then away again. 'I've never really talked about this before. Sorry.'

'No, I don't mind listening. It's interesting.' It is really, even if it's also kind of annoying she doesn't get how lucky she is.

'Well ...' She takes a breath and I can see suddenly how big a deal this is for her, like it's been chipping away at her for just about forever. 'School is so overwhelming. Then at home ... I get in and the house is empty. When my parents do come back, we'll have supper and they might quiz me about my day – but it's always what score I got in a test and if I didn't come first, where do I need to work harder, that sort of thing – and then I feel crowded again, like at school.' She holds up her hands. 'I don't know, it's ridiculous really. I seem to spend my time wanting space, but then when I get it ...' She trails off again, like she's trying to work it all out in her mind.

I'm so tempted to say something to fill up the silence, and, if I'm honest, there's still a part of me that thinks she's complaining her designer handbag's too heavy or something, but I don't. I wait.

'Sometimes ... no, that's not true. A lot of the time I feel ... it gets ...' She swallows, like she's pushing it all back down, and tries to smile.

'Lonely?' I remember Mrs H saying Annabel's not happy, and I'm starting to get why.

She nods and even though I know it's mad, I reach across the gap between us and touch her hand.

'It doesn't have to be that way,' I say.

Her hand is cold, but as I'm about to move, she curls her fingers up, so that they're squeezing mine.

We sit like that for a long moment before I come to my senses and gently ease my own hand away.

Cycling home, my hand feels hot and tingly where Annabel held it. There's a little voice inside telling me this is a bad idea, that I'm on the edge of something I don't want to get into, but I tell it to pipe down and pedal harder.

When I get in, the house has this strange sort of quiet to it. I go into the living room and can see by Dad's face something's up. Mum's sat next to him, holding a cup of tea.

'All right?' I say, but my voice has a prickle of anxiety in it.

Mum shakes her head. 'Your dad's had a bit of bad news about his work.'

Oh crap. I take a breath and hold it in.

Dad looks up. 'They're shutting down the warehouse. Moving everything to the other branch. We're all out of work from next week.'

Dammit, dammit, dammit.

I swallow hard. 'Next week?'

Mum pats Dad's hand. 'It's all right, love, we'll make do.'

I feel a sudden urge to cry. How will we make do? Even with mine and Jamie's wages as well as Mum's, it's going to be tight. I've got to find another job. I go over to give Dad a careful hug, and he grips me back extra hard.

'Don't worry, Dad, we'll get it sorted. You can always sign on until something else comes along, can't he, Mum?'

'Your tea's in the oven, love,' Mum says.

'Oh right, thanks, I – thanks.' I'm not sure now is the time to tell them I've just been scoffing a posh picnic with Annabel. 'Where's Jack?'

'In his room,' Mum says.

I speak without really thinking. 'Jack could get a job, a paper round or something?' It isn't that crazy an idea. I've had Saturday jobs since I was thirteen. And Jack's twelve now.

'Joni, not now,' Mum says.

'But –'

'Not now!' Dad's voice comes out in a roar that makes me jump. He pushes himself up, wincing, one hand on his back. 'I'm going down The Crown,' he says. Mum scurries after him and I hear her voice, low and wobbling, then him replying, 'I'll be back at ten, Marian.'

The front door slams.

Mum comes back in. 'You've upset your dad.'

'Sorry.'

Mum's eyes are too bright, her throat working. I shouldn't have said that, about Jack. But when I open my mouth to say sorry again, Mum shakes her head. We watch some nature documentary in silence, side by side on the sofa.

Much later, awake in bed, I finally hear the front door go, then the smell of cigarette smoke floating up from the kitchen. Mum and Dad's voices start quiet, but get louder, rising, then falling again when they remember we're all supposed to be asleep upstairs.

My door opens and Jack comes in.

'You all right?' I say.

In response, he climbs into bed next to me and I shove over against the cold radiator. I put my arm around his shoulders and we sit there, listening to the sound of arguing.

'What's going to happen?' Jack says.

'Nothing, don't worry. They're just a bit stressed out, money and all that. It'll be fine tomorrow.'

It always is, one way or another. Mum and Dad haven't had a row in such a long time. They only argue when money's tight, when worry forces itself out in an explosion, like an overinflated balloon. I get it. Doesn't mean I'm not scared though.

Eventually, we hear the living-room door thud and then Mum's tread on the stairs and Mum and Dad's bedroom door opening and closing. Guess this means Dad's on the sofa tonight. Before Jack tiptoes back to his bed, I tell him again it's all going to be fine, but after he's gone, I can't help lying there and wondering whether this will finally be the time when it's not.

In the morning, it's like nothing's happened. Dad must've shifted off the sofa in the middle of the night, because there's no sign he's slept there. Mum is already up, speaking on the phone.

'Can I pay twenty?' she says, her face pinched-looking. 'No, I can't manage that ... OK, twenty-five.' A moment later her face eases into relief. She reads out her card details and hangs up, then turns to me. 'Morning,' she says, overly cheery.

I raise my eyebrows and she says, 'BT. I'll pay the rest next week,' with a don't-tell-your-father look. Looks like we won't be getting broadband back for a bit. I take the free paper to the table with a coffee. A quick scan shows nothing doing except those work from home adverts everyone knows are a total con. I push it to one side, meeting Mum's eyes, then looking away before I can clock the disappointment in them. She hasn't had a text from work about doing any overtime today.

I still feel sick at school the next day and it's not helped by Miss Hills, my new English tutor, giving us a load of extra work, to catch up on what we missed when our teachers kept changing about.

There are only two bright spots in the week: I get a call from this new cleaning company saying they might have some evening work for me for a few weeks, and Annabel, who sends a couple of texts. Nothing things really, just asking how my week's going, a couple of library related questions that could've waited until we're next in together, but it feels nice seeing her name pop up on my phone.

I get to the library extra early on Saturday so I can sort out this homework Miss Hills wants – a comparative piece on language in tabloid and broadsheet newspapers. If I look online I won't have to pay to buy them. I bring up the *Guardian* and start scanning the headlines, but it's hard to concentrate because my mind keeps going back to Dad's work and whether we can pay the rent. Annabel's voice close beside me makes me jump.

'I didn't know you read the *Guardian*. Daddy hates it, says it's a leftie rag.' She gives this affectionate smile as she says it.

She's got on cropped trousers that make her legs look a million miles long today. And I might be getting used to the way she talks, but I don't think I'll ever think it's not weird that she still calls her parents Mummy and Daddy.

'Homework,' I say, and click the screen closed.

Annabel pulls a face. 'I have so much prep to do it's a wonder I'm getting any sleep at all.'

I realise I've never asked her what subjects she's doing. And that I want to know things about her. 'So what are your A Levels? Not French obviously,' I say.

'Maths, Further Maths, Chemistry and Physics.'

I gape at her. 'Bloody hell. I didn't know you were into Science and Maths stuff.'

'I'm not especially,' she says in an airy voice, but before I can ask why she's taking them, Mrs H comes in. There never seems to be the right opportunity for the rest of the day, so I just have to wonder.

I'm supposed to be going to Kelly's gig with the gang later on this evening. Mrs H starts complaining of a sore head and goes home ten minutes early, leaving me and Annabel to lock up. As we close the doors, I have a mad second where I wonder whether or not to invite Annabel along, but I can't picture her shooting pool and joking about with the gang, especially not Kelly, who'd be digging like mad for info or making a load of sketchy double entendres. It would be way too weird all round.

Annabel watches me pocket the keys and unchain my bike, not that anyone's likely to nick it, but still. I catch her looking at the rust and turn away to sling my leg over the saddle.

'Too big for me really, but I like it anyway, especially cos I get to be up high ...' I trail off, sure definite pity is showing on her face now. 'Right then. I'm off.' I get one foot on the pedal.

'Joni?'

'Yeah?'

'I thought ... would you like to do something tonight? With me?'

I blink. She flushes and then says, 'I thought we could go out to eat? Only if you'd like to,' she adds quickly.

I think again about asking her to come and see Kelly, but decide against it. 'I've got a thing on tonight.'

Her face falls slightly, then she shrugs. 'Oh well, perhaps next week?'

'Yeah, sure.' I'm about to push off when I stop and out of curiosity say, 'Like where were you thinking of going?'

She looks unusually flustered for a moment. I can practically see her spooling through places in her mind and she gets the same look, like she's thinking what I did about taking her to the pub. That I'm a bit of puzzle that will never fit.

'I'll see you next week, all right?' I start to push off.

'Wait!'

I wobble and tip the bike to one side so I can get my foot to the floor.

'What about ... would you like to have supper with me? At home?'

'Come to your house?'

She nods. 'My parents are away next week and Mary will stay out of our way.'

'For ... "supper"?' I say.

To me, supper means a bit of cereal or something before bed, but I reckon she means come for tea. This is definitely a mad idea. I can tell she's biting the inside of her cheek by the way one of her dimples folds into a crease. As for me, without me wanting it to, a smile has started somewhere near the balls of my feet and pushes its way up, until it's shining out through my eyes.

'All right then.'

Annabel brings her hands together and she looks so pleased I can't help laughing. 'Fantastic! I'll cook. Something vegetarian. Is there anything you don't eat?'

'Other than meat, I'll eat pretty much anything,' I say. 'Except mouldy cheese.'

Annabel laughs. 'Next week then,' she says, and there's something in her smile that makes my stomach clench. I pedal away, feeling her eyes on me as I go.

Later, I'm in the pub waiting for Kelly's set. The gang are all here, plus Ananya and few of the other Drama lot from school. Kelly sits next to me, gabbling extra loud the way she does when she's nervous.

'God, I wish I had more than Coke in this glass. Or a different sort of coke, haha. Not really, obvs. Shouldn't be drinking this anyway, I'll need a wee as soon as I get on stage.' She gulps back the last of her drink and turns wide eyes on me. 'I'm sweating bullets here. God, why do I do this to myself?'

'You'll be fine.' I pat her hand, which is definitely on the clammy side, but as soon as she goes on she's more than fine. She sings a short set of covers, accompanying herself on a keyboard. I've asked her before whether she ever wants to write her own stuff, but she laughed and said, 'I just like the singing. Glad Mum made me take all those piano lessons though.' I sit back, listening to the music and her amazing voice, remembering how Kelly made me do all these singing and dancing routines in her front room when we were little. She'd insist on us dressing up with glitter eyeshadow layered right up to the eyebrows and way too much lipstick and T-shirts tied in knots at the front to show off our bellies. She was desperate to be on *The X Factor*, back when it was a thing. I can't believe it's actually been going since we were in infants.

Kelly's just finished her latest song, a cover of 'Chandelier' that sounds really good with the keyboard. I think she's done, but then she leans into the microphone and says, 'For my last song, I have a helper today.'

To my surprise, Pete gets up from our table and walks to the space at the front. He sits on a stool next to Kelly, looking grey in the face, but determined. Then they start to sing 'True Colors'.

'Oh my God!' There's a massive grin on my face. I love this song. They work it perfectly, the harmonies and the keyboard going together just right. When they finish, I've got tears starting in my eyes and the whole pub erupts into applause and cheers.

I rush up to them. Pete's looking a little shell-shocked, while Kelly's beaming. 'I can't believe you never said!' I yell over the noise of the landlord announcing the next act, then lob my arms around Kelly and squeeze her tight.

'I know. I was dying to tell you, but Pete wanted to keep it a secret. We've been practising first thing …' Kelly stops because Ananya has come up.

'You were a-ma-zing,' she shrieks, drawing the word out. Then she throws her arms around Pete's neck and kisses him. I look at Kelly, smiling in an '*aw*, look at them' kind of way, but to my surprise she turns quickly back to her keyboard and starts taking the leads out, ready to pack away. *Huh*.

I help her with the keyboard out to Ed's car. Kelly's oddly quiet; usually she's buzzing after a gig. I open my mouth to ask what's up, but she gives me a look that says she doesn't want to talk about it. Then she says, 'How's you then?'

This would be the perfect time to tell her about going to Annabel's house, or that we went up the Downs together the other week, but for some reason I just say, 'Nothing to report.' I can't help giving her a significant look and adding, 'You?' But she simply shrugs and says, 'Ditto.'

The night carries on and we have a laugh like always, but underneath it is a new current passing between me and Kells, both of us thinking about other people, but neither of us saying a word. It feels strange.

CHAPTER ELEVEN

The following week I stop outside the gates to Annabel's place to catch my breath. She said I'd have to ring an intercom and I spot it to one side, but don't press the button just yet. First I try peering over the wall, but it's too high. Gates are solid too, no chance of anyone peeping in. All I can see are the tops of trees. I push my hand through my hair, rub my palms on my jeans. Get my phone out to check the time.

I'm early. I faff about, texting Kelly back to say I'm not coming out tonight. I don't say where I'm going though. I let out a massive yawn. A big part of me wanted to cancel tonight, because I'm knackered what with starting the new cleaning job this week. Mum's not happy, but it's six pounds an hour cash in hand so that's something. Hopefully it'll be enough for Jack's trip.

I put the camera on to selfie mode to check my hair, which is mad as always. I scrunch my fingers through it again, then wonder what on earth I'm doing.

I pick up my bike, sling one leg over, then get off again.

Stuff it.

I march back to the intercom and press down hard, before I can change my mind.

A moment later, Annabel's voice floats out. 'Joni?'

'Hiya.'

'Come in.'

The gates swing open and I wheel my bike through, then stop as they close automatically behind me. I'm on a tree-lined driveway that curves round so I can't see what's at the end of it, except the bend is so far away it's almost funny. I mean, I know she's minted, but this place is huge. I get back on my bike and pedal slowly. When I round the corner, I can't help stopping again.

The house is bloody gigantic. Like a stately home. Well, maybe not that big. A mini version, all red Georgian brick covered in wisteria. The drive ends in a perfectly raked gravel turning circle at the front, and an expanse of grass on either side with those stripes you get from a ride-on mower. Jack would love a go on one of those. Actually, stuff that, I'd love a go on one of those. I can see the roofs of a couple of other buildings and guess at least one must be a garage. It's about the same size as my house.

Holy crap.

Part of me considers turning the bike round and disappearing back the way I came in a spray of gravel, but a bigger part is totally curious. My mind gets made up for me a second later when the front door opens and Annabel runs out.

'There you are!' She comes right up and leans towards me. I realise at the last second she's going in for an air-kiss like she did with Charlotte and her mum in Waitrose the other week. Must be something about being on her home turf. I decide I'd better roll with it except I've now gone the same way she has and what I thought was going to be one of those *mwahs* landing into nothingness in the vicinity of my face actually ends up being right by the side of my mouth. Worse, I actually make one of those kissy noises, which sounds ridiculously loud in my ears.

Oh God.

I scuttle back a pace and the bike crashes down, taking a chunk of my shin with it.

'Crap. Ow.' I lean down to rub it and, I hope, cover up the fact that one part of me is shrivelling up and the other part's trying to finish off the first cringey bit, because who cares anyway? Since when did I give a stuff about air-kisses and that sort of thing?

'Are you all right?'

I risk a glance up at Annabel. If she thinks it's funny, she's doing a pretty impressive poker face.

'Yeah.' Her face is still all concerned so I cough and say, 'Where shall I put my bike?'

She flicks her wrist in a vague gesture. 'It will be fine anywhere.'

I guess I probably don't need to bother with the lock, unless someone's planning to ninja down from a helicopter, in which case I'm pretty sure my bike's about the least valuable thing in a two-mile radius. I prop it against the wisteria and follow Annabel through a huge entrance hall with a wide staircase and doors leading off it on all sides, then into a massive kitchen that smells like something's burning. A pot on the Aga hisses.

'Oh no!' Annabel rushes over to it and lifts the lid, letting out a stronger waft of burning. I come up next to her and peer in. Whatever the sauce was originally, it's now welded on to the bottom of the pan. She turns off the heat, grabs a piece of paper from an expanse of gleaming worktop and frowns at it. 'Ah. It says lightly simmer.'

She looks again at the pan, then at me with a completely tragic expression. I take it all in, the messy hair twisted on top of her head, her flushed cheeks, the million shining gadgets on top of the island counter thing with its huge stone sink, and there's only one thing to do. I start to laugh. There's a pause, and then Annabel joins in.

'It was supposed to be a creamy mushroom sauce,' she says.

'Let's have a look,' I say. I give the sauce a stir. 'That'll be all right.'

'Really?'

'Yup,' I lie. It's a bit of a whopper. 'What's it going on?'

She gestures to another pot, which is also bubbling. Inside is that fresh pasta stuff, which has been in there so long it's disintegrating into the water. 'OK. Er, this is fine. Where's your plates?'

She hands two to me and I ladle out a dollop of soggy, bloated pasta on each, then the sauce, trying to leave the burnt bits at the bottom of the pan.

'I forgot the salad.' Annabel goes to a giant fridge freezer and sticks her head in, emerging a moment later with a bag. She scans it, then says, 'This one's no good.' She drops the packet on the counter, and turns to rummage in the fridge again.

I pick up the salad, open it and sniff. It looks all right to me. Annabel swings round with another identical bag in her hand.

'The first one's fine,' I say.

'It's past its best before date,' she says.

'What? That was only yesterday. It's "best before", not "it'll kill you if you eat it a day after". It smells fine and it's not mushy or anything.'

'Really?'

'Yeah, of course. You weren't going to chuck it, were you?'

Annabel gazes at the bag in her hand. 'Well … yes, I suppose.'

I take it from her, shaking my head, and put it back in the fridge. 'Trust me, the first one's fine.'

When everything's ready we take the plates to a table over on one side of the kitchen and Annabel opens some wine. 'Do you mind eating here? The dining room is so formal. I never use it unless Mummy and Daddy are home.'

I take a mouthful of pasta, which tastes mainly of water and burnt sauce. Annabel pulls a face when she tries hers.

'It's disgusting, isn't it?'

I force another soggy mouthful down with a sip of wine. 'The salad's nice.' I say.

We start laughing at the same time. This buzzing feeling starts up inside, like on a fun night out with the gang, but with other currents going on underneath it too.

'Let's find something else,' Annabel says. We dump our plates on the side and I stand next to her to peer into the fridge. It's rammed with packets of ready meals, all with M&S labels on.

'Your parents got shares or something?' I say in a jokey voice. It's like our laughing together over her horrendous sauce has released something in me, let me be myself.

Annabel seems to feel it too, because she smiles. 'Oh probably, Daddy has shares in everything, I think.' She pushes a few things to one side. I don't think I've ever seen so much food in one place outside a shop; we'd probably eat for a month on all this. 'Do you like Brie?' she says.

'Uh …'

I actually have no idea. I've never had it.

'No mould this time, I promise,' Annabel says, smiling. 'We can always have one of these.' She gestures at the ready meals.

'No go on, I'll give the cheese a whirl,' I say.

Twenty minutes later, we're dunking our bread into the Brie, which turns out to be much less strong than the mouldy stuff. It feels odd against my teeth, kind of claggy, but nice with the bread. At first I only take a tentative bite, but when I realise it's OK, I start scooping out big stringy chunks, then Annabel does too, her piece of bread chasing mine. I look again around the kitchen, how shiny and warm everything is, the weirdly luxurious feeling of eating posh food, drinking wine and not fretting about cost, just enjoying myself.

When we've scoffed the lot, Annabel says, 'Would you like pudding? There's a chocolate cake.' She goes into a walk-in cupboard – a larder, I guess – and comes back with a tin.

'Did you make it?' I say, deadpan.

'No, Mary did. Actually, confession time, she made the sauce too – I only needed to heat it through, so I think she thought it would be safe – are you laughing at me?'

'Little bit.' I nudge her shoulder, only lightly but enough to intensify that humming feeling going back and forth between us.

Annabel smiles and cuts the cake. The wine is pretty strong stuff; I make a mental note to have just the one glass, especially seeing as I'm supposed to be cycling home. I don't usually drink at all; I don't like the way it makes me feel. Annabel's already polished off hers, mind – not that it seems to be having any effect on her.

I take a mouthful of cake, which oozes on to my tongue in this rich explosion. 'Oh my God. I could eat this all day.'

Annabel smiles. We seem to be doing that a lot.

I put away more cake, sliding the spoon slowly into my mouth, savouring each bite. And the silence doesn't feel weird. When it's finished I say, 'Why are you on your own tonight, again?'

'Daddy's in town on something work related and Mummy is away at a yoga retreat.'

'You didn't want to go?'

Annabel skewers a piece of cake with her fork. 'No.' Then after a moment. 'She didn't ask.'

She finishes her cake and stands up. I'm seriously full now; my jeans are digging into me.

'Want a hand clearing up?' I say. I look around for a dishwasher; they're bound to have one, but wherever it is, it's well hidden.

'Don't worry about that – Mary will do it tomorrow.'

Annabel has already moved towards one of the doors leading from the kitchen. 'It's such a lovely evening. I thought we could go to the lake.'

I'm still marvelling at the ease of just leaving it all for someone else to do, but now my mouth drops open. 'You've got a lake?' my voice comes out super high. This place is something else.

'Yes. Come on.'

I follow her from the room, the dirty plates forgotten on the table behind us.

Walking on that pristine lawn feels like stepping on to a massive mattress. The grass is so springy, so perfectly green and even, I almost want to reach down and pull a blade up just to check it's real. We pass a massive greenhouse ('Mummy's hothouse. She grafts orchids – I'll show you later,' Annabel says) and go through a gap in the hedge, then down towards a long lake, its surface broken by water lilies and the trailing branches of a weeping willow. A wooden jetty sits at one end and I wonder if they ever sail boats here. The lake is big enough for them. Yachts probably. For all I know her dad has one of those and all. There's a low building off to one side.

We sit on the jetty and look out over the stillness, surrounded by birdsong and the faint whisper of wind in the trees. Nothing else. No telly, no PS2 sounds, no neighbour's music coming through the walls or the noise of a motorbike being revved up. It seems like another world. Above us, the sky's going burnt orange. The breeze is soft on my bare arms. Every muscle in my body feels like it's relaxing while my brain's completely wired with thoughts about the food, the house, out here. And her.

'This is beautiful,' I say.

Annabel follows my gaze, to where the trees meet the water. 'Yes. I suppose it is,' she says.

'You suppose? Seriously?'

Not far from us is a water lily, its white flowers fanned out over waxy leaves, totally perfect. I stretch my fingers down so their tips touch the water. Ripples spread out into wide arcs.

'Look,' I say.

We watch in silence, Annabel close beside me. But when I lean further down, Annabel says, 'Careful, you'll fall,' and puts one hand on my arm.

I pull back, water dripping from my fingertips. Her eyes are really blue. I start to move, twisting my body so we're face to face and now there's this look in her eyes, like she knows what I'm thinking, and heat spreading up my arm where her fingers are still holding on. I know this is mad, but there's something in the stillness in the water, the way she seems lost, the hum inside me that's getting so loud now it's drowning out the evening birdsong, that's pulling me forwards whether I want it to or not.

And even though I know it's a total line, and Kells would be rolling her eyes at me, somehow the night makes me say the thing that's in my head without even getting embarrassed about it. Stuff the consequences. 'What's so bad about that?'

And I lean forwards and kiss her.

Her lips are warm and soft, and they fit perfectly with mine. For a long moment, there's just our two mouths touching, neither of us moving or even breathing. Then I part my lips a little and she does the same, so there's the lightest touch of our tongues against each other.

Inside, the hum I've been feeling all night stills into a something I've only ever experienced once before, kissing

Lara, but way stronger, like the answer to a question I didn't even know needed to be asked.

Like I'm coming home.

I pull away after a few long seconds, wondering if this is OK, what she's thinking, but she reaches for my hands so we're kneeling facing each other, our fingers interlaced at our sides and there's a look of wonder in her eyes. Her face is flushed in the fading light. I know I'm smiling with my whole body.

I speak first. 'Was that … OK?' I say.

'I … that was … I thought … I mean, I always wondered,' Annabel begins. I'm still quietly buzzing.

'Was that your first … you know? With a girl?'

She nods, still looking amazed. Then she gives a little laugh and there's this quality to it, like she's shutting down something. The look of wonder fades from her eyes and she speaks in her normal posh voice. 'Yes … there were one or two at school that I had, well, a crush on. Nothing ever happened. I suppose it wouldn't with someone from school, but I've always wanted to try it.'

She breaks off because I've let go of her hands. The sun's dipping down low, shadows spreading across the lake. 'Like an experiment?' I say.

Annabel laughs and flicks her hair back. 'And a very nice one too,' she says, still laughing.

There's a sudden clenching in my stomach, then my face is on fire. How have I read this so wrong? All evening, I've been thinking I'm here because she likes me, not because she thinks I'm someone she can play about with, then throw away. As though people like me don't really count.

Annabel's frowning now. 'Joni? I didn't mean –'

I stand. 'I think you did.' My voices catches on the last word and suddenly I'm near tears.

I've got to get out of here.

I'm up and running before she gets a chance to scramble to her feet. I spot a path to the side of the house and I run along it, hearing Annabel call after me, but I ignore her and keep going. She rounds the corner as I'm getting on my bike.

'Joni! Please wait!'

But I don't, I shove my head down and pedal fast, heart going hard. At the gate I punch the button to open it, hear her voice calling out my name as she runs around the corner, but I'm already through and into the country lanes. I don't look back.

It's almost dark when I arrive home and go in through the back gate to put my bike in the outhouse, then I stop and wipe my eyes before I open the back door into the kitchen.

I stop. Mum, Dad and Jamie are all sat around the table. I can see in their faces something's wrong. There's an open letter on the table in front of them.

'What?' My voice is rough.

'Would you like a cup of tea, lovey?' Mum says, and even though I can tell she's really worried about something, she gives me a close look and says, 'Everything all right?'

I ignore both these questions and say, 'What's going on? Where's Jack?'

'He's fine – he's at Dylan's,' Mum says.

I let out a small sigh of relief. 'What is it then?'

Dad's voice sounds defeated. 'We got a letter …'

'And I was right,' Jamie says, his eyes dark with bitterness. I go to the table and pick up the letter with its logo of a blank, white sun, and scan it.

'They've bought the estate?' I say.

'Of course they have. I told you all –'

'Yes, thank you, Jamie,' Mum says.

I swallow, then say, 'Well, it might be OK, right?'

'You haven't read the back. Rents are doubling, just like Dealo said they would,' Jamie says. 'To pay for "regeneration" – or to get us all out.'

I turn the letter over and wince at the figure. 'We can't afford this. Not now –' I snap my stupid gob shut, but it's too late to take back the words. Dad's face contorts.

There's a long silence, then Mum says without much conviction, 'We can work something out. I can ask for more overtime. And your dad –'

Dad grabs his coat and limps out the back door for a fag.

'So we'll move then?' I say and my voice has a wibble in it. I don't want to leave here.

Mum sighs.

Jamie still looks bitter. 'Yeah – and where do you think we're going to get the cash from for a deposit and three months' rent in advance? If we can even find anywhere around here with rent we can afford? We're already a month behind as it is. We'll be homeless. I told you all this was going to happen, but no one bothered listening to me. We could've –'

'That's enough, Jamie,' Mum says and rubs her hand over her forehead, then looks at me. 'You're not to worry, love.'

But how can I not worry when I see in her eyes that we're not going to be OK? Mum sighs, then goes into the garden. And though I know I shouldn't watch, I can't help following her to the door, and it seems like a piece of me breaks.

Because Dad is sitting in the back garden, Mum's arm around his shoulders as she talks into his ear, and for the first time in my life, I see my dad crying.

I meet her eyes and she gives a shake of her head. I know she's right; Dad wouldn't want me to see this. I pull the door quietly to, turn mechanically to the oven and get out a plate of shrivelled veggie sausages and mash; I never told them I was eating at Annabel's …

Annabel. I don't even want to think about her right now. Her laugh sounds in my mind again. It's people like her who've bought the estate and shoved up the rent. People like her who think they can play about with us because they've got all the power and we've got none. The anger pushes up from my chest and I clench my jaw against it, feel it wedged in the back of my throat.

'You want this?' I say to Jamie, in a shaky voice. He picks up a sausage and then plonks it back down and shakes his head. I scrape the food into the bin, the knife screeching against the plate.

As I sit back at the table, the anger begins to give way to fear. 'What are we going to do?' I say, my voice small.

Jamie's been staring out of the window to where the light makes a square on the patch of grass and dandelions beyond, but now he comes over to give me a hug. This is the big brother I need, the one who nailed boards and a rope ladder to the horse chestnut tree in our garden so I could have a base to sit in for hours, who took me out on bikes with his mates and cleaned the grit out of my knee when I fell over. The one who's always known what to do.

He pulls back and grabs some kitchen roll so I can blow my nose. 'Well, we're not going to do nothing, that's for sure. Me and Dealo have been talking about this for ages. There's other places this has happened to – I've looked it up.'

'Really?'

'Yeah. Mum and Dad are all like, "You can't stop it, these big companies always get their way", but that's not true. Other places have fought it, they haven't just rolled over.'

Jamie sits tall at the table, his face blazing with determination and suddenly I feel taller too.

'We're not going to let them kick us out. We're going to fight this, Joni, whatever Mum and Dad say. And I'm going to need your help.'

I listen to the sound of Mum's low voice out in the garden with Dad and feel my chest tighten, then I swipe at my eyes and look back at Jamie.

'OK. What do I need to do?'

Part Two

CHAPTER TWELVE

'Bloody thing! How do you make something your home page?'

We're in Jamie and Jack's room, grappling with WordPress on Deal's laptop.

'Click on the side bar.' Deal leans over Jamie to point. He's been round a few times in the last week and in between knocking on neighbours' doors, writing up lists of people to contact, making a website and the cleaning job at the office, I've barely had time to think about anything else, which is probably a good thing. My phone goes off and I check it, then chuck it back on Jamie's bottom bunk unanswered. Annabel again. She's texted every day, but I haven't replied.

'What do I put then?' Jamie says.

I look at my phone one more time, then shake myself and say, 'Pass me the laptop – I'll write it.' There may be a touch of exasperation in my voice. I wanted to set up something simple, but whatever.

An hour later we have a Twitter account, an email address, a WordPress site and a new blog post explaining what's happening to the estate. It was Deal's idea to set up a website first, so it can be a hub for people to find out more about the campaign. We're not sure what to call it yet: Deal wants 'The 99% Fight Back' but that sounds like those protests that happened years back when everyone camped in tents in London and stuff, and from what I remember, it all sort of fizzled out. I want the simple 'Save Cherry Tree Estate' but Deal reckons that's not got a broad enough appeal.

'Stuff broad appeal – we're only trying to stop a few people getting evicted,' I said to him the other night.

'You're not thinking wide enough. This could be a catalyst for something much bigger,' he said, but I'm not convinced. I'm not bothered about saving the world or anything, I just don't want to be homeless.

Deal takes hold of the mouse and I sit back to watch him and Jamie work. Now I'm getting to know him better, Deal seems OK. I wonder if the weird vibe I picked up off him when he first became friends with Jamie was him being shy. Maybe I'm a bit quick to jump to conclusions about people.

Like Annabel?

I squash that voice right down.

My phone goes again and I sigh. Maybe I should text back, clear the air. It's Saturday tomorrow so I'm going to have to see her then. We could forget the whole thing. Or I could see if there's more hours going cleaning, but I don't want to jack in the library job. It's regular money for one thing, so I can't risk it, not right now when the cleaning job's only for a few more weeks. And besides, the library … it was mine. Before Annabel came and made stuff complicated.

It's not Annabel texting this time though. It's Kelly. *Where are you? Thought you were coming over? Xxx.*

'Oh bollocks.'

'What?' Jamie says.

'I forgot I was supposed to go to Kelly's tonight.'

'Seriously?' Jamie's starting to wind up – he's been really stressed this last week, but to my surprise, Deal jumps in.

'I think we're done here for tonight. We've got work in a bit anyway, Jamie.'

'Yeah, OK ...' Jamie raises a tired face to me. 'We need to think about telling Mum and Dad, especially once we get the press involved.'

'The press?'

'Yeah – we've got to get the public on our side,' Deal says.

Jamie scratches at his stubble. 'Maybe we'll leave it for a bit though?'

I give a faint nod. The press? And public? This is all moving too fast for me. I grab my phone and leave them to it.

Kelly shrieks when she sees me. 'You're here! I thought you weren't going to come.'

'I know, sorry ...' Annoyingly, my eyes start to water. I was thinking about Annabel again on the way over.

'What's happened?'

I shake my head, not knowing which bit to tell her first.

Kelly reaches forward and pulls me inside. 'Come on, I'm making hot chocolate.'

We sit on Kelly's bed with our steaming mugs and I take a deep breath and then start talking. I tell her everything that's happened, with finding out about the house ... and Annabel.

She listens right through to the end, blowing on her hot chocolate and taking careful sips. 'Bloody hell. Why didn't you say anything before? Come here.' She gives me a hug, then sits back. 'Right. Which bit do you want to talk about first? And by the way, I knew something was up with Annabel. I know you too well.'

I take a sip of my hot chocolate, which is lukewarm now, but still comforting, and give a small smile. 'Yeah.'

'How's your parents?'

'Mum's working millions of extra shifts and Dad's pretty much in bed with his back. It's like he's given up. I think he feels useless.'

Kelly makes a sympathetic face. 'Right then, let's get going on this campaign.' I love how she doesn't say it with imaginary air quotes, but like it's a real, serious thing. 'You got any followers yet? Give me all the passwords and I'll start posting. We need a logo too. I'll make one, I'm good at that stuff. And some slogans.'

'Thanks, mate. I'll ask Deal for the passwords.'

She raises her eyebrows. 'You're getting on with him now?'

'Well, he's been pretty good with all this campaign stuff.'

'*Mmm.*' Kelly's only met him the once and apart from saying, 'Jesus, he's almost too good-looking, isn't he?' she didn't really have an opinion on him. Now though she says, 'Why's he helping so much?'

'For Jamie, I guess,' I say.

'You don't think those two … ?'

'Christ no. Jamie's straight.'

'What about Deal?'

'Who knows?'

'He rents a room at the pub, doesn't he? Where do you reckon he comes from? Where's his family?'

'Don't know. Does it matter?'

Kelly knocks back the rest of her hot chocolate, then scrunches up her nose. 'Nah, suppose not. Just curious, is all.' She gives a wicked smile. 'I could probably get to know Mason Deal a lot better, if he was up for it.'

I laugh, then say, 'Well, whatever, I'm glad he's helping. It's good to be doing something, although I'm not sure it's actually going to be much use.'

'Oh well, glad you're looking on the bright side. Positive mental attitude and all that.' She grins and I manage a smile back. Then she says in a softer voice, 'It'll be OK, Joni.'

'How?'

'I don't know but, well, no one's dead, right?' She gives me a careful look. 'Maybe your dad will get another job?'

We've had arguments before on the topic of money not buying you happiness. I know Kelly tries to understand, but it's not the same for her. Her parents can afford holidays, school trips, a new car every few years, God, even Walkers crisps not own brand, though I still remember her giving it out to Meghan West and her gang when they were teasing me about my lunch in Year Four. But Kelly doesn't really get what it's like to worry about every little thing. Right now, for instance, we're out of bog roll, milk, bread, shampoo … I'm going to have to use the money I got paid for the cleaning to get some stuff in, which means the Jack School Trip Fund still has precisely fifty quid in it.

But I just say, 'Hopefully he will, yeah.'

There's a pause, then Kelly says, 'Well, you can't fix it today, but as for this thing with Annabel … tell me again what she said.'

I do a swift recap and show Kelly the texts and she sighs as she scrolls through.

'Well … it seems to me like she was nervous and had a brain fart. She's said sorry about twelve times here.' Kelly tosses me back my phone. 'Mate, she clearly likes you. Question is, do you like her?'

I start to shrug, then turn it into a nod.

'Well then. You know, sometimes there's such a thing as playing it too safe.'

'You reckon that's what I do?'

Kelly's not smiling now. 'Sometimes.'

Huh. I think about this later on after we've said goodbye. Do I play things too safe? I guess I do feel most right when I'm at home, where everything's comfortable and familiar, but that's a good thing isn't it? To put your family first.

I mean, without family, what've you got anyway?

I can't deny it; I'm nervous on the way to the library in the morning. I texted Annabel back last night in the end. I deleted about fifty drafts before settling on: *It's OK, let's just draw a line.* (Thanks, Mum.) *See you tomorrow x.* She hasn't replied, but it was late when I texted …

Her car pulls in as I'm getting off my bike. I plaster a smile on my face and then do a weird little wave too, even though she's right there in front of me. Annabel waves back with the hand holding her car key fob thing, like she's embarrassed too.

I wonder if fate might send me one of those sinkholes round about now.

'Hiya.' My voice comes out weird and croaky. Oh yeah, sinkhole would definitely be a plan.

'Hello.' She's fiddling with her key fob, pushing it from hand to hand. We catch each other's eyes, both look away, then look back at the same time. There's a pause that goes on for eternity.

'I'm sorry –' We both begin at the same time and then stop again. I suddenly want to giggle and I reckon Annabel feels the same way.

Her face gets serious. 'I really didn't mean …'

'I know, you texted. Once or twice.' My mouth twitches. She's gone all pink, but then she smiles again.

I shake my head.

'We're a pair, aren't we? Come on, let's open up.'

All through the day, there's unspoken currents flowing between us. When Annabel passes me a book to shelve and her fingers touch mine, it feels like she's set off bursts of colour up my arm. I lean down to show her something on the computer and for a mad second all I want to do is touch her hair. At lunchtime, Mrs H doesn't even need to ask us if we want to sit out on the wall; we both head there in unspoken agreement.

I keep a careful gap between us as we sit and look out at the row of houses opposite. A woman appears in her window, watching, and I consider giving her a wave, but instead I open up the foil around my sandwiches.

'Peanut butter again,' I say, more to break the silence than anything.

'I love peanut butter.' Annabel examines her lunch. 'Olives.'

We look at each other and wordlessly swap. It seems to push us over some sort of barrier and I see Annabel relax as she chews. I munch the salad she gave me, including the olives, which are bitter and strong tasting, and wonder what next.

'So I know you said you want to draw a line, but last week …' Annabel begins suddenly and then trails off. I take a deep breath, let it out again slowly.

'Yeah?'

'I …'

'Girls?' It's Mrs H calling down the steps. I don't know whether to feel relieved or disappointed as we go in.

As soon as we get inside, Mrs H claps her hands together. 'Good news! We'll be opening every day, barring Sundays of course, over the summer holidays, thanks to your father, Annabel.'

Annabel nods.

'Joni, will you be able to do every day?' Mrs H says.

'Er …' I feel myself going red as I glance at Annabel and away again. 'Thing is, would it be, like, paid? Because I might be able to get more hours in somewhere else.'

'Yes, yes. Mr Huntington has kindly provided enough funding for us to have you here on a paid basis.'

I'm not sure how I feel about Annabel's dad paying my wages. I avoid looking at Annabel, my face still hot, as I nod and say, 'OK. I'll be here then.'

'Wonderful.'

We spend the rest of the afternoon sitting at one of the tables in a corner, brainstorming ideas for a timetable over the summer. Mrs H wants us to get the kids involved in a float for the annual carnival and summer fete, plus extra groups – including the dreaded toddler group, while Annabel's going on about art and yoga. It's pretty hard to concentrate though, because Annabel is sitting next to me and I can smell her perfume. At one point she shifts her legs, and her knee presses lightly against mine and I swear this is not helping the whole drawing a line business.

Just before it's time to close, Mrs H says, 'Could I have a word before you go, Annabel?' And a part of me falls inside, because I was hoping she'd leave early and we could lock up together, just me and Annabel.

Annabel gives me a fast look that I'm sure means she was thinking the same thing, before clearing her throat and saying, 'Of course.'

I shift out of there quickly, throwing one last look at Annabel from the doorway, still torn between wanting to see her, while my sensible head says this is probably a good thing. Kelly's take is to relax and see what happens, but I am feeling way less than relaxed right now.

At home, Mum looks even more tired than before; dark circles ring her eyes and her cheeks seem a little sunken. Jack's in the middle of shoving some fish fingers in the oven, while Mum sits with a load of paperwork, and the calculator on her phone open on the table.

I give her a hug, then go to take my own phone out of my pocket. 'Oh, boll–' I stop short, but Mum doesn't seem to have noticed.

'What's up?' Jack says.

'Left my phone at the library. I'm going to have to go back and get it – can't go all week without a phone. Can you keep my tea warm?'

Jack nods.

'Where's Dad?' I mouth at him and he jerks his head upwards. So Dad's still in bed. That's not good. Mum looks up through watery eyes, pinching the bridge of her nose.

'Did you say something, love?'

'I've got to pop back to the library. Won't be long. You've got it all under control, haven't you, Jack?'

He nods and Mum goes back to her paperwork.

'Back soon,' I say, just as there's a knock at the door.

'I'llgetit!' Jack shouts in one rush. He's always loved being the one to get the post or answer the door. I think it's got to do with him being the baby of the family. It's probably Dylan anyway; no one else is likely to be knocking this time of day. Jack bounds out of the room and I decide to take the opportunity to speak to Mum.

'You OK?'

'*Hmm*? Yes. Trying to work out some sums.'

'Look, Mum, you might not need to worry yet. Me and Jamie have got a pl–' I leave the rest of the sentence hanging because Jack's just come back into the kitchen, with an oddly shy look on his face, and behind him is the last person I was expecting to see here.

Annabel, my phone in her hand.

CHAPTER THIRTEEN

For a moment, I can't speak. I look around, at the hole in the lino, the stained roller blind hanging down on one side where it's come out of the wall, the dirty washing-up piled on the side. We don't even have a proper carpet in the hallway; just some rubbish mismatched offcuts Dave from our estate gave us that don't cover the gripper rod. I feel my face heat up.

Mum looks to me and then to Annabel and stands up. 'Hello.'

Annabel doesn't seem fazed at all. She holds out her hand to Mum, saying, 'Mrs Cooper. It's lovely to meet you. I'm Annabel. I work with Joni at the library.'

Mum shakes her hand, her eyebrows high in surprise, her old-fashioned reading glasses on top of her hair, which is gathered in a straggly ponytail. 'Nice to meet you,' Mum says, and then starts pushing all the paperwork together. 'Sorry, you've caught us at a … Would you like a cup of tea?'

'Ah,' Annabel looks at me. 'I only came to bring Joni back her phone.' She holds it out. Jack's looking from one face to another, clearly interested. I take it, avoiding Annabel's fingers.

'Thanks then.' I can only think I need to get her out of here now, before Dad comes downstairs or Jamie gets home. 'Shall I walk you out?'

'Joni.' Mum gives me a look that says I'm being rude. 'I'm sure Annabel can stay for a cup of tea.'

'I'll put the kettle on,' Jack says and I try to signal to him with my eyes to leave the damn thing where it is.

Annabel catches the look and takes a step backwards. 'No really, I can see you're busy. I wouldn't want to impose.' She probably wants to get out of here anyway.

'Well, if you're sure?' Mum says.

'Another time perhaps. It was lovely to meet you,' Annabel says.

I follow her up the hallway, wincing at every scuff mark on the skirting board, and the motley heap of shoes at the bottom of the stairs, then want to kick my own shins, because I don't usually care about stuff like this. But it's pretty hard not to compare, after seeing where Annabel lives. I wonder if she's thinking the same thing. I'm almost afraid to watch her too closely in case I see some telltale sign, a curl of the lip or wrinkle of her nose. Something that would make me feel small.

I lean past her and open the door. 'Thanks for the phone. Guess I'll see you next week.' I'm mumbling fast, wanting to hustle her out of here, get rid of this scratchy feeling, like my house is wrong, my family's wrong.

That I'm wrong.

But when I do meet Annabel's eyes, there's only confusion and something else … disappointment, I think. She steps past me, then takes a half step backwards and stops again, running her fingers through her long hair.

'I wondered … You wouldn't want to … ? No, never mind. Next week then.' She starts to go and it's only when she's nearly at her car – which is bound to be causing some curtain twitching from Lorraine next door – that I call, 'Want to what?'

'I don't know. We could, ah, go for a drive?'

'Now?'

She looks at me and that energy is there again, alive in the air between us. 'Would you like to?'

'All right. Give me a sec.'

I shout back to Mum that I'm going out, grab my phone, keys and coat and give the door a hard yank closed – it sticks, so you have to – before Mum can protest or start quizzing me on homework or worse, like what the deal is between me and Annabel. As I get into her car, I give silent thanks Jamie's not home, or this evening could've been even more awkward than it already was. Though judging by the shadow at Lorraine's window, he'll get wind of the 'swanky car' round ours soon enough. For now, I simply worry about getting my seat belt done up. It slides smoothly, not like the ones in our car, which always get stuck. The seat's really comfy too, with about an acre between where my feet finish and where the footwell ends. Annabel starts the car up and backs out carefully, then sits at the entrance to our estate looking left to right several times, even though there's no traffic.

'Where should we go?'

'It was your idea.' I feel a little mean about the short way I say it, but part of me is still smarting from how I felt earlier and even though I know she hasn't said anything, I can't help feeling like it is partly down to her. I mean, I never asked her to show up at mine, did I? If she'd asked, I'd probably have made some excuse to stop her coming. Preferably forever.

Annabel bites her lip, then says, 'Let's just drive and find somewhere to stop. It's a lovely evening, isn't it?'

I don't think she can see me shrug sitting next to her, but she pulls out anyway. We drive up the country roads, going slowly around all the bends, climbing towards the top of the Downs. I bite back an exclamation as I feel something warm underneath me. For a second it feels like I've had a horrific accident, then I realise the seat's heated. I don't think I like it. Finally, as the light is really fading, she spots a lay-by and pulls in, then switches off the engine.

I realise I've barely spoken all the way here, too preoccupied with running images of our two houses side by side, and then with looking at the narrow space between where my leg ends and hers begins. Plus the whole wondering if I accidentally peed myself and didn't realise. If Kelly had been in the car I would definitely have said something, because she would think that's hilarious, but I can't bring myself to with Annabel right now. I give a tiny sigh.

I reckon Annabel's feeling awkward too; she half turns in her seat towards me, but when I meet her eyes she looks down quickly, then back up again a moment later. 'I hope you didn't mind my coming to your home.'

What am I supposed to say to this? I mean, she clearly knows I do mind, otherwise she wouldn't be twisting her fingers in her hair all nervous like that. But it seems rude to say and even ruder to ask what she thought of it, like she'd tell me anyway.

Annabel gives a little cough. 'It's only I couldn't call you as I had your phone so it seemed like the simplest solution.'

'You just … surprised me, that's all,' I say and it comes out stilted. Why is this so awkward? Why do I care so much?

'I didn't mean to embarrass you.'

'I wasn't embarrassed.' I snap the words out louder than I meant to. 'Why, d'you think I should be?'

'God, no! Of course not. I only meant that you seemed … damn, I keep getting it wrong, don't I?'

She looks properly upset. I'm breathing heavily, my jaw aching where I've gritted my teeth. Part of me is thinking *I knew it*, and *This is stupid, it's never going to work, we're way too different*. But then she turns back to me, looking right into my eyes.

'I really didn't mean that at all. I promise.'

I hold her eyes for the longest time, trying to work out what I'm feeling, what I want. Then she shifts her gaze to the side and lets out a gasp.

'Look.'

I turn my head to where she's looking and suck in a breath through my teeth. The sky to one side of us is a brilliant pink. It's so luminous it's almost eerie, with the dark ridge of the Downs and a clump of trees in the distance silhouetted against the sky.

'It's beautiful,' Annabel says it quietly, on a long out breath, and her voice is so full of wonder I suddenly know that she does feel it too, the beauty you get out here. She sees it like I do.

I get out, hear Annabel doing the same, and then she comes to stand next to me and we're shoulder to shoulder, looking up at that amazing sky. Her house, mine, they seem to shrink down in front of it – not like they don't matter at all, but perhaps not as much, not out here. After a minute, her fingers find mine and we hold on, watching the colours deepen above us. The feel of her hand sends a pulse all the way through me. Then the pressure of her fingers increases and we turn towards each other at the same time. Our kiss isn't tentative this time, like by the lake. This is a full-on kiss, mouths open, tongues moving together, my body against hers. I'm on tiptoes, my fingers reaching up into her hair as she leans down and into me, her arms at my back. My heart feels like it's going to drum itself right out of my chest in a way I've never felt before, not with Lara, not with anyone. It's as though some sort of invisible thread is looping from me to her and back again, drawing us close, heat rushing through me at the places where our bodies meet.

Then a car goes past, its engine roaring from one of those souped-up exhausts on the back, making us both jump. Annabel immediately pulls away, one hand going to her chest. It's hard to read her expression in the fading light.

'That was loud,' she says.

I wonder for a second if that's the only reason she moved back sharpish. I haven't exactly asked her anything about, well, anything. Is she gay, bi, something else? Is she out to anyone? To herself? Does it matter at this moment?

I decide it doesn't have to. Not right now. 'Yeah, there's some proper dickweasels around here,' I say. She looks startled, but a moment later she laughs.

'Dickweasel. I like that word. In fact,' she gives my fingers a squeeze, 'I think I'm going to keep it.' And the look in her eyes seems to suggest it's not just the word she wants to keep.

We drive back in near darkness now. Annabel pops on some music but refuses all my pleas for her to sing. 'That was strictly a one-time only event.'

'Go on, you're not that bad,' I say, and Annabel risks taking her eyes off the road to turn her head towards me, presumably to give me a look I can't really see on these dark roads anyway.

'Joni. It would have to be an absolutely exceptional circumstance for me to ever sing in front of anyone. Even you.' I can hear from her voice she's smiling and I grin back, looking at the shadowy trees and the pool her lights make on the road in front of us.

'You saying I'm not exceptional, eh? I think I'm hurt.' I know she knows I'm teasing and it feels like we've taken a tiny step, together, joking like this.

She replies in a low voice I almost don't hear over the CD which, by the way, is the Beatles – apparently she likes the classics.

'I think you're just exceptional enough.'

I'm still grinning when I shove the door shut behind me. I go into the kitchen because I'm suddenly totally starving. Jamie's sat at the table and when I say hi he gives me a grunt and a dark look. I ignore him – I'm not letting anything wreck my mood tonight – and root about in the cupboard, coming up with a tin of beans at the back. There's no bread, so I put the whole tin in a saucepan on the hob; the microwave's busted, but it doesn't matter because beans taste better out of a pan anyway, especially if there's any cheese left which … yes! There is. I swing round with the last of the block in my hands, feeling stupidly happy. It's only cheese.

'Where's Mum?'

'Next door. Lorraine knocked about the letter. She was in a state.'

'God, I bet she was.' I can't see Housing Benefit touching the new amount of rent.

'You had a good night then?' Jamie says, and there is some definite barbed wire in his voice. I'm guessing he knows I was out with Annabel. I remember what he said before, about steering clear of people like her.

I decide to style it out and give a vague shrug, which would look more convincing if I didn't have to turn away to hide my smile.

Jamie's not letting it go though. 'You sure you know what you're doing?'

'I don't know what you mean,' I say, aiming for a light voice, but not really managing it. I give the tin of beans a hard shake over the pan.

'I think you do.'

'It's none of your business, Jamie!'

'What isn't?' Mum's come in. I give the tin another shake, but all the beans are stuck stubbornly to the side, so I huff and grab a spoon to scoop them out.

'She's seeing that girl from the library, Annabel Huntington,' Jamie says.

Oh my God, Jamie is so annoying sometimes. I swing round, fast enough that a big splodge of sauce drops from the spoon on to the lino. 'What are you, like twelve?'

Mum raises her eyebrows, which is enough to get us to stop. I give the floor a quick wipe, then stir the beans, pretending I can't feel Mum's eyes on my back.

When they're hot enough I start grating the cheese directly into the pan.

'Plate's an optional extra tonight, is it?' Mum says.

I take a big mouthful of hot beans and half-melted cheese. Wish we hadn't run out of Worcestershire Sauce, because then it would be perfect. 'Saves the washing-up,' I say through my mouthful.

Mum rolls her eyes. 'Chew and swallow first, then talk. Unless you're also twelve this evening?' She looks meaningfully between me and Jamie, who's still glowering at the table.

'I'm just looking out for her,' Jamie says in a sulky mutter.

'I can look out for myself.'

'*Without* your mouth full, Joni,' Mum sighs. Then she looks at me. 'Annabel seems nice. Why don't you invite her round properly? I could cook some tea.'

I choke on a bean and have to get some water, standing at the sink with my eyes streaming. It's nice of Mum to offer, but seriously, I think she takes the whole supporting-her-daughter-who-likes-girls routine a bit too far. Plus having someone round for tea might've been something I'd do once upon a time. In junior school. And Annabel sitting at our table? I can't picture it. It was bad enough her being round here for ten minutes earlier, let alone a whole evening. I wipe my eyes with a grubby tea towel that has a singe mark from where someone – possibly me, not that I'm owning up to it – left it too near the hob. Behind me I hear Jamie say, 'The Huntingtons are millionaires, Mum.'

'Yes, and?'

'And Annabel Huntington is not going to want to come here for "tea".' I don't like the way Jamie says it one bit. 'Joni knows it too. She'd be embarrassed –'

I drop the tea towel and whirl to face him. 'Wrong again, knobber. I'd love to have Annabel round.' I ignore the fact I'm definitely regressing to playground level. 'When's OK with you, Mum?'

'I'm not working a week Friday.'

'Oh good. Neither am I,' Jamie says, his voice a challenge.

'Great,' I say, with as much enthusiasm as I can rustle up. I dump the pan in the sink and fill it with lukewarm water, then decide to make my escape. I'm halfway out of the door before she says, 'You are planning to wash that up?'

'Uh, yeah? Just leaving it to soak,' I say.

'Good. And Joni?'

I stop in the doorway.

There's the hint of a smile on her face, but she tries to make her expression stern. 'Please stop calling your brother a "knobber".'

I flee upstairs to lie on my bed and contemplate how I'm going to ask Annabel round for sausage, egg and chips night in less than two weeks.

CHAPTER FOURTEEN

'So …' Jamie's shuffling his feet in my doorway. 'Can I come in?'

I'm in bed, balancing a worksheet on my knee. 'Well, anything's preferable to French comprehension. It's not due in until after half term anyway,' I say. I shut my dictionary with a harder thud than is strictly necessary.

Jamie comes to sit on the edge of my bed.

'Sorry about before.'

I shrug. He means the other night, but I don't want to get into it right now. I'm knackered from pushing a hoover around a deserted office earlier. It's kind of creepy, just me and a row of desks and blank computer monitors. I sat down at one of the swivel chairs and tried to imagine putting on a shirt and coming there every day, sitting at one of those desks and typing or whatever. Each one had a screen thing around it, covered with blue felt, and people had lists of phone numbers and rows of codes printed up, next to pictures of their kids or pets. Just sitting there made me feel like the life was draining out of me, even though plenty would say I'd be lucky to get a job in a place like that. I'd get sick pay and holiday and probably pensions and stuff. I can't help it though, the thought that what I should be aiming for is … Well, it's not what you dream of when you're a little kid, is it?

And then there's the next thought chasing the first one down hard: if not that, then what?

I don't know.

I realise Jamie's giving me a look, and wonder if he said anything. 'You what?'

'What?' Now he looks confused.

Just to wind him up, I go, 'What?' again and for a second he looks annoyed, then realises this is my way of accepting his apology and grins.

'What?'

We go back and forth a couple of times, our voices getting sillier as we do, until we're both laughing.

Eventually, Jamie straightens his face and says, 'So I was going to say, Dealo says the website's all live. And …' He runs his fingers through his hair, which has got pretty long even for him – longer than mine by a couple of inches now. 'I've emailed Douglas Lattimer and made an appointment. There's a surgery thing in a couple of days. You can just go and, like, chat to them or whatever.'

I make a face. Douglas Lattimer is our local MP, Tory as you come. Dad can't stand him, not that the woman who came knocking on our door for Labour in the last election got much of a hearing either. Dad's line is they're all the same: liars and out for themselves.

He's probably got a point.

'I want you to come and see him with me.' Jamie says.

'You reckon?' I mean, this is Jamie's baby, the housing thing,

I'm only helping out. I don't know how I feel about actually going and seeing our MP. It feels … committed, I guess.

Jamie spots the doubtful look on my face and scowls. 'Well, unless you're not bothered we're about to get kicked out.'

'That's not fair. You know I'm bothered. I'm just not sure what I'd say. What about some other people from the estate? Everyone else must be pretty upset too?'

'They are, but we can't have a massive group of us showing up. Well, at least not at first … Look, I'll do the talking. But if you're there too … you look pretty young for your age. And you're still at school …'

'Won't that mean he's less likely to take me seriously?'

'Or feel sorry for you.'

Oh right. Jamie wants me to use my youthful looks and boundless charm to convince the local Tory we shouldn't get kicked out. There's as much chance of this working as there is of me becoming an Olympic swimmer, which I totally wanted to be for about four weeks when I was seven and watching the Olympics on telly. We couldn't afford lessons. Actually, I still can't swim too well. About enough to not drown, if I got thrown into a lake or something. I think suddenly of the birds over Annabel's lake, the feel of her lips against mine, so surprising and yet not somehow …

'Hello? You coming then or what?'

I blink and focus on Jamie. 'All right.'

He smiles. 'Good. And I thought we should get some leaflets done, go door to door. Can you get some copied at the library?'

'I don't know. Maybe when Mrs H isn't about,' I say.

He stands, but before he opens my door Jamie gives me a funny look and opens his mouth to say something, then seems to think better of it. 'Let's not tell Mum and Dad yet, all right? Not with Dad so … well, we should wait till there's something decent to tell them.'

I'm pretty sure that wasn't what was originally on his mind, but I just say, 'OK then,' and let him go.

I look at my old dressing gown hanging on the back of the door. It's just about seen me through last winter, although it barely reaches my knees now and the sleeves stop somewhere mid-forearm. I add seeing the MP and working out how to do leaflets to my mental list of worries. Also keeping something like this from Mum and Dad. It's not like I tell them everything, obviously, but still – we usually discuss big things together. Jamie's probably right though. Dad isn't exactly doing too well since he lost his job and the buyout news. Poleaxed is probably the word for it. He needs something to start going right soon or … well, I don't know what will happen but I know it won't be good. I think again about Mum and Dad arguing, and how Dad gets this look like he wants to sleep forever some days.

I slump back against my pillows and lug the dictionary open again, but find the more I try to work out the language in front of me, the more other thoughts crowd to the front of my mind.

Douglas Lattimer's office is off the High Street, down a narrow cobbled alleyway between a tea shop and an antiques place, neither of which I've ever actually set foot in. They're more a tourist thing. I've got on my best jeans, my scuffed-up trainers and a clean shirt. Jamie's fiddling with his phone, trying to spot if we're too early.

'Let's go in,' I say. He pockets his phone, brushes his hand through his hair and pulls open the door harder than he needs to. I don't know whether to roll my eyes or cry at seeing my big brother all nervous like this.

Inside there's a reception area. The walls are dotted with prints of local scenery – views from the Downs, the old church, some black and white ones of the High Street with a horse and cart – and posters with slogans that say nothing meaningful at all. We give our names to the receptionist. Her smile is about as glossy as her hair, but she's definitely not what you'd call the chatty sort. We settle down to wait.

I flick through a couple of magazines, but it's all *Country Life*-type stuff, so I get out my phone instead. There's a text from Annabel about tonight, and I'm not sure if it's the MP meeting or later on that's giving me that scrunched-up feeling in my stomach, which then gives a massive gurgle like it always does when I'm anxious. I push one hand against it and avoid Jamie's eyes in case we both start cracking up. The woman at the reception desk approximately two feet away from me has definitely heard but is pretending she didn't.

Suddenly, a door opens and a lady comes through, a pearl clutcher type. She says thank you to the receptionist, gives Jamie's long hair a look that says she would most certainly be clutching her pearls if she was wearing them, and sweeps out.

Me and Jamie swap looks, Jamie's mouth pulled down, and I have to turn away in case I snort. The nervous feelings evaporate.

'Mr Cooper?' It's him. Douglas Lattimer, MP, complete

with balding head and sharp suit.

We stand.

'And Ms Cooper,' I add, stressing the 'Ms'. Mr Lattimer gives us one of those bland politician smiles, shakes our hands in turn, then motions for us to follow him. As we go, I flex my fingers by my side to check they all still work – he's got one strong grip.

We go into an office and sit across from him at a table.

'So …' He draws it out, his accent reminding me of Annabel's. He scans some papers. 'I understand you have some concerns regarding the recent purchase of Cherry Tree Estate?'

'Yeah – yes.' Jamie leans forward and starts to explain the situation. 'They've already said they're going to raise all our rents, and we can't afford it. They're doing it on purpose – they want us all out so they can sell the houses on and make a load of money. It's not right.'

Mr Lattimer steeples his fingers together as he waits for Jamie to finish. 'Unfortunately, my caseworker has looked into this and there is little we can do. The purchase and rent adjustments are perfectly legal,' he says with a patronising smile.

'But they're kicking us out!'

'White Light Holdings are within their rights to review the rental pricing structure. I understand the current rates offered are well below the market value.'

There's a smooth, smug look about him as he says this. He thinks he can blind us with his jargon, like we're just silly kids.

Jamie tries to interrupt, but Lattimer keeps talking, right

over him. 'They are committed to reinvesting much of the revenue into rejuvenating the housing stock, which I think you'll agree,' he gives a small laugh, 'is rather overdue.'

'So where're we supposed to go then? What about people like us? We can't afford to live anywhere else near here. My brother's in school, and my sister, she's in sixth form, aren't you, Joni?'

I nod. 'We don't feel this is fair.' I'm using my best voice, trying to sound grown-up and reasonable and stuff, but Lattimer's just giving me that same nod that's as good as a pat on the head.

'I do understand this is a difficult situation for your family and we're committed to supporting you where we can. My caseworker, Dev, has put together some resources – perhaps your parents would like to take a look?' There's a small but telling emphasis on the word 'parents'.

He slides a couple of leaflets and phone numbers for the Council Housing department and Citizens Advice towards us, then stands up. 'I regret I'm not able to do any more at this time, but if you have concerns on any other issue, I would encourage you to make an appointment to come and see me again. It's so refreshing to see young people engaging in politics.' He actually seems to think we're going to smile back. He's already at the door.

I look at Jamie, who's picked up the papers with a shaking hand. I can see in the way he clenches them in his fist, and how he's gone white, that he's struggling to stop himself lumping Lattimer one.

Lattimer's holding the door open now.

There doesn't seem to be anything for it but to go.

*

We're silent, walking down the street. When we get to the far end, Jamie suddenly bursts out, 'Stupid dick!' which is a bit startling for the two old ladies coming out of Laura Ashley. I give them an apologetic look, but they ignore it and hurry off in the opposite direction. 'Fat lot of good he was,' Jamie continues.

I let him rant the whole way home; it's probably best he gets it all out before we get in, because I've got something to say too. I stop at the end of our row of houses and say quietly, 'Jamie. I think we should tell Mum and Dad – you know, about the website and the leaflets, which I'm totally doing next week by the way. They'll be super pissed off if we don't.'

Jamie's rage has blown itself out and instead his face is grimly set. 'I will – soon. We've got to get those leaflets out. People are crapping themselves, but no one knows what to do. Let's get them together, have a community meeting next week. And find some stuff to fire Lattimer's way,' Jamie says, his voice loud like he's on a one-man mission.

I think again about that ridiculously painful handshake, and Lattimer's smug smile and I nod. 'I'll get Kelly to help. She always ferrets things out in the end.'

CHAPTER FIFTEEN

The Monday after half term, I'm sitting with Pete, Ananya, Stacey and Ed in the common room. I scowl at the History essay I totally didn't do when I should've, wondering again why I decided to subject myself to two more years' worth of dissecting the Nazis' rise to power. I pick up my phone, type and delete another text inviting Annabel for tea on Friday, then plonk my phone back down.

'It's too nice to be inside. I want to be on a beach somewhere,' Stacey says. It's true, the sun's out and there's actual warmth to it, heating up the room.

'Yeah, like Barbados,' Ed says.

'You wish.'

'Don't we all,' I add and then everyone's off on chats about holidays past, present and future. Kelly's been away to Paris over half term.

I don't have much to add on the holiday experience front, so I go back to my History essay, write a couple of notes – I'll type it up later on Jamie's laptop if I can nick it off him – and then pick up my phone again, angling it so no one can see while I type a fast message to Annabel and hit send this time. I could've just invited her face to face at the library on Saturday, but we were super busy and never got any decent time on our own. Plus, it feels safer doing it by text.

I've barely had a chance to see if it's sent when there's a shriek that seems to ping off all four walls and the ceiling at once. I don't need to look up to know it's Kelly.

'You guys!' I haven't even managed to get my phone down before she's on me, giving me a hard hug from behind. 'I missed you!'

'Steady on, it was only a week.' I grin as she pulls back. 'How was it?'

'Ar-may-zen,' she stretches the word out, her Wiltshire accent at full force. 'Well, Disneyland was a bit boring. There's only so many times you can go on Hyperspace Mountain, but we went to the Louvre, ate out a lot. I feel all cultured. Plus, hot French guys.' She begins a loud rendition of '*Non, Je Ne Regrette Rien*' while I flash back to the first time she went to Disneyland – the Florida one. God, you can get jealous enough when you're eight. Obviously, I'm over it now. Pretty much.

Kelly's still singing, giving it some welly. Her voice is so amazing. Stuff college, she needs to be on TV. She's got a YouTube channel, a few hundred subscribers, nothing massive, but she could be huge; all she needs is a lucky break. She grabs hold of Pete and swings him up, then does a twirl under his arm, choosing to ignore the stares and giggles from the basketball lot sat in the corner on the decent sofas. I glance at Ananya, but if she's fazed she's not showing it. Ed conducts in the air while Stacey laughs, until Kelly runs out of puff and drops into the seat next to me. Behind her, Pete's kind of pink in the face.

'What's the news then?' Kelly says.

A chorus of 'Nothing' greets this.

'Well, we've got that Drama audition thing,' Pete says from his perch on the table near Ananya.

She smiles up at him and adds, 'Yeah, there's bursaries going for the summer drama school at Edrington. Part of their outreach programme.'

My ears prick up at the mention of Annabel's school. 'Oh yeah?'

Ananya grins, her face alight. 'I really hope I get a bursary – there's no way my parents are paying for it. Did you know they're sponsored by Mr Huntington?'

'Are they?' I'm aiming for casual here, but I can feel tell-tale heat creeping up my neck.

'Yeah. And I hear they've got some famous director coming. You do workshops and rehearsals through the summer then there's going to be a showcase performance in September. You should audition too, Kelly – it's going to be a musical.'

'Which one?' Kelly says.

'*Grease*.'

'Seriously?' She mimes an exaggerated yawn. 'I'd be an excellent Sandy though.'

She would and all. Kelly sings a few bars of 'You're The One That I Want'.

I groan. 'Oh God, she's off again.'

Kelly shimmies at me and sings louder.

'You're all going to come to the showcase if we get in,

right?' Pete shouts over the top of her.

I give a half-nod. Part of me is totally dying to see Annabel's school and another part really doesn't want to. Stuff already feels complicated enough.

Kelly spots my expression and stops singing, to zero in. 'What about you?'

Luckily for me, the bell goes. Stace grabs her stuff. 'Dammit, it's never ten, is it? Come on,' she says to Ed. Ananya and Pete head off to what's laughingly called the Drama studio. They've been fundraising to get some proper new lights and seats in there for forever.

When it's just me and Kelly she sits down, puts her chin on her hands and gives me a Look. 'Out with it then, Cooper.'

'Out with what?'

'Whatever it is. I know you.'

I think about Annabel, feel my face heat up and swerve for the other main news which, amazingly, feels less complicated. 'Well, we've started the campaign. You still up for helping?'

Kelly's face lights up like I knew it would. She loves a good Cause, does Kelly. Over the years she's cycled through animal rights, nuclear disarmament, global warming and a ton besides, usually dragging me with her, though ironically I'm the one who kept up being a veggie. 'Definitely.'

'Thanks. By the way, Mum and Dad don't know yet.'

'Won't they see it online?'

'They're too old school. I had to explain what Tinder was to Mum the other day and she definitely didn't get it.'

'Why were you on Tinder? Looking for a date? Has anything happened with you-know-who?'

I'm about to tell her, I really am, but something holds me back. This … whatever it is, with Annabel, feels like a bubble floating in the light – if I poke it too hard it's going to pop, and I'm not sure I'm ready for that yet. I kind of want to float with it, just for a little while. My phone pings and I grab it before Kelly gets a look at the sender. *I would love to. What time? A xx.*

I shove the phone in my pocket. 'Nope, I think imminent homelessness is enough. Plus I haven't done my English.'

Kelly lets me switch the subject but as we half study, half piss about, I touch my phone in my pocket every so often, like I'm trying to reassure myself. I catch Kelly giving me a thoughtful look. It's one that says there's something different about me, but she can't quite make it out.

Which would make two of us, because whatever this thing is that's going on with Annabel, I already know life's about to get even more complicated.

Whether that's good or bad is anyone's guess.

I'm nervous, Friday on my way home from school. Annabel's due in, ooh, about an hour and I've got no idea what state the house is in. I poke my head into the lounge. Dad's in front of the TV, in the big armchair that's always been his, a cup of tea resting on the arm. I give him a hug. On the floor by his feet is the free paper, folded back to the job pages. Dad's ringed a load and then scribbled them out, the scribbles getting increasingly vicious the further down the page you look.

'You all right, Dad?' I say to his balding head.

'Yes, love,' he says and I can tell from his voice he's in pain. I wish they'd give him disability benefit. Lorraine next door gets it, even though she seems all right to me, but apparently Dad's back doesn't give him enough points to qualify. So he's got to apply for a load of jobs he can't do, every week, to get jobseeker's allowance, which is tricky given we've got no laptop other than Jamie's, and the library only has a couple of PCs. Plus the jobcentre's a forty-minute bus ride away, which knackers his back and costs £4.20 for a return. Mum needs the car for work because she has to drive all over the place to get to each client – not that she gets paid petrol or travelling time. She practically cried when unleaded went up to £1.20 a litre.

'Want a fresh cuppa?' I say.

'That'd be smashing,' Dad replies and gives me a smile though his eyes are hazy with pain.

'You taken any painkillers?'

'Yeah, I've used up all the ones from the doctors. Got to get myself down there again if they'll give me an appointment.'

'I'll call for you in the morning.'

Dad squeezes my arm. 'Thanks, love.' I pause at the door. He looks so small suddenly, hunched in his chair, and I know it's not just because of his bad back.

There's a couple of cups perched on the arm of Dad's chair as well as the paper on the floor. I should tidy up before Annabel gets here. Although running the hoover round the lounge isn't going to make much difference to the ragged carpet edges or stains anyway. Nope, to make this house look in decent nick we'd need some sort of fairy godmother.

In the kitchen, Mum's whacking the grill.

'You all right?'

'Damn thing won't switch on,' she says.

I twist the knob all the way round and hit the ignition button, but it doesn't give its usual *whoomp*. I sniff; no smell of gas.

'Er … have we paid the gas bill?' Mum leans closer and sniffs too, then looks in the oven where there's a tray of pale chips. 'Not all of it, but I called up and paid them something – the woman said it was fine.'

'Then maybe the cooker's knackered?'

Mum sighs. 'Probably.' She looks to the ceiling and blinks rapidly, then says, 'I'm sorry.'

'It's OK, we'll sort something out. What else have we got in?'

'Beans. That's about it,' Mum says and I don't know whether to sit at the table with my head in my hands or start laughing, because I know they're not even Heinz, just those watery ones that we all lie and say we prefer anyway.

Before I get the chance to do either, there's a voice from the doorway.

'Is there anything I can do to help?'

Annabel's standing there, holding a bunch of flowers, Jack hovering behind her. Oh crap. I look at Jack and realise he's got his best T-shirt on and his hair carefully gelled. And then my heart contracts because I spot he's swapped his jeans with the hole in the knee for his school trousers, about the only ones he owns that aren't an inch too short. He sees me looking and goes pink so I give him a faint wink. Seems like I'm not the only one who wants to put a good face on it for our visitor. Unless Mum told him to scrub up – probably she did, but whatever, I think I love Jack even more for it.

Mum plasters a smile on her face. 'Hello, Annabel.'

Annabel hands over the flowers and Mum goes all pink with pleasure. 'Thank you, they're lovely,' she says. Dad shuffles in from the lounge and Mum turns to him. 'We might have to do a rain check – oven's packed up.'

Dad's face is expressionless. Now he's up I can see he's made an effort too; he's combed his hair anyway, and got dressed. Mum's definitely had a word. I'm picturing her rushing home from work with the carrier bags, telling Jack and Dad to be on their best behaviour, getting everything out and fretting over the time. She's even got the paper tablecloth out and a little milk jug of wild flowers Mum must've got from the garden.

We all look at each other and then Mum says, 'Sorry, Annabel, it seems we've hit a problem with the cooker.'

Annabel takes all this in her stride, saying, 'Don't worry, I'm sure we can arrange something!' in this voice that reminds me of talking to teachers at school, but more easy and practised. She turns to Dad and holds out her hand. 'Mr Cooper. It's so lovely to meet you.'

He takes her hand a little awkwardly, but she's got on a face you can't help smiling back at and I relax as I see him manage to stand a bit straighter, despite his back, and tell her, 'Take a seat while Joni's mum and me sort this out.'

Jack slides into a chair next to her.

'Hello,' she says, still smiling. 'You must be Jack.'

I edge my way over to where Mum and Dad are having a whispered debate by the sink.

'I can't give the girl beans on toast, Derek,' Mum's saying.

'Well, haven't we got anything else?'

'Have *you* done any shopping?' Their voices are starting to carry. I glance back at Annabel and Jack, who seem deep in conversation. I think Jack's telling her about Dylan's new Xbox – or to be precise, his new Xbox One X Project Scorpio, as Jack's still insisting on calling it.

'Look, we'll do it another night,' I say, my voice low because I'm trying to catch what Jack's saying. Annabel has an intent look on her face as she listens to him. Then she decides something; I see the click as a plan slots itself into place in her brain. She stands up.

'I'm sorry for interrupting, but I wondered if you would mind … well, I thought it would be fun to order pizza.'

I whip my head towards Jack. He's a total gannet for pepperoni and loves Domino's when we can afford it, which is not too often. To be fair, we probably should've just done that the night of his birthday. He grabs a glass quickly to avoid looking at me and lifts it to his mouth before realising there isn't any water in it and lowering it again, his face sheepish. I'm trying to think of a decent excuse, because there's no way we've got the spare cash for ordering pizza.

'I'll pay,' Annabel says like she's read my mind, then on seeing Mum and Dad's faces change she adds quickly, 'I'd like to. As a thank you to Joni for teaching me in the library.' Her face softens when she looks at me, in a way that makes me swallow nervously.

This does not go unnoticed by Mum. Dad's already saying, 'Sorry, love, we can't let you waste your money –'

when she cuts across him. 'That's really nice of you. Only if you're sure though,' she says.

A faint *whoop* from Jack, who then pretends he's dropped something under the table so I can't glare at him.

Annabel gives him a conspiratorial smile. 'What about Domino's?'

We order. Every time Mum says she's not hungry, or I say we can share, Annabel waits for us to tell her our favourites and then adds them quietly to the order, angling the phone screen away from where I'm peering over her shoulder, trying to work out how much it's all costing. It's better than thinking about the look on Dad's face as Annabel started ordering, because if I do, I might howl.

'Can I have double pepperoni? And those garlic breads with cheese and bacon? And maybe some Fanta?' Jack's saying in a rush.

'Jack!' We blast him from both sides; me and Mum's eyes meeting helplessly over his head as Annabel gives that smile and taps away. I'm trying really hard not to mind, but there's this weird itchy feeling starting up inside, one I can't help. I'm ashamed. I know Annabel doesn't mean it to be like that, but it is anyway. She keeps glancing at me, her eyes asking if this is OK and I get the sense she really wants not only me but Mum, Dad and Jack to like her. It should help, but there's this horrible question scratching away at the back of my mind.

Does she think she can buy them? Buy me?

The next moment, Jamie walks into the kitchen.

Oh double crap.

To his credit though, after looking at my mortified face, he goes up and says hi to Annabel.

Then Jack says, his voice squeaky with excitement, 'We're ordering pizza and we can have anything we want.'

'Jack!' Dad's shout fills the room. Everyone stops for a second. Dad pushes a shaky hand through his hair, his face mottled. Annabel looks uncertainly at me and I try and give her a reassuring smile, but I suspect it doesn't come out right.

Jamie's eyes narrow. Oh no. Then he looks at me again and in a passable attempt at a polite voice says, 'That's nice. I'm not staying though. I'm meeting up with Dealo to talk about that stuff.' He gives me a meaningful look.

I glance at Mum. Usually she'd have something to say about Jamie skipping off out when we had someone over, but she seems to have picked up on the tension in the room and says mildly, 'Don't be back too late.'

Jamie goes and I take a deep breath. Mum starts to unwrap the flowers.

'Shall I help you with these?' Annabel seems to be done with the pizza order and puts her phone back in her handbag. It's a small pink tote with big buckles that I bet Kelly would kill for. We don't have a vase tall enough, so wind up chopping a good few inches from the flower stems and divide them between a tiny vase that used to be Nana's and an old pint glass. Mum pops the vase on the table, swiping the little jug of flowers away. She goes to the back door, about to tip them out in the rhubarb patch when Annabel says, 'Those are so beautiful.' She walks over and touches the purple petals where a flower looks as though its mouth is open and says, 'Mummy's a super keen gardener. She used to take me to the Chelsea

Flower Show, but she's too busy this year …' She trails off, clears her throat. 'I can't remember the name. *Prunella* uhhh …'

'*Vulgaris*.' We all turn to stare at Mum, who gives Annabel a gentle smile, like the sort I usually see her give to Jack, then looks at our jaws hanging. 'Your nana used to know the Latin for all the flowers about. It's also called self-heal or heal-all. You can eat it, you know.'

Jack screws up his face and Dad says, 'Eat flowers? We'd have to be right down on our uppers for it to come to that.' But there's not the usual twinkle in his eyes as he says it. Instead he sounds like Jamie. I cough and move over to Annabel who is looking at Mum under her lashes, this odd expression on her face, like the echo of her pleased look, but sad somehow too.

Suddenly, an almost unbearable urge to be alone with her hits me square in the stomach. It's not like there's anything wrong with how she's being or anything, but at the same time, my family on their best behaviour, Dad's expression … Annabel working so hard to seem at ease … the pizza. Nothing fits right. Is this what it'll be like if we … carry on with whatever it is we're doing? Awkward? Me feeling small next to her? And if so, can I live with it or should I put whatever there is brewing between us to bed now?

Can I, if I even wanted to?

'You want to go and look at the other flowers?' I say and for some reason add, 'In the garden?' like a dumb-ass.

'Sure,' Annabel says.

We wander down past the cat toilet/rhubarb patch and the overgrown bushes laced with brambles, ducking past a couple of mouldy-looking socks hanging from the rotary where no one has got them in for weeks. The garden's narrow and lumpy, full of dips concealed by weeds. The bits that were supposed to be grass were taken over by dandelions years ago. We've long given up trying to sort the lot out and now it's a kind of wildflower meadow at the bottom, a haven for bees at least.

'Watch your step,' I say, just as Annabel stumbles. I shoot a hand out to steady her and don't take it away. We're nearing the bottom of the garden and I gesture to an old pile of bricks Jamie used a couple of years back to make a barbecue, a little way from the horse chestnut tree. We sit, the tops of our legs inches from each other, and I tip my head up to the wide branches. From here you can see the bit of board Jamie nailed on to make a tree house of sorts, and the remains of the old rope ladder with its broken top rung. That cracked under me actually, a few years back, and I landed butt-first at the bottom. Not recommended. No one climbs the tree nowadays except Jack sometimes and me when I need somewhere to hide and think.

'Do you still climb it?' Annabel says, like she's reading my thoughts again.

'Only usually Jack these days,' I say.

Annabel shudders. 'I'm terrified of heights. I don't think I could even climb that.' She gestures to the rope ladder.

'It'd probably collapse if you tried anyway. But I love this tree. I swear I used to spend a zillion hours up there with books and stuff. All those animal stories – I had all Mum's old ones. *Watership Down*, *The Animals of Farthing Wood*. It was like my own little world.'

Annabel shudders again. 'I don't think I've ever even climbed a tree.'

'You are kidding me.' I jump up, put one foot into the bit where the trunk makes a V and pull myself into the branches. 'Come on, climb up too.'

She shakes her head, half smiling, her eyes worried. I stomp on one of the boards and a bit chips off and falls. 'Heads!'

Annabel takes a step back, then screws up her face. 'Come down.'

'Come up. It's safe, honestly. Look, I'll pull you.' I hook one arm around a branch and lean down so my hand's dangling, but that really seems to freak her out. She shuts her eyes.

'I can't watch.'

I lose the smile and swing down, landing with a thud right next to her. 'Sorry. I didn't realise.'

Annabel lowers her hands. 'You must think I'm completely pathetic,' she says.

'No I don't. There's plenty of stuff I'm scared of.'

'Really? You don't seem afraid of anything,' she says.

I think about losing our home, how someday soon I might never be able to climb our tree again, about how I'm getting to feel about her. 'I get scared, believe me.'

She doesn't ask of what and part of me is relieved, because how do I tell her that not only can't we afford Domino's, but also we can't even afford to live here at all?

I change the subject. 'You never needed to order the

pizza, you know, but thanks. Jack thinks all his Christmases just came at once.'

'He's so sweet. And you don't need to thank me.'

'Yeah, I do.' I pause, then I add, 'It might not be a big deal to you, but it is to –' I substitute 'me' for 'Jack'.

Annabel nods, and suddenly I know I have to be myself with her if this is ever going to go anywhere. I take a big breath and look her in the eye. 'Thing is, you know we're pretty skint. We can't afford stuff like you can.'

'I know,' she says and I can see she's trying hard to be all inclusive or whatever the word is, but that she doesn't really get it. It's like Kelly but twenty times worse.

'Yeah, you say that but you don't. Do you know what a zero-hours contract is? Or how much a loaf costs, even? I'm betting you've never taken a cleaning job to pay for your brother's school trip, have you?'

Her mouth falls open and then she closes it again.

'I'm happy to do it, that's not my point. The point is …' I look up at the new leaves on the tree. 'That life's not easy for us like it is for you, and stuff could get a lot worse.'

I'm about to tell her about the buyout and the campaign, but she's giving me this odd look, her head on one side. Then she says quietly, 'You're right, I don't understand all that. But having money doesn't mean life's easy.'

'Seems it from where I'm sitting. My family would be totally sorted if we had enough cash,' I say. I'm not saying it in a horrible way, but it feels good anyway, to let her know what I think.

But to my surprise, Annabel's eyes are full of tears. 'Yes, I think you would.'

I'm about to ask her what's up when Jack's overexcited voice comes down the garden.

'You guys! PIZZA!'

Later, with everyone stuffed and the leftovers shoved in the fridge, me and Annabel go up to my room. She looks around as I fiddle with my docking station. It's only a cheapo one and the sound's pretty tinny, but I shove it on random and turn to Annabel just as Rihanna's 'Diamonds' comes on, which makes me think of the time I caught Annabel in the library singing. I reckon I already knew, right then, but I don't say anything. I look around too, trying to take in through her eyes the clothes hooked over the back of my chair, the spare books stacked up on the floor because there's no room on the bookcase for them. Annabel touches one of my blue WALL-E curtains and I laugh to cover up my embarrassment. 'I loved that film. Got the curtains for my ninth birthday.' I don't add we haven't had the cash to replace them since; pretty sure Annabel's twigged that.

'They're sweet. And they go with your rug. It's beautiful. Where did you get it?'

She means the rag rug, done in blue and purple, my favourite colours when I was little. 'My nana made it. It took her months,' I say.

'Wow. I couldn't imagine my grandmother making anything like that.'

'No?'

Annabel laughs. 'Definitely not. We don't see her often in any case; she stays in the Toulouse house mostly.'

'How many houses have your parents got, exactly?'

'Well, home of course and the Toulouse house and a little flat in town for Daddy.'

'Town? What, like, London?' I pause, then say, 'How little?'

'Only three bedrooms, so we don't often …' She stops, probably remembering we're currently in one of three bedrooms. Or two point five really, given there's only about enough room between my desk and bed for the rag rug.

Annabel sits on the edge of my bed and because there's nowhere else except the loaded up chair, I sit next to her. Jazzy hops down from my windowsill and comes over to investigate. Annabel tickles him behind his ears.

'You've got his seal of approval. He doesn't let just anyone stroke him, you know,' I say, smiling.

When her phone buzzes for the third time since we went up to my room I say, 'You going to look at that?'

'It's just everyone on SnapChat,' she says, but doesn't say anything else, and I realise apart from that Charlotte girl, she's never mentioned any friends. It's like this massive part of her I don't know anything about.

Then again, how much have I told her about Kelly and the gang? Cuts both ways, I guess.

I'm thinking about this and wondering yet again if it's all just too complicated when she says, 'Joni?'

I look at her.

'I wanted to …' She swallows, then gives me this tentative look and leans towards me. I stay still, letting her come to me, liking that she's moved to kiss me, not the other way around, and then I'm getting lost in this kiss that goes on forever. We pull close together, enough so I can feel her chest pressed up against mine and my heart is beating hard, heat spreading right through me in a hot rush. I put one hand up to the back of her head, feel her hair soft under my fingers.

Me and Lara were seeing each other for three months in all and the most we ever did was kiss, but this … I want to do everything. I want to touch her. The sensation's so powerful I actually feel myself starting to shake and I pull back and take a deep breath. Bloody hell. What is happening to me?

Annabel breathes hard too, her face flushed. She's so beautiful. 'Is this OK?' she says and there's something so sweet about the way she says it, how she bites her lip after, the words I said after our first kiss echoing back to me, that I smile. 'I think … let's go back downstairs, yeah?'

For a second she looks disappointed and that sends another shot of excitement through me, but there's a bit of my brain that knows this is moving really fast, that I'm thinking with my pants and not my head here. I take her hand, give it a squeeze. 'It was more than OK. But let's just … take it steady.'

She nods and lets me lead her downstairs.

At the front door, she says, 'I'll see you tomorrow?'

Obviously she will, it's a library day, but I know what she's really trying to do is check in. It makes her seem less … I was going to say posh and scary, but I realise as I wave her off I haven't really been thinking about Annabel that way for a while now.

CHAPTER SIXTEEN

Work the next day is almost painful. Not because it's a tricky day or because of anything Annabel does – she's great actually, relaxed and smiling loads more than usual. She's come up with this plan to do a seniors' yoga class, which of course Mrs H loves, and we spend some time making up posters and updating the library website. First lesson will be next week, taught by none other than Annabel who, surprise, surprise, has had private lessons. I don't feel snarky about it though.

No, work's painful because of last night, how all these feelings seemed to leap up and ambush me, and how much I keep thinking about kissing her … so much so, it's kind of hard to concentrate on much else.

Even Mrs H notices. Me and Annabel are sitting next to each other working at the PC and she leans over me to point to something, her leg pushing up against mine, a second before Mrs H comes up.

'Are you feeling OK, Joni? You look very flushed. You're not coming down with a cold, are you?'

'Er, no, I'm good, thanks. It's just a bit hot,' I say and Mrs H goes off to open a window. I look at Annabel and quickly look away, but not before I catch her eye and see her smile.

'Gonna go to the store cupboard for … something,' I say.

I take a little while in the cupboard, telling myself I need to get a grip. I've got too much else to worry about without getting so hung up on someone I hardly know: the community meeting and how behind I am with my school work, for starters. But it all seems to fade to the back of my mind when I think about Annabel. Which is pretty much most of the time right now. And even though I should have seen this coming, did see it really, it still feels overwhelming, like climbing right to the top of a huge tree and then looking down and not knowing whether to be exhilarated or scared.

All of a sudden I want to chat to Kelly. I send her a quick text to see if she's about later, and go back out.

Annabel's disappeared, but in her place is a group of girls and lads about my age I've never seen in here before, looking around the place and talking loudly.

'Do you think they'd have it?'

One of the girls laughs. 'Why don't you ask?' The way she says it sounds like a dare.

My stomach drops. It's the black-haired girl from the restaurant, along with the two lads and another girl I don't recognise. One of the boys spots me and walks over casually. I flash back to the restaurant, his chair tripping the waiter and the feel of the sundae spreading across my lap. 'Hello. We were wondering if you had a particular book?' he says.

His voice is polite, friendly even, but I'm sure I catch something in his eyes. But these are Annabel's friends, so I smile and say, 'I can have a look. What is it?'

'It's called *The Plum in the Golden Vase,*' he says. 'I don't suppose you've heard of it?'

'Er, no … I don't think we have many Chinese authors, but I could look? Was it published recently?' I notice I'm doing this weird thing with my voice, making sure I pronounce all my words carefully. I sound like a pale imitation of Annabel.

The black-haired girl says something to the other girl and I swear she looks like she's about to burst out laughing. I get the uncomfortable feeling something I don't quite get is going on, but I sit behind the computer and do a quick search of the catalogue. Nothing comes up.

'Sorry, no, we don't have that,' I say.

'What about *The Fabliaux*?' he says. I pause and look up at him. He has this totally innocent expression, but the black-haired girl is smothering a laugh.

'Henry!' Annabel has appeared out of nowhere.

The boy turns and then they're all saying hello and *mwah*-ing each other. I take the opportunity to do a quick Google search.

Yeah, so they're both dirty books from medieval times. What a knobber. I do another quick search and scribble down something on a piece of paper.

Annabel's in full-on posh mode, chatting away to the girls, flicking her hair and laughing. She looks like she's grown about an inch somehow; she's holding herself totally differently. I sit behind the desk, trying not to go red. The black-haired girl, whose name I gather from their talk is Izzie, says, 'I don't know *how* you're managing it, Annabel, I really don't.' She says it like Annabel's working in some Third World sweatshop or something.

'Oh, you know Daddy, he always gets his way,' Annabel says with a laugh. 'And besides, if he hadn't intervened the library wouldn't be here any more.' She gets this proud look on her face.

The two boys are standing closer to me, so I catch Henry say lazily, 'Or his name on the crest outside.'

I don't think Annabel hears. She turns at something Izzie's asked and says, all smooth, 'That's Joni. Joni, come and meet everyone.'

I tear the paper off the pad and go over.

'Joni, this is Henry, Max, Izzie and Helena.'

'Hi,' I say, trying not to sound awkward. They all say hello back.

Helena looks at me. 'Don't mind Henry, he's a total bastard. He's forever teasing us all, aren't you, Henry?' She gives him this big-eyed flirty look while he does what's quite possibly the smuggest grin I've ever seen. Honest to God, I don't know how he's never had a smack in the chops. It also didn't feel much like teasing to me, but I think she's trying to be nice, so I just smile. Then I push the paper into his hand. 'Here you go. Sorry we didn't have those other books but you might want to check this one out. The Amazon reviews say it has a good section on masturbation.'

There's complete silence for a minute, and I get the satisfaction of seeing the smug look wiped right off his face. Then they all start laughing and this time it doesn't feel directed at me. Izzie gazes at me with new respect. Annabel looks confused.

They go soon after, in a flurry of more kisses. Izzie says to Annabel as if I'm not there, 'She's fun, isn't she?'

Annabel says something indistinct to this and as they walk away she turns to me and makes a face. 'Was Henry … ?'

'Being an arse? Yep.'

She sighs. '*Urgh*, sorry. He's such a dickweasel.'

I grin at her use of the word. 'That's all right,' I say. But it's not really.

Later on, we lock up and say bye to Mrs H, then stand in the car park watching her go. I turn to Annabel. 'Do you like him? Henry?'

I may have been stewing on this all afternoon.

She pauses. 'I know he takes it a little far sometimes, but he can be good fun. And his father's got something to do with Daddy's business. We have them over for dinner parties fairly regularly. I think Daddy would love it if Henry and I were – you know.'

'Seriously? *Eww*. He's a prat. Henry, not your dad, I mean.'

'Yes, a lot of the time he is. I remember this one dinner party, Henry came with his parents, made a load of ridiculous jokes, got pissed and I found him throwing up into the lake. He tried to kiss me straight after he'd vomited.'

'Nice. What did you do?'

'I sidestepped him.' She smiles like this is funny, but I keep my face straight and her expression fades. 'I suppose he is a bit ... He celebrated when Donald Trump got elected. He's really into winners and losers, "survival of the fittest"' – she puts on a deep voice – 'that sort of thing. It's irritating.'

I give her a long look. Sounds more than 'irritating' to me. Annabel's face has clouded over.

'Do you remember the Grenfell Tower disaster the other year?' she says.

I nod. We did a bake sale for the appeal at school. Mum and Dad scraped together the money for ingredients for an epic chocolate cake. Jamie helped me bake and decorate it.

'Henry's father was talking about how some of the survivors were going to live in a luxury block nearby – and how it was so ridiculous they were being given those flats for nothing, when people had worked hard to buy them, and I remember sitting there, listening to Henry agreeing, and no one said a word. I had to excuse myself and say I had a headache. That's when I first started thinking … Oh, I don't know.' She makes an impatient gesture and I can see she's about to say she's being silly or ridiculous or whatever the word is she always seems to use to put herself down.

'It'd be weird if that didn't hack you off,' I say, my voice careful.

'Yes. And it made me feel like, well … that I don't fit.' There's a long pause, then she shakes herself and says, 'Anyhow, I'm sorry if he was rude to you. Don't pay him any attention.'

We leave it at that, but the conversation has let me know another thing about her I was pretty sure of anyway: her parents definitely don't know she likes girls.

Which is going to be a problem, sooner or later.

I sigh and start to unchain my bike, and Annabel gives this little squeak. 'I almost forgot! I have something for you.' She pushes me gently back up the steps so I'm in the doorway to the library, her car just out of sight around the corner. 'Wait there. And close your eyes,' she says.

I hear her rustling around and some banging, then the sound of a boot slamming.

'Open your eyes,' Annabel calls in her clear voice.

I do.

The next second she appears at the bottom of the steps on a bike.

A gleaming red mountain bike. She dings the bell and grins at me.

'*Huh*?' I manage.

Her smile widens. 'It's for you!'

'*Huh*?' I say again. Articulate as always.

'Do you like it? I had the saddle lowered so it should be just right for you, but I didn't know exactly how high. It's not a problem though, we can alter it if we need to ...' She trails off.

I come down the steps slowly, and put one hand on the handlebars. She's got a bike? For me? This is way more than pizza. Too much more.

'Annabel ...'

Her smile fades. 'Oh no, don't look like that, Joni, please. I just wanted to say how much I ... I wanted you to have something ... nice.'

I close my eyes for a second, feeling a sudden urge to cry. 'And it is, it really is. But you've got to know I can't take it.'

Her eyes shimmer.

'I'm sorry, Annabel, but I can't. It'd be like charity or something.'

'That isn't what I meant though, not at all.'

'I know you didn't, but –'

'A loan then.' Her voice sounds almost desperate. 'I didn't buy this. Daddy got it for me a year ago and I've never ridden it. I wanted you to have it, but what about if you borrow it? Just for now?'

I hesitate, but she looks so worried I end up saying, 'OK. But only for a bit, all right?'

She smiles.

'It's properly smart,' I admit, and hate the wistfulness in my voice.

'Why don't you go for a ride?'

I do a couple of circuits of the car park. The bike's smooth, fast. So much easier to pedal than Jamie's with the knackered gears. I could probably ride for miles on this. I hear myself laugh as I whizz past Annabel, see her face light up. Maybe it's OK, for someone to do something nice for you, just because they can. But still, I feel a twinge of unease as I come to a stop in front of her.

'You know you don't have to –' I stop myself saying 'buy me', because that seems harsh and I don't even know if that's what she's trying to do. 'Do this, Annie.'

Annabel blinks, then says, 'What did you call me?'

'Oh! Annie. I just call you that sometimes, like, in my head.' It seems like a big thing to admit somehow. As if it makes her mine in some way.

This smile blossoms over her face. 'I like it.'

I look at the two bikes chained up side by side. One familiar and rusty, the other sparkling new. 'Um, how am I going to get two bikes home?' I say.

'We'll ride them. Both of us,' Annabel says, her eyes shining.

'What about your car?'

'I'll call a taxi from your house.'

For a rich person, Annabel definitely knows how to waste money. 'Or we could put one in your boot? Save the cash,' I say.

'I want to ride with you. Please? It will be fun.'

'Go on then.'

She insists on taking Jamie's bike, and rattles off in front of me.

I hop on to the new bike to follow and Annabel pauses at the entrance to the car park, and looks back. Her blonde hair tumbles down her back and her eyes are sparkling.

I get a sudden mischievous impulse. 'Race you!' I sprint past her, laughing at the surprised look on her face. She drops back, but starts to gain again on the first big hill, until we're neck and neck, gasping for air. Then we're at the turning to my estate and I cut in front of her, hear her yell as I shoot around the corner and pull up in front of my house a few seconds before she does. I put my feet on the ground, raise my arms up like I've scored a goal, then give her a smug grin. 'Looks like I'm the winner.'

Annabel is breathing too hard to say anything, sweat running down her forehead. For once, her make-up's smudged, eyeliner in a greasy line under her eyes, her hair properly messy, not designer messy, her face bright red.

She looks real. And hot as anything.

'You'd better come in and get a drink,' I say.

We lock both bikes away in the shed and go in through the back door. I listen for a moment, but there's only the tick of the kitchen clock and an odd high-pitched squeal from the fridge. Something else on the way out. A note on the side from Jamie tells me he's out with Jack, Mum's at work and even Dad's managed to get himself down the shop. We have the place to ourselves. I remember the other day, how these huge feelings came up out of nowhere, like they were this massive wave ready to sweep us both away. I swallow and grab some water for us both – tap, not bottled from the fridge like at her place.

Annabel goes over to one of the finger paintings next to the flower calendar on the wall and touches it. Above are the loops of fairy lights we put up one Christmas and decided were too nice to take down. 'I love this. Whose is it?'

I squint. 'I think that's one of my baby masterpieces actually. Mum's kept ones from all of us.' I gesture to the row of pictures with bits of crispy, yellowed Sellotape holding them up. 'She's got boxes and boxes of stuff in the loft.'

Annabel raises her eyebrows and for a minute I feel all defensive, then she touches a picture of us all together the day we went down to Weymouth. Jack's about two and is wearing only a nappy because he got covered in this huge chocolate ice cream. You can see the ring of it around his mouth like a mini beard and moustache. Jamie and me are both doing stupid poses with huge grins on our faces, me with a T-shirt tied over my head because we forgot a hat, and Mum and Dad have their arms around each other's waists. The whole beach is heaving.

'You all look so happy,' Annabel says. I'm trying to work out the expression in her eyes. Were there any pictures of her family at her house? I can only remember one or two of those glossy studio ones, plus pictures of her parents' wedding and graduations. There was one of her on a horse, I remember now, super smart in a jacket, the horse shining in the sun and a yellow rosette that said 'Third', but she wasn't smiling. Then I think about that feeling I had looking round her giant house. Not quite envy, more a sort of wistfulness. I realise suddenly what Annabel's eyes are saying.

Maybe we've got something in common after all.

'So I pulled up his voting record – did you know he voted three times against gay marriage?'

We're back in Kelly's room, having a look at some of the stuff she's dug out on Douglas Lattimer. I'm still tingling from the time me and Annabel spent in my room, kissing, before Dad came home. I'm not sure what might have happened if Dad hadn't banged on the door fifteen minutes or so after we got in.

I pull my attention back to Kelly. 'Figures. But people round here would probably like him for that.'

Kelly frowns. 'You really think that?'

'It's true, isn't it?'

'Maybe for some of the old biddies or whatever, but people like us would mind he's a raving homophobe, wouldn't they?'

I shrug. Probably they would, but then the voices of people like us don't count for as much next to the Edrington type.

And at the thought of her school, Annabel, Annie, is back in my head again. Another thing I've been thinking since her friends came to the library is how to talk to her about coming out. I don't want to put pressure on her or anything, but at the same time, she's going to have to tell her family sooner or later …

'Joni?'

I haven't been listening again. 'Sorry. I was thinking about Annabel.'

She leans forward. 'Details, please.'

Kelly grins as I bring her up to date. Then she says, 'Just remember, once things get physical it all gets a lot more complicated.'

Kelly's had sex with a couple of people so I guess she'd know better than me, but she always makes out like it's not that big a deal. I wonder what's got her so serious all of a sudden. Then I realise, and could give myself a swipe to the back of my own head. I've got so wrapped up in myself, I haven't been paying attention to my best mate.

'Is this about Pete and Ananya?'

'Them? Nah. They're welcome to each other.' She grabs a nail file from her cluttered desk. 'Got a snag.'

I watch her draw the file over one perfect nail, and wait.

Eventually, without looking at me, she says, 'I mean, I just guess I never realised, until they got together ... Pete's always just been *there*, you know?'

'But now you've changed your mind?'

'Something like that. Ah well, them's the breaks,' she says with a grin that totally doesn't convince me.

I shuffle up the bed towards her and she puts her head on my shoulder briefly. That's about the nearest Kelly gets to bawling.

We sit like that, both of us thinking about other people, about what ifs and complications.

CHAPTER SEVENTEEN

The leaflets are ready; Kelly's new logo looks cool. We've gone for: S.O.S. – Save our Streets, which was Deal's idea. I wasn't that keen but got outvoted. He wanted to use Comic blinking Sans for the lettering and all, but Kelly shoved her foot down over that. We've written a bit about the buyout, put in all the social media links and a list of actions to take. So far we've got:

- Visit or write to MP
- Sign the online petition
- Write a letter of complaint to White Light Holdings
- Come to the meeting at The Olde Inne

Me, Jamie, Deal and Kelly are having another meeting, the leaflets spread out over Jamie and Jack's desk.

Deal picks one up. 'We'll go knocking on doors tomorrow. We shouldn't just do the estate but some of the other streets too. We could put a poster and leaflets up in shops, pubs, the library. How many have we got?' he says.

'Fifty leaflets and ten posters,' I say. I didn't have enough money to pay for printing any more.

'Well, it's a start. Let's see what that gets us.'

Kelly says, 'What we really need is a celebrity or someone to get on our side. I'll look into it. We should get the rest of the gang involved too.'

Deal scribbles on some paper while I shoot her a grateful look. I'm glad we told each other about Annabel and Pete respectively. I feel bad for neglecting her recently; Kelly's the best mate I've ever had and I want her to know it.

I turn to Jamie. 'What about telling Mum and Dad?' I say.

Jamie twists his lips together. 'I don't know. Mum's pretty knackered.'

This is true. She managed to pick up some more shifts and she only seems to be in the house to eat and sleep these days.

I start to say, 'Dad?', then stop. I think about him crying and how much he stays in bed or slumped in his dressing gown in front of the TV. I can't bear that look on his face, all helpless humiliation.

Jamie shakes his head. 'Let's try and catch Mum first.'

'All right. I'll do it though, yeah? Probably best coming from me.'

At this, Jamie grins.

So that evening, when Mum comes in from work, I'm waiting for her with a cup of tea and the leaflet and poster. Dad went straight to bed after *Pointless Celebrities*, but he forgot to turn the TV off and it's still blaring out, which is unlike him because he's usually a fanatic about turning off lights and stuff when you're not using them. It's like he's just given up.

I turn the TV off.

As I push the door to, I see Jamie hovering halfway up the stairs, listening. He makes the 'OK' sign with his finger and thumb.

'What's up, Joni?' Mum says from the sofa, her voice heavy. Maybe I shouldn't be bothering her with this, but surely she'll see a poster or speak to one of the neighbours at some point.

I take a deep breath and go for it. 'Well, it's about the buyout,' I say. I show her the leaflet and poster and explain what we're doing. 'And we've got stuff going on online too. We're starting to pick up followers. We already have fifty signatures on the petition.'

Mum sits still, taking this in. She smells like antibac gel and faintly of sweat and I know she just wants a bath and sleep. But she makes an effort to focus on me and sighs again. 'This is all lovely, Joni, and I can see how hard you've worked, but I don't want you to spend so much time on this when you should be studying.'

What?

I suck in a long breath through my nose and then let it out slowly. 'So you want us to give up before we've even tried?'

'It's not that, it's just, I'm a bit older than you, sweetheart. I've seen a few more things. You've got to remember, people round here … They're not used to, well, this sort of thing.'

'You reckon no one will come? This isn't only about us, Mum. Most of the people round here can't afford the new rent either.'

'Yes, but others can. There'll be plenty of people who'll want to move in when –' Mum breaks off and looks around the room, lips pursed. 'And a big company like White Light? There's no fighting them.'

'You don't know that.'

Mum puts her hand on my arm. 'I do, love. I've been to the Council and Citizens Advice and they've said there's nothing they can do. White Light aren't doing anything wrong, legally speaking.'

I didn't know that; she never said.

'But it *is* wrong.' It bursts out of me. 'You've got to see that. It's like what Jamie said, about those billionaires and the rest of the world.' I know I'm not making much sense, but I plough on anyway. 'Other people will see it's wrong if we explain what's happening. And then it'll be, I don't know, like bad PR or something, right? And White Light might back down on the rent stuff.'

Mum gives me this sympathetic look, but doesn't say anything. It makes me even more angry.

'I just don't think you should be getting your hopes up. We've got to be realistic,' she says.

I think about all the times Mum and Dad have said not to rock the boat, to be happy with what we've got. But this time it's different, surely she can see that? Why shouldn't we at least stand up and say it's wrong? Even if it doesn't get us anywhere.

I clench my teeth together and breathe out hard. Then I square my shoulders. 'You can't stop us doing this. We're going to anyway. I don't care what you think.'

I never talk to Mum like this and her face works to stay calm as she looks at me.

Eventually, she says, 'Well, as long as you get all, and I mean all, your coursework and revision done, there's no harm in it, I suppose. Just understand these things rarely go how you want them to. We've got to prepare ourselves for, well, what's probably going to happen. And you're not to tell your dad. He's got enough on his plate as it is.'

What – like staying in bed all day? I want to say, but even I know that's too cruel. As much as I want my normal Dad to roll his sleeves up and start fighting with us, I also know he just can't at the moment. And I know Mum's picking up so much slack she's permanently shattered, even with me, Jamie and Jack getting in the shopping and doing the cooking, but I can't help it; I can feel my temper pushing up and up until I have to let it out.

'Fine. You do that. I'm going to save my energy for actually doing something, not just sitting about waiting to get screwed.'

'Joni!'

But I'm already walking out of the room.

Jamie's looking down from his perch on the stairs. 'Blimey. And I thought I was the only one with balls in this house,' he says.

The next day is my last one at the cleaning company. I meet up with the woman, Grace, who hired me, in the little coffee shop tucked up one of the side alleys at the end of the High Street, away from the main tourist bit. She gives me my last week's money – just over thirty pounds, which isn't bad going – and says if she needs cover again she'll shout.

Part of me is relieved to get out of the creepy offices and have more time, but the other part is conscious Jack's school trip fund is going nowhere. I made the first instalment, but the second is due any day and I need to stop off at the shops on the way back home for washing powder and tea bags. There always seems to be things we're running out of. And last week I gave Mum some of my library wages for petrol, so she could get to work.

Deal comes around later and with Jamie we make the rounds of the neighbours. Some of them don't want to know, or don't answer their doors, even though it's not that late in the evening, but most are worried, and angry. Dave's at Number 26 and when we knock on his door and tell him about the meeting he nods several times. 'Yeah, I'll be there.'

One old lady I don't know smiles at us and offers us a biscuit from a packet of broken Rich Tea. 'Good on you. About time someone stood up to this nonsense,' she says, before Deal or Jamie have even had a chance to really get into their spiel.

By the time we've finished, at least twenty people have said they'll come and some have said they'll help spread the word too. I save Lorraine next door for last and say to Deal, 'I'll speak to her on my own. She'll be more likely to listen if –' I stop, not wanting to say if he's not there, but I reckon she'll respond better to someone she knows than a stranger.

Deal nods.

Lorraine answers in tracky bums and a big T-shirt, which isn't like her. 'You've caught me at a bit of a bad time. Although you've not got a tea bag, have you?'

I run home to get one and then we go into her kitchen, which is similar to ours but with loads and loads of plants everywhere so it's like a jungle. We sit at the table with a cup of tea. I have to shunt a heap of washing over to one side to make room. Lorraine heaves herself down with a low groan, one hand on her back. When she got the sugar down I saw rows of boxes of pills and medication for her diabetes in the cupboard. I get a twinge of guilt for judging her: I can tell from her face she's in pain because she's got that same shadowy look to her face Dad gets. So that makes another time I jumped to a conclusion and got it wrong, just because I was jealous someone had something I didn't.

'How's your Jack?' Lorraine says.

'Good, thanks.'

'And your mum and dad?' She looks at me closely and I weigh up what to say in my head, knowing whatever it is will be round the whole street before you know it. But that's sort of the point, isn't it? If we can get Lorraine on side she'll bully and cajole everyone into joining in. I still remember the street party for the Queen's Diamond Jubilee Lorraine organised when I was twelve. It was kind of epic. I smile, remembering the bunting we put up, all the food, everyone laughing together and setting off fireworks in the evening. We even rigged up a net to play volleyball in the street and Lorraine organised face painting and dragged out a massive ancient stereo for dancing. It was one of those days you could feel like part of something. Maybe we can get the whole community together again.

So I give her the edited highlights of the last few weeks: Mum working and Dad so down, plus our ideas for fighting the buyout.

Lorraine listens through without interrupting, then gets out her letter. 'I spoke to your mum about this. She's been up the Citizens Advice and they said there was nothing doing.'

'Well, we don't think so. We want to do something.'

'You reckon it'll make a difference?' I see the lines on her face, the scepticism in her eyes, mixed with a kind of wary tiredness and for some reason Dad's face when he got back from his disability assessment comes to me.

'Yeah, I do. We can't sit here waiting until half the people round here are gone who knows where. Do you remember the Jubilee?'

Lorraine's face brightens. 'Lovely day that – we were lucky with the weather, weren't we?'

'And with you. You organised all that.'

'It was a while ago,' she says.

'I know.'

There's a silence and I can see her thinking. 'If this rent rise goes through, me and Dylan'll have to move out. Loads of us will.'

'It might not, if we all kick up enough of a fuss.'

Lorraine's nodding now and I feel a surge of triumph. 'Right, when's this meeting? Give me the rest of them,' she says and I hand over the leaflets. Lorraine scans through one and then nods, her face determined. 'We'll be there.'

I go back to my house, where Deal and Jamie are waiting, and give them a thumbs up. It feels good to be out doing something, talking to people. Trying to get everyone to see we're all in the same boat. And with Lorraine on board, I know we'll get a decent turnout at our meeting.

Question is, will it ever be enough?

I work all week on social media, checking in with Jamie, Kells and Deal. Kelly says she's got a plan, but won't say what. I think it involves a celebrity – she's been tweeting everyone she can think of but so far no one's answered. I've barely been bothering with homework. School's starting to feel less and less relevant these days.

I got pulled up on it by Miss Lund in French the other day. She stopped me on the way out with that look teachers get when they're about to tell you that you need to start working otherwise Your Whole Future Will be Ruined. Like I haven't been hearing that crap since Year Six SATs. Schoolwork is just there, something to get out of the way so you can get on with your real life, like seeing mates, going up on the Downs, going out. Seeing Annabel …

I try and push thoughts of her out of my head. Remember Miss Lund saying, 'You need to buckle down, Joni. I know you can do better than a D.' She was waving my last practice paper in front of me.

I said sorry, explained there was some stress going on at home, which usually does the trick, and escaped, but I'm still left with that scratchy feeling, like everyone at school and at home is trying to wrestle me into this big costume marked *Uni for the Win* and I'm not sure I want to wear it at all.

CHAPTER EIGHTEEN

The meeting is in the back room of The Olde Inne. I'm still worried no one will show up, but when I walk through the door with Kelly, the place is already half full and as Jamie goes around talking to people and handing out leaflets, more come through the door. I reckon there's a good thirty people by the time Deal starts talking.

I sit next to Kelly and watch him in action.

'Hi, everyone. Some of you know me already.' There's a general murmur at this. 'I've been living here the last three years and I love this place.' That gets some smiles. 'If you don't know me, you'll all know Jamie and Joni here.' He pauses to look at us and everyone else follows suit. I feel myself going red, but he's already launching into his speech.

He's good. Really good. He's toned down the swears and the ranting side I sometimes hear with Jamie, but he still talks with passion, setting out all sorts of stuff, like how expensive houses are to rent outside the estate, using words like 'social cleansing'.

'Who do they think is going to do the care work, or the bar and restaurant work?' He nods to someone who's come in late at the back and I realise with a leap inside it's one of the TAs from school. 'Or work as teaching assistants, if we all move out? Loads of you have been here for decades.' He looks at the many grey heads in the room.

Jamie's nodding, his expression similar to Deal's: fierce, alight. 'Our family have been here all my life. We're people too and we matter,' Jamie says, his voice rising at the end.

There's a chorus of approval at this.

One lady speaks, the TA. 'But these big companies never back down, they always win in the end.'

Jamie's about to speak, but Deal slides in smoothly. He's walking up and down, filling the space like a natural, all six foot of him. 'That's not true. They fought it on an estate in London. Same thing – company came, bought the houses, jacked up the rent and expected people to go quietly. But they didn't. They had sit-in protests at the Town Hall, picketed the company's offices, the works. And they won. There've been others too.' He reels off a list. 'We just need to show White Light we mean business. We're going to have a march, right here in the town. We'll force them to listen. And if that doesn't work, well, we'll keep going. What you've got to understand is how people like White Light think. And I know about that.' Deal's gaining momentum now, his voice getting louder. 'People like the men in charge of White Light only believe in money. They don't give a shit – excuse me,' he says to the lady with the biscuits from the other day but she waves a hand and smiles up at him. 'You're right, this is a time to be angry, so I'll say again. They. Don't. Give. A. Shit. Not about you or me or anyone but themselves. But we can make them. And we will!' He shouts the last bit, then adds in a voice that seems almost menacing, 'Believe me, we will.'

I feel a momentary chill, then look around the room. People are nodding, their faces determined. One or two are smiling, exchanging comments with the people sitting next to them. There's a buzz in the air as the meeting wraps up.

'Wow,' Kelly says to me. 'He's pretty woke, isn't he? You reckon this lot will be though?'

'I don't think they were ever asleep. it's just they didn't know what to do before,' Deal says from behind her. He's still pumped up, his face flushed.

'And now they do,' Kelly says.

'Yeah. Now *we* do. All of us,' I say.

I'm smiling too.

Later on, I'm on my way to Annabel's house. It feels great to be whizzing along, no sticking gears or falling-off chain, just the air running across my bare arms and the smell of summer approaching. The tree tunnel above me is an explosion of green shadows as I whip by. I'm still buzzing from the meeting earlier. Loads of people signed the petition and took down the web address, said they'd tell their friends about the march or write to Lattimer.

There's only one thing that's bothering me as I go up the driveway to Annabel's house. I haven't actually told her about the campaign yet. I'm not sure why, except my impulse to keep things separate seems to be winning out. But it's also starting to feel odd to keep something this big to myself, now that I'm more comfy telling her stuff.

Annabel is waiting on the front step, wearing shorts and a vest top. Her legs are about a mile long.

'Hello!' She gives a big grin and I know there's an equally wide one on my face. We don't do the stupid air-kissy thing, just hug for a long time.

'Your parents in?'

She shakes her head and gives me a look that makes me go hot. I know we're moving more and more each day to a point we're not going to come back from and still be the same people.

When we're inside she says, 'Shall we go to my room?' I gulp.

It's predictably gigantic, with an enormous double bed you can easily walk all the way round. The bed has pillows and a duvet that match and look like they've been ironed on. There's a throw over the foot of the bed in the same pattern as the cushions. One corner of the room has this huge antique-looking oak desk. I touch the warm grain of the wood.

'Daddy had it custom-made. He has a matching one in his study. Well, larger, but you know,' Annabel says.

'It's nice.' I'm having trouble getting the words out because my eyes keep sliding towards the bed. I'm pretty sure my face is still tomato-like so I turn away to look around again.

Everything is nice, understated but in a way you can tell costs a mint. All cream walls and thick rugs on beautiful floorboards, and that desk. That bed. I'm wondering if coming up to Annabel's room was a good idea.

'This place looks like a magazine or something,' I say.

Annabel gives an embarrassed cough. 'Mummy had it all decorated. I didn't actually choose any of this. Except the poster. Daddy got it for me, and some other things. One for each A star at GCSE.'

It's a framed signed picture of the Beatles record 'Love Me Do'. 'That's not real, is it?' I say.

She gives a faint nod, looking sheepish.

Bloody hell. Again.

'Definitely beats my place,' I say.

I don't mean it in a horrible way, it's just the truth.

Then because there seems to be no way to avoid it, I leap on to the bed and start bouncing up and down, pushing the covers wonky and revealing a layer of pillows. The mattress is awesome, deep and smoothly firm, no sagging bits or springs you'd have to curl your body round. 'Come on. Bounce with me.'

'No, I don't –'

'Come *on*!' I snatch a pillow and chuck it at her.

Annabel laughs and lets me pull her up and then we're jumping up and down and lobbing pillows, her hair flying up behind her. We bump into each other and fall to one side, so I'm half on top of her, still laughing, and then we both go really still.

I am lying on Annabel's bed. With Annabel.

I'm about to pull back when she reaches up and puts one hand around the back of my head, drawing my mouth down to hers. I can feel her underneath me, her body, her tongue against mine, and it's there again, bursts of colour behind my eyes, my head light with it. One of my legs is between hers. I push up so I can look at her. Then with my face close to hers, checking she's all right with my eyes, I reach down and put my hand on her stomach over her vest top and move it up. She makes a little noise, pulls me in for another kiss, so my hand is kind of squashed between us, but it's OK, and there's a huge part of my brain that's just going *OMGOMGOMG*, because I've never touched anyone's boob before. We roll on to our sides and she reaches for me too, and it feels so good, amazing, her fingers light and then firmer, our legs still tangled up together.

After forever, we stop for breath. Annabel's smiling and I am too.

Part of me wants to keep kissing her, touch her again, to do more, but I sit up instead, knocking a pillow on to the floor.

Underneath is a tiny bear with matted fur and one ear missing.

I pick it up. 'Who's this?' I'm still smiling.

Annabel goes red. 'It's nothing. Ridiculous. If Mummy thought I'd kept him …'

I stare as she tucks the bear away, then turns to face me, her bottom lip caught for a second under her top teeth. 'The only other person who's seen Barney is Mary, when she makes the beds. She knows to keep him tucked away.' She gives a laugh. 'It's ridiculous really,' she says again.

But I don't smile back. 'Why do you hide him?'

Annabel jerks her chin up; her version of a shrug. 'Mummy thinks he got thrown out years and years ago, when I went to boarding school. She said I was too old for him, that the other girls would tease me.'

'Did they?'

Her smile is an odd one I haven't seen on her before. 'I know how to keep things hidden. If they need to be.'

Like me? I don't ask.

Instead I let her pull me towards her again, but as we start kissing, a voice floats up the stairs.

Annabel pulls back so fast she almost falls off the bed. I have to shoot out a hand to stop her.

'That's Mummy,' she says, looking horrified.

'Want me to climb out of the window?' I'm half joking and half hurt.

Annabel gives me another panicked look and then she squares her shoulders and says, 'No. Come on, we had better go down.'

I follow her down the wide stairs. There's a woman in the hallway with a suitcase, who's the spit of Annabel if you add on a few years. Not many mind; I wonder if she's had work done.

'Mummy!'

Annabel runs over and they air-kiss twice. Then Annabel's mum spots me lurking at the bottom of the stairs. I swallow hard, think, *showtime*, and step forwards.

'Mummy, this is Joni from the library.' Annabel says, in a pretty normal voice considering.

I feel like I should wipe my palms on my jeans before I take the hand Annabel's mum holds out to me, saying, 'Eleanor.' Her hand is cool, just like Annabel's. They're so similar up close; it's properly freaky, and I stare into Annabel's mum's eyes a bit too long as I mutter, 'Nice to meet you.' This seems to be the wrong thing to say because I can see I've failed some test I didn't even know I needed to revise for.

My stomach churns. I never feel nervous like this with anyone's parents – Kelly's mum is a right laugh and even

Lara's parents were nice enough – but then, I've never really met anyone like Annabel or her mum.

Eleanor says, 'Mary's left something for supper?' Annabel nods and Eleanor turns to me. 'Well then, why don't you stay for supper too? I always like to get to know any friends of Annabel's.'

Annabel gives a twitch, like she's thinking this is a bad idea. I look down at the frayed laces on my boots. 'Um, thanks, but I'd best get off. I don't want to put you out or anything.'

'Nonsense – I'm sure Annabel would love you to stay.' This time her mum's voice is firm. Annabel's shoulders seem to slump forward but I don't feel like I've got any choice except to say, 'OK, thanks.'

'That's settled then. Perfect.' She suddenly purses her lips and looks Annabel up and down. 'Would you like to change into something a little less …' She wafts her hand at Annabel's shorts, which I guess are on the skimpy side.

Annabel flushes and says, 'Sorry, Mummy.' She runs off up the stairs. I stand awkwardly in the kitchen as Eleanor goes to the oven, opens it and clucks her tongue, then wrenches a knob around quite hard. Then she turns to me. 'You like salmon?'

'Er … I'm a veggie – vegetarian actually,' I say. 'Sorry.'

'Really?' Her eyebrows arch. 'Surely not fish though?'

I try to smile. 'Sorry,' I say again.

'Well, I'm sure we can find something for you. It's no trouble.'

I'm pretty sure it is, but she goes to the fridge and gets one of those M&S ready meals out, then smiles at me. 'Here we are. Mushroom en croute.'

'Lovely, thanks,' I say and hope I can eat it, because I've no idea what that is and I'm not a massive mushroom fan.

Annabel comes back into the kitchen. She's changed into a below-the-knee floral dress which looks nice but somehow seems to make her stand taller and stiffer than usual. I don't think I've ever seen her in a dress before.

Eleanor gives her a once-over, lips pursed again. 'I'm not sure that colour does anything for you. And it rather cuts you off at the knees.' I thought the blue was kind of nice – goes with her eyes – but I don't dare say it. Annabel looks down at her legs. 'I saw this gorgeous dress in Browns last week. I'll pick it up next time I pass,' Eleanor says.

'Thank you,' Annabel says and I swear her voice is posher.

I go with Annabel into the dining room. The table's big enough to get half my History class round. 'All right?' I say, in a low voice. Annabel lays down a cloth serviette and smooths it over with the tips of her fingers, then darts a glance up at me that says it all. She's terrified.

'I won't let on anything, you know, about us. I take it your parents don't know?'

She shakes her head.

We've got to have a proper talk about this. 'It's nothing to be ashamed of, being gay, you know,' I say in a whisper, then add, 'I'll make an excuse.'

I don't wait for Annabel's response before I go into the gigantic kitchen, where Eleanor is opening the Aga.

'I think I need to get off after all. I've got … um …' My brain goes totally blank, just white space where an excuse should be. 'I'm sure you want to have Annabel to yourself,' I say finally.

She turns, holding a dish. On her left hand a diamond above her wedding ring catches the light. 'Not at all. It will be lovely to hear all about the library.'

There isn't much arguing with that, without seeming completely rude. I slink back to the dining room where Annabel's finished setting the table with proper serviettes and both wine and water glasses.

'Shall we sit?' Eleanor calls. 'Annabel, why don't you get some water.'

I follow Annabel into the kitchen and watch as she gets a jug and starts slicing a lime. 'Need a hand?'

She pulls a face. 'Could you get some water from the fridge?'

I grab a couple of bottles and she decants them into the jug, adding lime slices and ice.

Eleanor's already sat on one of the lounge sofas, holding a glass of white wine. I sit gingerly on the other one, while Annabel brings in a tray and puts it on a shining wood coffee table near me. The jug's heavy and as I pour, two ice cubes plonk out, sending water sloshing over the table.

'You've put too many in, darling,' Eleanor says.

'I'll get a cloth,' Annabel says, but I've already grabbed a slightly grubby tissue out of my pocket and started mopping up. We both kind of freeze and I say, 'Sorry,' yet again. Eleanor gives another wave of her hand but I'm sure I catch her lips going tight.

We sip our drinks. I scan my brain for something to say. Eventually, my eyes land on that photo of Annabel on an orange coloured horse. 'Is that Puzzle?' I say.

Before Annabel can reply, Eleanor gives a laugh. 'Oh, you did love that pony.' She looks at me. 'Annabel insisted on riding her every day. I used to worry about her up on the Downs on her own.' This sounds like something my mum would say so I smile, but then Eleanor turns to Annabel. 'I never understood the fuss you made about getting something more forward going. Puzzle was such a plodder.' She looks back at me. 'Annabel grew so tall so quickly. Her feet must have been at poor Puzzle's knees. We had to sell her while Annabel was away at school.'

'I wasn't too heavy for her,' Annabel says.

'Yes, but your legs, darling. I've never seen a more gangly child. It really did look ridiculous.' She laughs again and I glance at Annabel, whose face seems frozen into a smile. I suddenly hear echoes of Annabel saying she's ridiculous in my head. She takes a sip of water and I want to reach out and touch her hand, but I don't.

Eleanor seems to be enjoying her reminiscing. 'I am glad we finally got you out of the habit of slouching though. I always think if you must be tall, wear it well,' she says and smiles at Annabel. I think I catch something in Eleanor's eyes then, like the shadow of an old worry mixed up with softness and it makes me think of Mum again, but Annabel hasn't seen because she's staring at the picture of Puzzle. She's also sitting really upright.

When tea is ready we go into the dining room. Eleanor insists I sit down so I watch as Annabel brings in a dish of baby potatoes, creamy yellow, the faint smell of mint floating across the table, the fish and this plate of baby corn on the cob and other veg.

Eleanor dishes out the food. I notice she only puts a really small portion out for her and Annabel. Mine, on the other hand, is massive and I wonder if I can eat it all. I put a big forkful in, burning my mouth. I chew and swallow as fast as I can and take a long slug of water, the inside of my cheek stinging. At home, I'd have been waving my hand in front of my open mouth and laughing, but no way am I doing that here.

'I understand you've been doing some wonderful work in the library,' Eleanor says after a moment, in this voice that reminds me of the mums at toddler group. When they're trying to get their kids to talk to some-one new.

'Er, well, I guess. Annabel's been a real help.'

'Has she?' She leaves a tiny pause, almost as though she doesn't believe this. 'And you've been working there for some time?'

'Yeah, a few months now.'

'You're local?'

'Yes – I live on Cherry Tree Estate?'

Eleanor says, 'Oh. Yes. Lovely.' It isn't, but for a moment I get the sense she's floundering, unsure what to say next. 'Ah, what does your father do?'

Seriously? My mouth's hanging open, but nothing comes out for a moment. It's like she's sniffing me out, making sure she knows exactly where I fit. Or don't. But why? Why does it matter so much?

'Joni's doing A Levels,' Annabel says quickly and her mum's face clears, like this is a conversation she can handle.

'Really? Which subjects?'

I tell her and she makes a face. 'I suppose you'll have to do an arts degree. Have you thought how that might affect your career prospects?'

'Not really.'

She gives a small shake of her head as if this is confirming something. It's kind of patronising. 'Annabel's father wants her to take a Maths degree. I understand it's the most useful thing in the City these days. What is it Daddy always says, darling?'

'"It's brains not balls",' Annabel says quietly.

Eleanor gives one of those braying laughs while I stare at Annabel. She never said. I can't exactly imagine her as a banker or something. Jeez.

We limp on, Eleanor asking me clipped questions, but I'm on edge, a rerun of that out of place feeling I got at the restaurant we went to for Jack's birthday. Also, I seem to be talking in a really weird fake posh voice. Annabel looks uncomfy too, even though it's not like I'm about to blurt out, 'Oh, and by the way I'm gay and I'm pretty sure your daughter is too. We've just been doing some serious snogging upstairs.'

I'm getting beyond full, but I don't want to seem rude, so I plough on through my food. We're nearly finished and I'm thinking about making my escape with a pretty large sense of relief when a door slams. A second later a man comes into the dining room, talking into a mobile. 'No, tell Amir that's not good enough. I need stats tonight. Yes. Right. Dominic has those. Tomorrow then.' His voice is clipped, tired. He reminds me oddly of Dad, his face crumpled with that same look of pained weariness Dad gets. He finishes his call and looks at Eleanor.

'I thought you were on the seven o' clock?' she says, a hint of something, maybe irritation, creeping into her voice. Annabel has gone completely motionless: obviously she hadn't expected either of them. Oh Jesus.

'I got the driver to bring me down. Bloody protesters on the train in First Class. And I'm going to have to let Dominic go if he doesn't buck his ideas up.'

'Oh dear,' Eleanor says. 'I'll get you some supper.' She goes into the kitchen.

He looks again at his phone.

'Hello, Daddy,' Annabel says, her voice quiet, and he finally seems to notice we're both in the room.

'Hello, darling,' he says. She turns her face up to him and smiles the same sort of tentative smile I've seen on Teddy's face when he's after a toy or biscuit in the library, all big eyes and shy charm. Then her dad looks at me and raises expectant eyebrows.

Annabel says, 'This is Joni from the library.'

I get the same feeling he's assessing me like Eleanor was. I reckon he comes to the same conclusion, but this seems to relax him; the frown he was wearing smooths out as he says in a jolly voice, 'Ah, hello. I hope Annabel's been pulling her weight?' He smiles at her.

'She has, yeah. She's a trouper,' I say.

'Wonderful to hear.' He pats Annabel on the shoulder. 'And the Maths score this week?'

'Joint first,' she says.

He smiles properly at this. 'Excellent stuff.' He reaches into his suit pocket. 'Dominic ordered too many,' he says as he hands her a small box with the Apple logo on the front.

'Thank you,' she says.

I can't help thinking she probably would've preferred a hug.

Eleanor comes back with another plate of food, but he's barely started eating when his phone goes again. Ignoring Eleanor's frown, he picks it up, gives a few instructions then ends the call and puts it back on the table. It's the latest model, light glinting off the metal around its edges.

'Edward,' Eleanor says in this jokey voice to make it sound like she isn't really telling him off.

His finger strokes the side of the phone once, then he pushes it away and starts to eat. He's a good-looking bloke, even I can see that, with the sort of greying hair Mum calls 'distinguished' and strong features. You can totally imagine him in an office behind a giant desk, with lots of minions.

For a minute, I think we're going to sit there watching him in silence. Annabel and Eleanor seem to be waiting for him to speak. It's easy to see why Annabel is so tall. I feel like a midget next to the three of them.

Finally, he says, 'Damn protesters. What do they think they're going to achieve?'

'Why the trains?' Annabel asks.

'To make a nuisance out of themselves. They want all first-class carriages abolished. Pure spite and envy,' he says.

I've only been to London a couple of times: once on a school trip and once with Kelly last year. She badgered me into going shopping on Oxford Street and I went because she agreed we could visit the Natural History Museum too. We had an ace day, but walked about a zillion miles. The train home was rammed; we wedged ourselves into a space between two carriages. I was crapping myself the plates we were standing on would somehow shift apart and I'd disappear through the gap. First Class was silent, peaceful. And pretty much two-thirds empty.

Annabel is nodding like everything her dad says is coming down from on high. I speak before I've thought it through. 'They might have a point about First Class.'

Every head swivels to me.

Annabel's dad's eyes go hawk-like. 'You think so?'

I swallow. 'Well, yeah. I mean, you'd fit a load more people in, wouldn't you? Then they wouldn't have to stand up or get squashed.' His eyebrows are much darker than his hair, thick and low as he gazes at me. 'It'd be fairer,' I finish lamely.

Annabel closes her eyes for a second.

Her dad gives me a long look, then laughs suddenly. It makes his face so much younger, softer. 'I admire your idealism. Completely unrealistic of course, but that's the prerogative of the young.'

It's weird, even though I know he's kind of talking down to me, there's also something about the way he smiles when he says it that makes you want to agree with him. Annabel nods.

I open my mouth, trying to work out a counter-argument, but it's like my brain goes blank under his gaze. Then he smiles again, his eyes crinkling at the corners. 'Let's not spoil supper with a discussion on politics. What I really want to know is how's the library? Putting my money to good use?'

I guess that lets me know who's in charge of the conversation then. His tone is friendly, but I get this sudden image of a lord handing out coins to the commoners.

'Um, yea– yes. I think so. I was saying before, we're doing new classes in the summer holidays and we've got the toddler group. Plus all the books and that.'

'You have enough resources?'

I nod slowly.

'Wonderful. Well, you let me know if there's anything you need. Libraries are another thing the Tories can't get right,' he begins.

'I thought we weren't going to talk politics, darling.' Eleanor smiles, but Annabel's dad ignores her; he's off on some speech about meritocracy and a load of other stuff, like he actually cares. Annabel and her mum smile in agreement, but Eleanor's eyes seem strained, maybe because he keeps barrelling past any contribution she tries to make. Annabel doesn't even bother trying. But her dad doesn't stop. It's like he's so sure of his opinion, he can't even consider the thought that anyone else might have one. For a moment, I feel sorry for all of them.

Finally, Annabel's dad finishes and stands up. 'You'll have to excuse me – I have a lot of work to do.' He pats Annabel on the shoulder and she smiles up at him. I'm staring. I don't mean to, but I can't square the version of the bloke who hates people for wanting to get rid of First Class with the one who is happy to give his cash to the local library.

He clocks me looking and I feel the beginnings of a blush. 'Er, yeah, nice to meet you,' I say. He nods his head, gives Eleanor an indecipherable look, then leaves the room.

'Well!' Eleanor says, her voice bright. I can't tell if she's putting it on or not. Annabel seems to take this as a sign and stands up, looking at me to follow.

'Right. OK, I'll get off then.' I get up too and give Eleanor an awkward smile. 'Thanks for tea,' I say.

Annabel walks me out into the hallway. Her dad's study door is ajar and through it I catch a glimpse of him in a chair behind a huge desk, his legs stretched out as he talks on his phone, frowning into the distance.

'Well, see you Saturday then,' I say as we go outside, and Annabel nods, her face suddenly miserable. I wish I could take her hand but we're in full view of her dad's study so I just wave and get on my bike. I think I see him looking out of the window, but I pretend I haven't, shout another bye to Annabel, then whizz off up the drive.

On the ride home, I think about them all in that massive house, of the strange undercurrents between Annabel and her parents. And for the first time since I've met her, I don't feel even a tiny bit jealous of Annabel.

CHAPTER NINETEEN

The two weeks before the march go by in a massive blur. I see Annabel every night if I can or we speak on the phone. I haven't been back to her house although she comes to mine one night and we watch a DVD, holding hands on the sofa.

The more time I spend with her, the more I want to. Even with everything else going on, she's on my mind pretty much 24/7.

I'm listening to all the romantic Beatles songs on repeat.

I am so in trouble.

The one downer is that even though it's getting easier to talk to her about stuff, I know there's still so many things I'm not saying. Like whether she's going to come out to her parents.

And I haven't told her about the campaign.

One evening we take a drive up to Avebury. We park at the Red Lion, which is quiet apart from a few bikers, and hold hands as we wander towards the stones. It's warm out, the sun skimming the undersides of pale clouds. I can smell fresh air and grass and also sheep poo … I check the ground carefully before I sit, resting my back against one of the stones.

We lace our fingers together.

'Joni? I was wondering something. Are you going to apply for university?' Annabel says.

I reckon she's thinking of the conversation with her mum.

'Because you really should,' she adds. 'You've got more brains than half the people in my year.'

'How do you figure that?'

'I see it,' she says. And I remember what I thought the day I first kissed her, that I saw her too. It makes me smile.

'You sound like my teacher. Or my mum. They're all on at me to decide. I guess I'll have to soon-ish.'

'But don't you want to go?'

'Plenty of reasons not to. Money, for starters. And what for? I mean, yeah, if I was going to be a nurse or a lawyer or something, but to be in that much debt for three more years of essays and exams, and still not get a job at the end of it … What's the point? There's not that many jobs round here anyway.'

'But surely you won't always live here? And university isn't only about the career you get at the end. You could study something you love.'

'What, like Maths?' It's a low dig, but the words fly out of my mouth anyway.

She flushes. 'That's …'

'Different? How? I'm not stupid. I know everyone says you should "do what you love".' I put air quotes around it. 'Which is great if you can afford it. Some of us can't.' I look her dead in the eyes. 'You could though. You can afford to do whatever you want, go wherever you want. And you're doing Maths? You hate it.'

Annabel shifts as if to stand up, then she sits back again. Her face has gone from pink to really pale. 'It's not that simple.'

'Why not?'

It comes out loud enough to make a couple strolling past look over, but I can't help it; it's not like I'm trying to start a row, but I could shake her right now. It's the lake all over again. Why can't she see she has all the choices in the world?

As if reading my mind, she says, 'I don't have a choice, not without … There's things to consider … people to consider.'

'Like?'

Annabel sighs as though this should be obvious. 'My parents have all these plans for who they want me to be, the things they want for me.'

'What about what you want for you?'

She tries to laugh. 'They'll be paying my tuition fees and living expenses after all. Daddy could easily decide not to.'

'So? Get a bloody job then, Annabel. Put yourself through uni like the rest of us.'

We've moved apart to face each other, the evening air cool on my face. How has this blown up so fast? I guess that's what happens when you don't say the stuff you really want to; it builds up inside until it comes crashing out whether you like it or not.

Annabel raises her voice too. 'But you just said yourself you can't afford to go to university. Well, neither could I, if Daddy didn't pay.' I open my mouth, but she's shaking her head. 'Truthfully? It isn't only that. It's also …' She dips her chin so the next part is aimed at her shoes. 'I – I don't want them to be disappointed in me.'

'But –'

'You're so focused on the external things I have – the money, the house, the school. Don't you see I'd swap them all in a heartbeat, for a family like yours?'

She walks off so fast it's almost a run.

I stare into the sky, breathing hard. I never realised Annabel might feel trapped too. I think back to the look she gave her dad, her eyes screaming out a question he didn't notice she was asking. Even I stress about not letting Mum and Dad down and I know they'll always love me whatever I do.

These last weeks, I've thought I get her, but I guess people are harder to work out than you think. Maybe you're not supposed to know everything about someone.

I go after her, through a little gate and up to where she's gazing at this huge tree with its roots all sprawled out overground. Dangling from it are hundreds of coloured ribbons, swaying in the early evening breeze.

Without looking at me she says, 'What are they for?'

'I think they're wishes. You tie a ribbon on and make a wish.'

Her face is hurt, but open. 'What would you wish for?'

'Right now?' I look into her eyes. 'For you. I'd wish for you.'

We sit under the tree and talk properly this time, no shouting.

'You're wrong about the house and car and stuff. It's not about having all that, it's that I think – thought – money gets you freedom. Choices. But maybe it doesn't,' I say.

'Not always.'

'But …' I'm feeling my way, trying to think about things from her point of view too. 'I still reckon it helps. You're right – I've never doubted my parents love me and I love them. And my brothers – well, apart from Jamie when he's driving me crazy – but having no money … it stresses you out. Always having to worry about the next bill. It gets hard to plan so far ahead when you're worrying about how to afford the food shop. You see, your dad's not going to see you homeless, is he? Or your mum, or that rich gran of yours in Toulouse. But for me, well …' I take a deep breath and then I explain what's happening about the estate and the campaign. I finish up with, 'So we really could be homeless. Probably will be. Best thing I could do right now is quit sixth form and the library and get a full-time job.'

'My God, Joni. Why didn't you tell me?'

Seeing as we're being the most open with each other we've ever been, I say, 'I was embarrassed. I didn't want you to think – to be – ashamed of me, I guess.'

Annabel reaches out for my hand. 'I could never be ashamed of you.'

'Are you sure?'

She looks me in the face. 'I'm sure. I promise.'

'Then do you … when will … Are you going to come out? To anyone?'

She hesitates.

'I mean, I'm not trying to pressure you. I knew my family and friends would be OK and it was still a big deal for me. But at some point, you have to start being you. Properly you, you know?'

'That's not the –' She bites her lip. I don't want to push; it's enough for now to know I've said it.

'I think the same for you. Without arguing again,' she gives a faint smile, 'I really think you should consider university.'

'I know.' I sigh. 'Maybe if I could find something I really wanted to do.'

'I understand what you said, about money. I respect that. But just imagine for a minute that's not a concern. What do you love?'

I think about this in a way I've not let myself before. 'Here. I mean, not just home and family, but here – the Downs, Avebury. We used to go to the Arboretum all the time and I loved looking at the trees. I guess I like, you know, nature and stuff. Wildlife.' Then I give a laugh. 'Not many jobs in that though, are there?'

'What? Of course there are. Ecology, conservation, arboriculture … Have you done any research?'

OK, she's sounding like a teacher again. 'No-o.'

'Then that's your prep. I challenge you to research five careers in nature you'd like to do, in the next week.'

Just as I'm about to get annoyed again, she leans over and kisses me on the nose, as if to take some of the sting out of her words.

It works.

I can't help smiling around her.

'All right, I will. But "quid pro quo, Clarice" and all that.' Not sure it's the most romantic thing to be making *The Silence of the Lambs* references – she looks confused. I silently curse Jamie for showing me all those old horror films when

I was Jack's age. Although, the bollocking he got from Mum when she found out what he'd shown me was pretty funny. He was grounded for about a million years. 'What do you want to do?'

'Horses.'

'Eh?'

'I love horses. I was never any use at competitions, but I love being around them. And I love the library, the children.'

Actually, she's not that bad with them. She brought in a load of craft stuff for the kids to do last toddler group and they're really warming up to her.

'I thought when Daddy sold Puzzle I'd never ride again, but recently, I've been feeling differently. I would love to open a riding school.'

'There you go then.'

'But it takes money, premises. And it isn't exactly prestigious. Daddy would never let –' She breaks off. 'We were supposed to be talking hypothetically, weren't we?'

'*Uh-huh*. And like I said before, you work on your parents. Tell them what you want. Bet you anything they see it your way eventually. And if they don't, then you get a job, work for it.'

She nods. Looks like we've got a deal.

It's turned serious again here, but I've got an idea of something that will lighten things up. 'Right, come with me.' I lead her back to the stone circle, stopping at the deep ditch that rings the stones. I lie down. 'We're rolling.'

'You are joking?'

'Not even a bit.' I grin. 'Double dare you.'

This doesn't have the same effect as with Jack; she just screws up her face in confusion.

'Watch me, then,' I say and push off. I roll all the way down the hill, seeing flashes of sky, then earth; grass grazing against my arms as I pick up speed, and land with an *oof* at the bottom, breathless.

'Are you OK?' she calls.

'Come down!'

'No.'

'Go on. *Carpe* whatever it is.'

She lies down gingerly. 'I'm not sure this is quite …'

'Don't think, do!'

She shuts her eyes, pushes off and comes flying towards me, shrieking. She lands in a heap and lies there with her eyes shut.

'Annabel?'

No answer.

'Annie? Oh crap.' I scramble over and see she's moving. She's OK. Thank God for that. If I'd got her hurt … hang on. 'Are you laughing? Oh my God, you are as well. I thought you'd hurt yourself …' I stop because she's looking at me now and she's giggling so hard she can't stop. She reaches up and pulls me down and now I'm laughing too, arms round her.

Eventually, we calm down. Annabel picks a piece of grass out of my hair. 'That was amazing. The last time I did something like that was … do you know, I can't remember?'

'Good.' I love seeing her have fun. I remember thinking how she just needed to unwind a bit, and I reckon I was right.

We make our way back up the bank, holding hands. I notice Annabel doesn't pull hers away even when she sees the older couple coming back. We're not speaking, just being together. I feel as though we've come through something, like I've shown her another side to me, and she's shown me herself too, the real her, and I love her even more for it …

Wait. I love her?

I stop.

'What is it?' Annabel says.

I'm about to answer when I hear a trilling noise above our heads. I look up and there's a skylark rising into the air and down again, singing its heart out. 'Look.' I whisper, so as not to frighten it away.

Annabel follows my gaze.

'It's a skylark. They're getting really rare – you never see them around here.' I'm still whispering, but I squeeze her hand tighter and we watch the bird as it flies high above us, singing like it's the only thing in the world that matters. And I feel it – not just that things here are beautiful, but that life can be beautiful. That there are possibilities.

I turn to Annabel and I don't say it out loud, but my eyes are telling her I'm falling in love with her and I think hers are saying the same thing back, and then we're kissing under the skylark and the ancient stones and I know suddenly that what we have, where we're going, is real.

Real and beautiful and free.

CHAPTER TWENTY

'You are not going to believe it!' Kelly is hopping about in the doorway to my room. She texted ten minutes ago. *AMAZING NEWS!!* Then, *I'M COMING OVER*.

'I didn't know you meant you're coming right now,' I say. 'Who let you in?'

'Jack. But shut up and listen to who might be coming to the march. Only Jemima.'

Blank pause. 'Who?'

'Je-mi-ma?' She stretches out each syllable. 'She's that singer – she was just nominated for best breakthrough artist at the Brits. How do you not know this?'

'Err …'

Kelly shakes her head. 'Anyway. I've been chatting to her on Twitter and she's retweeted a load of stuff and then she said she'd come. She only lives like twenty minutes away.'

'But the march is tomorrow.'

'Yeah and?'

'So it's a bit short notice. You sure she's going to come?'

Kelly flashes her phone at me. 'Said she would. And look how many people have replied. I reckon we're going to have a crowd.'

'Maybe. Just don't get your hopes –' I stop abruptly. Mum's words still come out of my mouth on occasion, out of habit, but I'm starting to feel differently these last few weeks. My parents don't know everything.

I scroll through the likes and comments and RTs on all the feeds, and realise something: this thing that started with a little blog in Jamie's room is building up to be something way bigger.

Annabel texts as we're getting ready the next day. *I'm so sorry. Mummy is insisting I come with her to the brow bar for a 'tidy up'. Pray for me. xxxx.*

So that's Annabel out of the picture, but I don't let it wreck my mood. Instead I say to Jack, 'You ready?'

'Yep,' he grins.

Me, Jamie, Deal, Kelly and Jack are all going to the meeting point we've set, by the old church. The plan is to meet whoever shows up there, then walk to Lattimer's office to deliver a printout of the online petition, which so far stands at two thousand signatures, thanks to us working like mad to feed stuff out on social media. It might get to a lot more if Jemima shows up today, even though I secretly still think it's a big if. Then we're going to march up the High Street and stand in front of the Town Hall with our signs.

'Are you?' Jamie says to me.

'I am, actually.' I grab my sign, one of the twenty or so me and Jack made late last night. Deal's brought some too, although his have a more, er, assertive theme. One of them has a picture of a pig in a bloody top hat. Our *S.O.S.* and *Local Homes for Local People* signs seem slightly tame in comparison.

We pile the signs into Deal's car, then all squeeze in, Jack wedged between me and Kelly in the back. The car is so loaded down I'm wondering whether it'll actually make it up the hill, but it does, engine screaming, the windows open and Deal's stereo blaring out some music with a heavy beat, that I don't recognise.

Deal pulls up and it's not until he turns off the music that I look over towards the church.

There's complete silence in the car.

Jamie speaks first. 'Holy crap.'

There's got to be at least a hundred people. And a woman with massive sunglasses and a megaphone who I assume is Jemima.

'I believe we're going to need more signs,' Kelly says, her smile smug.

We bundle the signs out of the car while Kelly goes over to Jemima. She's only a few years older than us. I can hear Kelly saying thank you in this high-pitched squeal.

'No problem. I grew up near here – I know what it's like. You should be proud of what you're doing with all this,' Jemima says. Kelly looks like she's about to implode.

I go over and Kelly introduces me. Deal's handing out placards and instructions. Jack's hopping about at my shoulder.

There's so many people here. Loads from the estate, of course, and their families and friends. I spot the rest of the gang: Pete and Ananya holding hands – I glance at Kelly but she shrugs – and Stace, perched on Ed's shoulders, holding a banner. There's others from school too, and – oh my God, my French teacher. I recognise Theresa and Mrs Jenkins, the nice woman from the newsagents I chat to sometimes. But also loads of people I've never seen. Some are Deal's friends, with a seasoned protester air about them. A big group of Jemima fans are queuing in a messy line to get stuff signed, which she does super fast. We're a strange mix, but that doesn't matter.

People are here for us.

Then a battered car with a different coloured door panel on one side pulls up.

'Mum!'

She comes over, smiling in this amazed way at the crowd.

'You came,' I say.

Mum gives me a hug. 'I thought about what you said.'

I nod.

'I can't believe you've done this, got all these people here.' Mum has actual tears in her eyes.

'It was the others more than me,' I say. 'Did you tell Dad?'

She shakes her head, then says, 'But I will, when we get back. I can't believe it,' she repeats.

Before I can answer, Deal's shouting, 'Let's go!' and everyone starts to move off. Jack scampers to be with Mum, who gestures to me to go on ahead, so I walk fast up the line until I'm with the group at the front – Jemima and her entourage, plus Deal, Jamie, Kelly and the gang.

'Gonna have to put you down,' Ed grunts to Stacey.

'Why, are you saying I'm too heavy?'

He grunts again and she swats him over the side of the head, then clambers off his shoulders. Me and Kelly raise our placards and then Deal gets a chant going as we walk up the High Street.

The pavement's wide and we walk four in a row, linking arms. Shoppers step back to let us past, some looking confused, others interested in the signs. One or two seem hacked off, but I don't care. With the crowd behind me – singing, chanting, our feet stomping on the pavement together – I don't feel small any more. I feel like I could lift up into the sky any moment. Kelly's singing the loudest of all. When I look at her she grins – the same exhilaration I'm feeling, mirrored on her face.

And in the middle of it all, I realise something. This is my home. Not just the estate, or the library, school or the Downs, but this town. I never completely felt like it was my place, like I belonged. But today I do. I fit. The adrenalin pumps through me, making my voice loud and powerful. And I'm suddenly filled with this rushing sense of things opening up, here with all these people behind me. Like we're a proper community.

We get to the alleyway leading to Lattimer's office and Deal stops. Me and Jamie are going to be the ones to deliver the petition. The same blonde woman is behind the desk but she's not looking so glossy today; she seems pretty alarmed.

I smile at her and say, 'We're here to deliver a petition.'

'I'm afraid surgery is by appointment only.'

'Oh. Well, could you give it to him?' I say.

'Hang on.' It's Deal, behind him a man I recognise from his picture in the *Evening Gazette* and a woman holding a camera.

'Hello, Evelyn,' the man from the *Gazette* says. 'Mind if we take a few pictures? These youngsters have gathered quite a crowd. I'm not sure we've seen the like of it for years.'

Am I dreaming it, or does he wink at me?

Evelyn snatches back the hand she'd been holding out for the petition. I don't think she factored in being in the local rag today. 'Wait here, please. I'll speak to Mr Lattimer.'

She disappears through a door and there's the sound of voices rising and falling. The reporter looks at me, Jamie and Deal and says, 'Can you tell me more about this protest?'

Deal's off straight away, the reporter asking loads of questions. He looks like someone just gave him a winning lottery ticket. I guess this is more exciting than reporting on escaped cows, although that story was pretty funny considering they took a nice long amble up the High Street and stopped all the traffic.

A door opens suddenly and a sharp-suited Douglas Lattimer strides out. He shakes hands with everybody, saying, 'I apologise. I was busy with another constituent. I understand you have something for me?'

I stand next to Jamie and try to look confident as Jamie hands the petition over, the photographer taking a million pictures. Lattimer doesn't stop smiling through the whole thing. It's kind of freaky. Then he says, 'Well, I'll certainly give this my full consideration.' He pauses as though he's just remembered something and says, 'I do hope you cleared this little gathering with the police? Got the correct permits in order? Under the usual procedure, I'd be notified you see.'

'We don't need them, we're not blocking the road.' Deal says.

For the first time, Lattimer's smile gets thin. 'Let's hope the police agree with you.' Deal's eyes flash and something seems to pass between him and Lattimer. Interestingly, Lattimer looks away first. Jamie bundles us out of there.

'Is he right?' I whisper.

'Who? Lattimer or Dealo? Don't actually know, but it's a bit late now. Come on,' Jamie replies and we rejoin the crowd, who are definitely spilling out on to the road now. My stomach starts up a nervous growl, but then we're all marching again, Kelly shouting in my ear, 'What did he say?'

Then we're at the Town Hall and we gather in front of Deal and Jemima on the steps. The people from the paper are definitely excited now, taking loads of pictures of Jemima, who makes a short speech. She says the word 'solidarity' a lot and clenches her fist to the camera. There's phones out everywhere; this is going to be all over social media. Then Deal makes a speech and Jamie hops up too to say more about the campaign, but I shake my head when he holds the megaphone out to me. I'm happy listening to the ripples around me, people echoing what Jamie and Deal have said: that the buyout's not fair, that we're part of the community too. That we deserve a place to live that we can afford.

'It's a crying shame, is what it is,' one older man shouts out and others around nod.

A few minutes later, the first police car shows up.

CHAPTER TWENTY-ONE

I know it shouldn't, but seeing a police officer always make me feel like I've done something wrong. The woman seems quite smiley considering, as she asks who's in charge. Probably helps she's asked Mrs Bartlett from up the road, who is about as unthreatening as you can get. I notice one or two of Deal's friends muttering to each other though and I'm sure one says 'Pig' but Deal goes over to shut them up, which they do, looking sulky.

'Right then, I'm PC Smith. What are you lot all doing?'

'Peaceful protest. We're just finishing up,' Jamie says.

'We've had a complaint you're blocking the road.'

'That was an accident – we're not now. Who was the complaint from?' Jamie says.

'I'm not able to say,' PC Smith answers. She has this stern face on, but then she spots Jemima and goes pink. 'Oh my … I didn't realise … My daughter's a huge fan.'

'I can sign something if you want,' Jemima says.

The police officer's face lights up, then she seems to remember what she's doing and says, 'I'm afraid that won't be appropriate.' She raises her voice. 'I'm going to have to ask you all to leave.'

There's a few mutters at this, but then Jemima switches on the megaphone and shouts into it. 'We've done what we needed to do today. Thanks for coming and remember to keep spreading the word. Watch this space!'

The crowd starts to drift away. Someone brings round a couple of cars and after we've all said thanks, Jemima climbs in and gets driven off. I kind of wonder if we'll ever see her again, other than in the paper.

I watch people go, then look up into the sky, where a couple of birds are making their way across the blue.

'Brilliant turnout. Now we need to keep the momentum going,' Deal's saying, but for now I'm happy to just watch the birds and think about all the people who came today. I look over to where Mum's standing at the edge of the thinning crowd and I meet her eyes, see my own thoughts reflected back there, along with what I reckon is an apology.

She underestimated what we could do, what people would do, but I guess right up until today I was still doing that as well. I didn't really believe people like me, or Jamie, Deal and Kelly could make a difference to anything. And perhaps nothing will come of this, but now I can feel that belief is there, soaring just like those birds in the sky.

Maybe I can believe there's hope. And that it's worth standing up and fighting for ourselves.

The next few days seem to prove me right, at least in a small way. There's a decent front-page article in the *Gazette*, and more interest on social media. All our accounts are picking up followers, helped by Jemima who's been steadily RTing pictures from the march with slogans like 'Poor but not Powerless', so that proves me wrong on that front. We plan another community meeting, and more people say they'll come.

And we finally talk to Dad, now there's something good to tell him.

He's in his dressing gown in the lounge when we show him the picture in the paper of Jamie handing the petition over to Lattimer.

He scans the article, then looks from Jamie's face to mine and back again. 'Bloody hell,' he says. And for the first time since I saw him cry, I catch some of the old Dad back in his face. 'I'm proud of you both. You look all professional.' He smiles suddenly, then screws up his nose. 'Although you could do with a haircut.'

I laugh. Dad's forever on at Jamie about his hair, but I reckon Jamie's aiming to get it as long as Deal's. I feel a surge of gratitude when I see Deal in the background of the picture, fist clenched. I can finally see what Jamie likes about him.

I'm pretty relieved they didn't print one of me; my hair needs a cut too and I've got a massive spot on my chin. Anyway, I never photograph well. Obviously, it's the camera's fault and not my actual face that's the problem.

The next day, Dad's up and about, job hunt renewed. Mum hums along to the radio when she's cooking dinner. They've got it too, a light feeling inside, like the brush of a feather. Best of all, they both come to the next meeting.

It's packed this time, people standing three-deep at the back. I find a chair for Dad and then someone taps me on the shoulder.

It's Annabel. I give a shriek and go to hug her, then remember and look around in case any of her posh friends are here, but of course they're not, although there are definitely a few posher-looking people from the town and even the local vicar. We're gaining momentum, as Deal would say.

'I'm so happy you came,' I tell her.

Annabel gives a wide smile. 'I didn't think I was going to get away, but then Mummy needed to go to town for work, so here I am.' She looks around and I can tell how impressed she is. It makes me stand tall, even if I do still only come up to her shoulder.

'Still got your eyebrows then,' I say.

Annabel grins. 'It was a close-run thing. I thought I might have to kick the technician at one point.'

'You look good.'

We stand together near the back as Deal jumps on to the makeshift stage we made and holds up his hand.

Everyone quietens down and there's a pause, then Deal begins. 'Thank you for coming. It was brilliant to see so many of you at the march last week –' He breaks off because someone gives a whoop and there's a burst of clapping and cheers. Deal smiles as he waits for it to die down. He's a natural in front of the crowd, like he was born to it. 'Last week showed what we can do when we all stand together against the elite, the people who run White Light, the bankers and the politicians. They don't want to listen to you, to us.' For one second his face seems to contort into something approaching hatred. Then he gives that boyish grin and raises an arm. 'But we will make them listen. There is hope!' His voice rises and there's more whooping and applause. I glance at Annabel, who's staring at him, her eyes thoughtful.

'This campaign is quite rightly focused on you. On your homes, your town. But there are wider issues at stake in all this too. Inequality. The NHS. Schools. Opportunities.' He's ticking them off on his fingers. 'Is it fair that some people get everything handed to them on a plate, with their private schools, their internships and their parents' connections, while others leave university with debts of forty-grand plus? Did you know that only half of politicians went to state schools?'

I shift from one foot to the other as Deal continues like that for another couple of minutes, finishing with, 'But we can create something new, something better. And it starts local, it starts here with our homes, our jobs, our town. It's time to rise up and take what's rightfully ours!' This time the applause is slightly less enthusiastic from some sections of the crowd and I spot one or two confused faces, but Deal's friends from the march cheer.

I turn to Annabel. 'Well, that was a bit more than I was expecting.'

'*Hmm?*' She's still looking at Deal, then she turns her head to me. 'It was interesting. I wonder if ...'

It must've felt weird for her, standing there listening to him basically slagging off people like her dad. Like her. Maybe I shouldn't have asked her to come.

'I reckon we should just stick to the houses though. That other stuff … I don't know. It's not like I don't care, but it's just too big, isn't it?' I say. 'What if it puts people off?' There's a chance I'm also asking whether it's going to put her off, and maybe she senses it, because she touches my arm briefly and smiles.

Deal and Jamie come over as we're clearing up. I wonder about trying to catch Jamie on his own; tell him what I just said to Annabel. But Deal's stood right there, so I introduce Annabel instead. He gives her a smile but it doesn't seem as friendly as usual and I realise he's taking in her expensive bag, her earrings and the sunglasses on top of her head.

Before I can say anything, Kelly and the gang come up. I give Kelly a 'behave' look and say, 'This is Annabel.'

Kelly says hi in a totally natural voice and I stand back to watch Annabel chatting easily to them all. Ananya's going on about the summer drama programme at Edrington's – both her and Pete got in, while Annabel asks all the right questions. I wish I had that much confidence. I can only think of one other person who seems to have stacks of it the way Annabel does, even if it is an act, and that's Deal.

I frown again, wondering. I thought it before but it seems clearer from his speech tonight: he's got an agenda and I don't think it's just to save our estate.

The next evening, I meet Annabel at the pub. The gang aren't there, but it still feels like this huge milestone, to show her another one of my places. And they all seemed to like her the other day.

Annabel wants to get in the drinks, but I shake my head. 'I can stand a couple of Cokes, you know.'

She opens her mouth to disagree, then nods and lets me buy them. When I sit down, she gives me a close look. 'You know, you seem …'

'What?'

She smiles. 'More yourself.'

'Is that a good thing?'

'It's the best thing.'

It's true too, I do feel different. 'Maybe it's all the stuff with the campaign.'

'What's the plan next? Will you have another march?'

'I don't know. Keeping up the pressure on social media. Deal's been muttering about more "actions", whatever that means, but maybe we won't need to.' I leave out my uneasiness about it, or the fact that some days I feel like we're shouting into the wind and the wind's always going to win. And I definitely leave out some of the messages we've started to get on social media. Trolls, pretty much, saying the usual crap – calling us libtards, scum, peasants, jealous – all sorts. Jemima's had the most abuse – I know because she RTs them with funny takedowns. I can't help noticing how many of the ones directed at her seem to feature words like 'bitch' and 'whore', or are threats to rape her, murder her. Stuff that'd probably make me want to live in a cave for the next fifty years if it was coming my way. I've kind of ducked a lot of it, as our accounts are all campaign ones rather than personal ones, but it still makes my heart clench whenever it's my turn to go online and do the usual checking, blocking and deleting. I don't know how Jemima does it. Maybe she's got someone to do it for her.

I pull my attention back to Annabel, and catch this fresh lemony scent from her hair as she turns her head. 'You about tomorrow?' I say. I'm thinking we can go out for a walk, or she can come to mine, or I'll go to hers when her parents aren't about, and maybe we could …

'I'm sorry. I can't. I have the sixth form supper tomorrow evening.'

'Sixth form supper?'

'Didn't I tell you? It's really boring. You have to go in for supper with the teachers and the old boys – past pupils. They usually have people from business and industry, sometimes politicians or artists. I can't remember who the guests are this term.'

'What do you have to do that for?'

'Well … it's tradition. And I suppose it helps us to make connections …' She trails off, her face thoughtful. 'It's really nothing.'

But it isn't. I think back to Deal's speech and wonder if Annabel was taking any of it in. I can't imagine sitting down to some posh dinner at school with an artist or successful businesswoman. Knowing that was the future I could have too. And suddenly there's a pressure in my chest because I don't want to feel jealous or resentful, but I think about how easy it all comes to her, to talk to any adult and seem confident, like she knows her opinion matters. That she matters. It's … I don't know the word. Like she's meant to have all this. But someone like me, well, we don't get too many visitors to our comp. No wonder Annabel's sort always seem so … shiny. They get it dripped into them their whole lives.

I'm still thinking about all this and trying to get my feelings under control, but Annabel's clearly forgotten it already. She leans forward. 'So … I have a surprise for you.'

Something about the way she says it reminds me of the bike and it sets off a tiny panic inside, like there's this pendulum between us that was briefly hovering in the middle, but is now inching back her way.

She hands me a piece of paper, beaming. I scan it and feel my mouth drop. 'Paragliding? You want us to go paragliding?'

'Yes, on the Downs. You said you would love to fly, and apparently this is the nearest thing.'

'But …' I look more closely. The cost is over one hundred pounds. Each. 'I can't afford – wait, you're coming too?'

She nods and smiles, although there's a definite look in her eyes, like she's just volunteered to muck out a lion's cage. 'Yes.'

'But you're scared of heights. And anyway, I can't afford to pay you back.'

'I don't want you to. I wanted to do something to show you how much I –' She's blushing. 'How much I think of you.'

'You're really coming too?'

That look again. Lion's cage. She can't be serious about this. But somehow it's that look, the thought she's prepared to do something that terrifies her, all for me, that makes me decide.

'All right then. Thanks. But you're going first.'

By Sunday morning, I'm not sure this was the best idea, even for me.

'Oh Jesus.' I stare up into the sun's glare as the first paragliders run along the hill, then soar upwards into the sky.

Annabel is rigid beside me.

'You don't have to do this, you know,' I say, but she squares her shoulders and sets her chin.

'No, I'm doing it,' she says and I think I love her for it.

Maybe we're both learning to be a bit braver, together.

We've already had the safety talk and handed in our disclaimer forms and now this is it – we're really going up there, into that pale blue sky. Mick, the main instructor, comes over with helmets. Then we get into the harnesses.

'You're with me,' he says to me. Annabel's going with Guy, a man with a strong Wiltshire accent, sun-beaten face and kind eyes. I see Annabel open her mouth, look to me uncertainly, then shut it again. She's not going to go for it, there's no way. I'm waiting for her to say she's sitting it out, but she doesn't, just watches with her arms hugging herself, breathing hard as Guy sorts out the yellow parachute thing. It's called a 'wing', like we really are going to get to be like birds.

My heart's going pretty fast too as Guy checks the ropes and gives Annabel some last-minute instructions. They're almost back to back, Annabel's fists clenched, her eyes half-shut. She looks at me again and suddenly I realise she's beyond scared. That she probably would rather be anywhere than here.

'Annie. You don't have to …' I trail off as she shakes her head. I have to admire her. She's not backing down. Then it all happens super fast: the wing fans out over their heads, the instructor turns, and they're running. They lift gently up into the sky, like a miracle. Annabel's blonde hair fans out behind her. It might be majestic or profound or something, this girl flying high on a wing for me, except for the fact that she's screaming blue murder.

'Think she's gonna be all right?' I say to Mick.

'Guy's very experienced. So are you ready then?'

'OK, let's do this thing.' I'm sounding braver than I feel, because all of a sudden, my legs have gone wobbly.

We repeat the process Annabel followed, our wing inflating, then Mick is moving, pushing me forward and suddenly my legs aren't connecting with the ground any more but running into nothingness. We rise, my legs hanging free, only the harness under me, my fingers welded on to the ropes. My stomach swoops and then I open my eyes really wide to take it all in.

'Oh my God.' The words come in a gasp as we climb, the air rushing at my face. I let out a whoop and then I fall silent and just breathe.

Sometimes when you look at the hills from a distance, you can make out these huge blocks of shadow moving over them as the clouds pass overhead. Now I see the shade everywhere: the lighter green of the track, the scoop of dark shadow to our left, running over the hills, while we float up here with the clouds. Jack used to call broccoli 'trees' when he was little and it pops into my head now, how the treetops look just like that. It seems impossible. I relax my death grip on the ropes ever so slightly, feel the comforting bulk of the straps underneath me. As we go higher, the fields become little squares, villages and roads shrinking down and over them all, a shadow like a dragon's wings blossoms. Light and shade spread out in a way I've never seen before, could never have seen – except on a plane maybe, if I'd ever been on one. The ridge of the hill we started on looks like a tiny piece of plasticine with thumbprints pressed into it. We soar higher on thermals, like birds. Everything below us is so small. We're so small. And I'm thinking, how come I didn't know how big clouds are before? How the shape of shadows can be so beautiful?

I've never been one for religion, but up here in the air everything feels almost spiritual; bits of me seem to fade into nothingness and melt, like I've become part of the sky and the trees, the sun and the clouds. I'm insignificant and bigger than I'd ever thought it was possible to be. My breath, huge in my chest. Every bit of me alive, like I've never really been awake before. Happy. Flying.

Just like in dreams.

Every so often, I catch a flash of Annabel's yellow wing as they make turns, then she disappears from view again. I hope she's feeling at least some of what I am. She's stopped screaming anyway, which has to be a good sign.

Finally, too soon, it's time to come down. I brace myself as we approach the ground, but my legs connect with only a small jolt and I run for a few steps, then that's it. We're down.

'That was brilliant! I want to go back up again. Oh my God.' My face feels split in half by the biggest smile ever. Mick, who's been so matter-of-fact and professional in the air, stops to nod and smile at me.

'You did well – you've got a feel for it. You should come up again sometime, do a course.'

I would love to if I could afford it, but I know I can't. Not right now, but one day maybe. No. Make that definitely.

Annabel and Guy are coming in to land now. They hit the ground harder than we did, and I hear Annabel yell out, then they both tumble over. My smile disappears as I run to them, Mick next to me.

I get there a second after he does. 'You OK?' My voice is panicky, heart clenched tight with fear. But Annabel sits up, holding her ankle. She stares at me and says, with a trace of disbelief in her voice, 'I think I'm here.'

I launch myself at her, tumble down half on top of her. 'I thought you'd hurt yourself, you muppet. It was amazing. Thank you,' I say in a rush.

Then I kiss her.

And she kisses me back. No pulling away, no looking round to see if anyone's watching. Just the two of us, full of adrenalin and wonder, on the side of a hill.

We're grinning as we sit up to see Guy and Mick busying themselves sorting out the equipment. I help Annabel stand and she takes a few short steps, then gives a half-smile. 'Well, it doesn't seem like anything is broken.'

A while later we say bye to Mick and Guy and get into Annabel's car. She winces as she puts it in gear.

'Your ankle all right?'

'I just wrenched it a little. It will be fine,' she says, but I think she's putting on a brave face.

She drives slowly through the country lanes. I put the window down to feel the wind on my face, reliving the flight, wondering whether I'll ever afford to go back again.

As we get closer to her house, she says in a quiet voice, 'My ankle is starting to hurt rather a lot.'

'Is it?' I focus on her, realise she's in way more pain than she's been letting on. 'Oh Christ, Annie, you should've said.'

She bites her lip.

'Look, don't worry about dropping me off. We're near yours – just get home and I can get a bus or something.'

Annabel gives a tight nod and a few moments later we pull up outside her gates.

'Your parents home?' I say. I'm not sure I want to run into them again, but on the other hand, someone needs to make sure she's all right.

'I don't think so.'

'I'd best come in with you for a minute, do you think?'

Annabel nods, her face white.

We go up the long driveway and park in the turning circle.

When Annabel puts her feet on the ground she lets out a small cry of pain. I go over to her side and kneel in front of her to help her ease her boot off. Her right ankle looks puffy, the beginning of a dark bruise already forming over the top of her foot. I frown.

'I'm not sure about this. What if it's broken?'

'It's not, otherwise I wouldn't have been able to drive.'

She's probably right. 'Come on then. Let's get you in.'

She leans on me and half hops, half limps to the front door. We go into the cool hallway.

I can't help standing and listening, feeling myself getting twitchy. 'Definitely just us in, is it?'

She gives me a quick look, a little sad, and says, 'Mary doesn't come at the weekends usually. And Mummy said she was going to be at the town house. Daddy had to go to town – some crisis again to do with his company, I'm not sure what.'

I help her to one of the lounges, where two enormous sofas are lined up opposite each other like they are about to do battle, a massive stone fireplace in between them. I sit her down on the closest sofa, then go to the kitchen for ice. The fridge freezer's rammed; there is no way most of it's going to get eaten, but I find the ice eventually.

In the lounge, Annabel is pressing gently on her ankle and wincing.

I chuck her a tea towel filled with ice cubes. 'Here, put that on it.' When she has, I pass her a Diet Coke and a grab-bag of crisps.

'You got any painkillers?'

Following her directions, I locate some paracetamol in a mini chemist's in one of the bathrooms. She necks a couple, then lies back and shuts her eyes.

'You sure you don't want that looking at?' I say.

Her eyes spring open again, a faint look of panic in them. 'No.'

'Why not? You're not scared of hospitals, are – hang on. You worried about what your parents will say? Weren't they keen for you to go today?'

She gazes at me until I twig.

'You never told them. What about the form thingy?'

'I didn't think they'd agree, so I signed it myself,' she says.

'Oh.' I think about this, then a slow smile spreads over my face. 'I think I might be a bad influence on you.'

She raises an eyebrow. 'I don't think so.'

'Oh yeah? So you usually do stuff behind your parents' backs?'

Annabel purses her lips. 'Not generally, no,' she says, her voice thoughtful.

'You looked like you were about to wet yourself on that hill.'

'I did not!' Her face is indignant, then her mouth twitches and her face starts to glow. 'I suppose … maybe a little. I was frightened to start with. But then, once we were up in the sky … it was so beautiful and I felt really … I don't know …'

'Free?'

'Yes.'

I know what she means.

'I felt like I was minuscule, but also like I could do absolutely anything I wanted. None of the usual worries mattered at all. And –' her voice catches, 'I thought about you. About us. I didn't want it to end.'

I scoot along the enormous sofa and reach out my arms. I need to ask her – did she mean the flying, or us, or is it the same thing, because as we kiss and hold on tight to each other, that's how it feels, how it has been feeling these last few weeks. Like flying free.

We sink closer into each other, and I'm thinking about how huge the sky was, and how my heart feels big enough to fill it right about now.

I pull back to look at her.

And then she says it before I do.

'Joni. I think … I love you.'

This massive pulse goes through me and then I'm laughing with it, taking hold of her arms so I can feel how we're both shaking.

'I love you too.'

CHAPTER TWENTY-TWO

I feel like we've been here together for an eternity. We take it slow, both of us nervous. She sits up and I pull her top off over her head. It gets caught in her ponytail and she has to stop me and tug it off herself, and we both start giggling, then I go serious again as I look at her. I sit back and take off my own top, then my jeans, and hers, which takes forever because they're skinny ones and because of her bad foot, and I'm whispering all the time, 'This ok?' and 'I love you,' and stopping to kiss her. Then it's just our underwear between us, which feels like nothing at all, and I'm on top of her, fumbling about with her bra and I can feel her trembling too.

I stop. 'Are you OK?'

In response, she reaches around and unhooks it herself, and I can't even speak. She's so beautiful, the curves of her body, the half-nervous, half-happy smile on her face. My hand shakes as I reach out for her, feel her skin soft and hot beneath me, and she gives a small gasp and pulls me in close.

We're both breathing really hard, moving with our legs between each other, like we did that time in my room, and I'm so turned on, I'm pretty close to … I let out a weird noise and that sets her off and she's giggling now, fiddling about with my bra, but she's having the same trouble I did.

'How is this so hard?' I say, and we're both laughing, my bra finally off.

We stay like that, our bodies pressed together, barely moving for ages, just kissing, getting used to the feel of skin on skin. My whole body feels like its singing, like we're still up there together in those clouds.

I want to stay like this and never leave.

'I love you,' Annabel says again.

'I do too. I love you.' I look at her, and I'm on the edge of tears. 'You're beautiful.'

'You are.'

Then I start to smile. 'No, *you* are.'

We're giggling again, then Annabel stops smiling and gives me a look I'm sure I'm going to remember until I'm ninety or something. 'You really are, Joni. You're beautiful, inside and out. And I want to …' She bites her lip and I know what she means, because there's so much more I want to do too. But we've got time. We've got a whole universe of it.

'We will,' I say, and I really feel it, that everything is open to us now.

A while later, we're dressed again and cuddled up on the sofa, scoffing crisps. I've gone to the bathroom and when I looked in the mirror it seemed so weird it was the same me looking back. Except, maybe it wasn't. There's this light there in my eyes, made up of the last few weeks: the library, the campaign. Annabel.

I knock back the last of my Coke and as I put it down I notice the screen of my phone flashing with a text, but I don't look at it, just snuggle closer to Annabel. I don't care if I have a hundred notifications, everything else can wait.

'Should we go again?' I say and Annabel gives me this smile I've seen on Kelly when she's taking the mick, eyebrows wiggling. I burst out laughing. 'I meant paragliding.'

Annabel laughs too, then says, 'Yes. To all of it.'

I'm about to answer, when there's the sound of the front door opening and closing.

A moment later, Annabel's dad walks in.

We've already sprung apart and Annabel's halfway through pushing her hair back into a ponytail. I'm sure I must be looking guilty. Then I flush bright red as I see him take in our feet, which are still bare, our socks kicked off somewhere or other.

He goes over and gives Annabel a kiss. 'Hello, darling.'

'Daddy! I didn't – you remember Joni? From the library?'

I sit up straighter, wondering if I should stand and call him 'sir'. His gaze flicks from me to Annabel, the pouches under his eyes creasing in a thoughtful squint.

Then he says, 'Ah yes, hello again,' but his tone isn't exactly friendly. I feel Annabel stiffen beside me.

'Uh, I need to be getting off, actually,' I say. I grab my socks, shove them on and jump up. Annabel comes too, trying not to let her limp show. Her dad doesn't notice anyway; he seems lost in some thought.

He follows us into the hallway and says suddenly, 'Joni from Cherry Tree Estate, wasn't it?'

'Um, yeah, that's me.' I smile. He smiles back, but his eyes stay cold.

'Well, lovely to see you again.' He disappears into his study, but not before giving Annabel a look.

I turn to her and whisper. 'Oh crap, do you think he's mad?'

She shakes her head, an expression I can't quite work out on her face. 'I'll need to call you a cab. I don't think I can drive.'

'That's all right,' I start to say, then there's this feeling of dismay, because I don't want money to come up between us again. The last few hours have shown me it doesn't matter, not if we don't let it.

'You're not walking. I'm going to call one now,' Annabel says.

When the taxi arrives, she insists on giving me a tenner and I do my best to accept it without being all weird.

I wish I could kiss her goodbye, but with her dad in the next room, it's probably not the best idea.

Still, as we drive away and I look back to see her framed between the pillars either side of her doorway, I can't help thinking how one day soon, she'll have to tell her parents. Then we won't have to worry about getting caught, like we're twelve and we've done something wrong.

Because what we've got is the opposite of wrong.

CHAPTER TWENTY-THREE

The text was from Kelly and it's not her normal chirpy one. I phone her once I've got in. 'What's up?'

Her voice sounds like she's been crying. 'It's Pete …'

I bike over and she lets me in, her face puffy. We go to her room and I sit cross-legged next to her as she sniffs. 'I went to rehearsal today, and just seeing him with Ananya … I've made a mistake, like, a huge one.'

'You definitely like him then?'

She nods.

'Blimey. It's a shame –' I shut up. Nicely done there, Joni.

'Yeah, I know, I could've worked it out sooner.'

'Maybe they'll split up? Not that I've got anything against Ananya but …'

Kelly blows her nose. 'I want him to be happy. I just wish it was with me.' Then she flicks back her hair and gives a laugh. 'No use moaning about it now. I've had my cry. Time to move on.'

I wonder about this, but I let her turn the conversation to other stuff. I tell her about the paragliding and she shrieks. 'That sounds awesome. You should've taken up a selfie stick and filmed the whole thing. I've seen people doing it on YouTube.'

'Maybe next time.' I've been trying not to, because of Pete and Ananya, but I'm finding it really hard to stop my mind going back over the past few hours. I smile before I can help myself.

'What else have you been up to?' Kelly says.

I tell her. It's weird – before, I wanted to keep me and Annabel in a bubble, separate from everything else. Now I want to shout her name to everyone I see, tell them we're together and we love each other.

Kelly gives me a hug. 'Right, I want to meet her properly, OK? We barely had time to say hi at the meeting. Get her down the pub next weekend.'

This time, I don't hesitate or worry how Annabel might fit in, because it doesn't matter. She fits with me.

Instead I smile.

The week seems to zoom by. Annabel's ankle is getting better. She ended up telling Mary and going for an X-ray – she said she'd tripped over – but it's just a bad sprain. We don't see each other though. Her dad's gone back to London for some work stuff that's come up, but Mary tells her mum about Annabel's ankle and Eleanor decides to work from home all week, so I steer clear.

I imagine what it will be like when Annabel comes out to her parents. I think about how maybe they'll be a bit shocked, but soon enough they'll come around, and then I can start spending time with her whenever we want, without worrying about who might see. I picture us all sitting at that big dining table, her parents properly getting to know me. Her mum smiling at me, pleased me and Annabel have found each other. Because once her parents see us together, properly see us, they'll know it's right, won't they?

It could happen.

The only dark spot is that I've missed an instalment for Jack's trip. I meant to pay it, but then we had nothing in for a food shop. I spend hours wondering how to get more cash. We could take out a loan, but I'm not eighteen so I'd have to ask Mum and Dad, and I can just picture the look on Dad's face, a mixture of hurt and pride.

'We pay our way in this family,' he'd say.

Sometimes, I want to argue back, ask why it matters so much. Loads of other people get loans. Why should we always miss out? Then I think about how much stress it would cause, having a loan hanging over us, and that seems totally unfair too. I'm also feeling guilty about the paragliding, because that money could've gone on something else.

Halfway around Lidl one day, a voice snakes into my ear.

You could ask Annabel.

I stop. Part of me is seriously considering it for about three seconds. Annabel would say yes, I know she would. And I so want Jack to go on his trip. I imagine his face when I tell him, how happy he's going to be …

And then I think about how Mum and Dad would feel when they find out where the money's come from, the look on Dad's face when Annabel bought the pizza. How small I would feel, having to ask, and how she wouldn't have any option except yes because that's the sort of person Annabel is. It would shift things between us, make that pendulum swing so far in her direction I'm not sure it could ever come back.

I sigh and pull my mind back to comparing prices on toilet roll.

But I can't stay down for long. By Friday, I'm counting the hours until I can see Annabel, although I don't even know how I'm going to manage being around her all day in the library and not being able to do anything without Mrs H spotting us. I try to distract myself with homework and the tons of texts flying back and forth between us.

She calls lateish, her name on my phone giving me a big goofy grin. I wonder for a moment about what song would be good to have as a ringtone for her, before shaking my head. I'm not *that* far gone.

'How's the foot?' I say.

'Almost better. I've told Mummy I'm coming to the library tomorrow whether I can walk or not.'

I smile at the resolve in her voice.

Annabel continues. 'I need to go in a moment, Daddy's just come back from town and he says he wants to speak with me. I hope it isn't to do with my grades.' Her voice catches and I picture her putting one finger up to her mouth to bite the nail and then stopping herself, like she sometimes does.

Annabel has been getting double the number of practice papers I do, and believe me, her dad keeps track.

There are times I am beyond glad my parents are 'as long as you do your best' type people.

I wish I could show her it's OK to stand up to him, that she's enough on her own. 'You know, one day we'll be little old ladies with white hair, and our grades will so not matter,' I say instead.

'Speak for yourself. I intend to dye mine,' Annabel says and this time I can hear a proper smile in her voice. Then she adds, 'I've been thinking about something since I came to your meeting. Would you mind if I spoke to Daddy about it? Only because he may be able to help. Not with money, I know you don't want that,' she adds quickly. 'I just thought, well, he knows people. He could speak to some connections. What do you think?'

'I think … Thank you. You don't have to, but if you reckon he might be able to help, I guess it can't do any harm.'

'Wonderful. I may not today – I don't think he's in a brilliant mood. I heard him talking to Mummy about bringing something forward with his lawyers and the *Guardian*. Although, he's always distracted about something at work. I should just talk to him now, shouldn't I?' I can practically hear her wearing a hole in her carpet as she talks.

'Whenever you think's best. But you don't have to, you know.'

'No, I definitely will. I'll do it now.' There's that determination in her voice again. It makes me oddly proud. 'That's him now. I need to go,' she says.

'OK. See you in the morning. Love you.'

'I love you too.'

Next morning, I wake up early with the birds. There's loads of them now it's summer and it seems like they're celebrating with me. The holidays are around the corner; soon it will be Annabel and me every day at the library. Long evenings for us to wander the Downs together. Maybe we can find somewhere to go, just the two of us, overnight. I can't afford a hotel, but we could scrounge a tent from someone and pitch up somewhere. I'd love to lie next to her all night, to wake up and have her right there.

It feels like the only blip in the sky for miles is the campaign. It's growing, but not fast enough. And the dodgy stuff on social media's kind of ramping up. I had to block a good twenty people the other day and Kelly phoned to say she's disabled comments on the blog after she got fed up wading through all the haters. It makes me feel so helpless and angry, then irritated with myself for letting them get to me. But it does, and I wish they'd just stop.

As if someone's read my mind, my phone pings. I already know from the egg symbol on the person's profile what to expect, but I can't help looking anyway. *diaf you fucking plebs.* I really wish I didn't know 'diaf' stands for die in a fire.

There's others too. I sigh and hit *block*. I don't get it, why people have to be that way. And it's hard not to take it personally. Jamie and Deal seem to think it's almost a good thing. 'It shows we're getting somewhere, people are taking notice,' Deal said the other day, when he came over for tea. 'And it's naive to think you can make an omelette without smashing a few eggs. We've just got to give out more than we get.'

I wonder who the eggs are in Deal's scenario. He's not exactly likely to get rape threats, is he? And he talks about smashing stuff a bit too much for my liking, these days.

But I refuse to get down about it. I lie back and listen to the birds' songs merging in this brilliant symphony, and for a second it doesn't matter. Even if it doesn't work, even though the thought of having to move somewhere, leave this house – which might not be a contender for some posh magazine shoot like Annabel's, but is our home – sends little shooting fingers of worry right through me. Somehow, knowing I'm in love and that Annabel loves me back makes me think I can tackle anything.

Besides, this morning I am an optimism machine. It's flooding through me in the shower, at breakfast where I smile so many times Jack starts to look around like maybe there's something funny in the room he's missing, biking on the way to the library with the sun already warm on the back of my neck. And I know it *is* going to work. I can feel it somehow, in the same way I do out on the Downs with Annabel.

Not that life can be beautiful.

But that it already is.

I'm hoping Annabel gets in early so we can sneak off to the store cupboard before Mrs H arrives. She didn't reply to my text this morning, but I can see a car I'm assuming is hers, although it's a Jag. Maybe she had to borrow one of her parents' for some reason. Then I realise Mrs H's car is also here.

I check my phone: 8.30 a.m. Why's everyone so early?

Everyone except me, it seems.

I chain up the bike, taking care to lean it carefully so it doesn't get scratched, and go up the steps.

My key won't turn in the lock. Someone must've left theirs in the other side.

I peer through the glass, but can't see around the corner. I think I can hear voices though, or at least Mrs H's, sounding a bit urgent for her, coming through one of the windows.

I give the door a sharp rap and the voice inside stops.

Still, no one comes out. I knock again and call out, 'Annie? Mrs Hendry? It's Joni.'

The only sound is a bird wittering overhead.

I take a few paces back down the steps, aiming to go around the side and peer in through the window, and then the door opens suddenly.

I look up, already about to exclaim, 'You left the key in,' when I stop.

Looking down at me, framed in the doorway in his dark suit and wearing an even darker expression, is Annabel's dad.

'Oh! Hi. Is Annie – I mean Annabel – in there?' I say. I've crossed my arms over my chest. It doesn't take Einstein to realise something's up.

Then Mrs H appears.

There's an awkward silence. I can't make out the expression on her face. She looks mainly … disappointed.

'You're early,' she says, and is it me or is that a wobble in her voice? Annabel's dad is still looking at me and I have to crane my neck back to meet his eyes.

I slowly move mine to stare at Mrs H. '… What's up?'

'I think we should do this inside –' Mrs H begins, but Annabel's dad makes a small movement and she stops.

'Do what? Where's Annabel? Is she OK?' There's a strange sense of dread flooding through me now. I run up the steps, but Annabel's dad is blocking the door; I'd have to barge right past him to get through. I stop. I still have to tip my head back to get a proper look at him.

Then I realise he's waiting. Not for me, but for Mrs H. And she twists her hands together and takes a breath, and then in a firmer voice says, 'I'm afraid I need to let you go.'

I squint at her. For a mad second, I'm about to ask, 'Go where?' but then I realise what she means. I just about get out an, 'Oh.'

There's another pause as I hold Mrs H's eyes, my heart racing, pushing blood up to my face, and then she looks away.

My voice comes out louder now. 'Why?' I'm not looking at her any more, I'm looking at Annabel's dad. He stares right back and the expression on his face is trying to make me about three foot tall. And I get it suddenly. 'You know, don't you?'

His nose wrinkles slightly before he says, 'Mrs Hendry has terminated your employment with immediate effect. You should leave.' He adds a curt, 'Thank you.' And he's actually turning on his heel, glancing over at Mrs H as if to say, 'Follow me,' like she's one of his lackeys, which I guess she is, and I can't believe he thinks that's it.

'I don't fucking think so.' I say it loud enough to startle some birds pecking at the ground nearby. They shoot up with a panicked flap of their wings. 'Where's Annabel? Is she here?'

Annabel's dad turns back, his top lip curling. His voice is danger-zone quiet. 'It's in your best interests to leave now. Before I take things further.'

'Take what further? What are you talking about?' I'm shouting now.

Mrs H is looking between us and I can see in the way she's got her lips pinched together, the corners turned down, that she doesn't understand exactly what's going on. That she feels bad, but not enough to stand up to Annabel's dad. She's not going to fight for me.

He nods to the bike chained up. 'That, for one thing. I believe you have been extorting things from my daughter.'

'What? You know that's bollocks. Is she here? I want to speak to her.' I'm still shouting and now I yell, 'Annabel!'

'I'm warning you, I could call the police about this. You people – don't think I don't know what you're up to.'

Then I see Annabel in the doorway behind him.

She looks pale, like she hasn't slept.

She's also having trouble meeting my eyes.

The pounding in my ears seems to get louder, then fades down, like I'm in the centre of this massive bubble of silence, because somehow the fact that she can't look at me is already telling me what I need to know, but I have to try anyway.

'Annabel … Annie. What … ?' I take another breath and Mrs H says, 'Perhaps we should all go inside?' but that makes me flare up again.

'Why?' I shout. 'You think it's shameful too, being gay? Because it's not. Jesus, we're in the twenty-first century here. It's not a crime. How can you stand there and let him tell you what to do? And you?' I look at Annabel and this time she meets my eyes. 'Why can't you see …' I trail off because there's a look on her face, a sort of pleading mixed with horror, and my stomach twists. I go brighter red as it dawns on me I've just outed her for sure and no matter how angry I might be, there's no excuse for that. It's not my thing to tell.

'God, Annie, I'm sor–'

'I can assure you, I am not homophobic in the slightest. I'm surprised Annabel didn't tell you her aunt is happily married. To a woman. I was her best man.' Annabel's dad is speaking clearly, his voice clipped, driving each word home.

I stare at him, then back at Annabel.

'Then … why does it –' I'm cut off by his scornful laughter.

'Don't play that game. I told you, I know. You've been trying to use my daughter against me. It's not going to work, I can assure you of that. The estate sale will continue as planned. Your pathetic scheme has failed. Now, I'm telling you one more time to leave.'

I feel like someone's sucked all the blood out of me. 'The estate? What –'

I stop, because I suddenly understand the look on Annabel's face.

Realisation comes over me like my skin's turning inside out.

She was never worried about being with a girl.

She was worried about being with the wrong sort of girl.

With me.

'Oh my God.' I say it really quietly. Then I look at Annabel. 'Did you know?' She shakes her head as though she's unable to speak.

There's that white bubble of silence all around again, like I'm about to faint. I wait to fall.

But I don't. I'm still standing there, so small. And I can't feel anything.

'Joni.' One word, but I can't bear to hear her voice, see the apology that means nothing, in her eyes.

It does one thing though. It loosens up my feet and I'm whirling down the stairs, tripping at the bottom. I crash to my knees, but I barely feel it because I'm up again and I can't hear a thing except the sound of my breath and my feet hitting the pavement as I start to run.

Part Three

CHAPTER TWENTY-FOUR

I don't look where I'm going. I just run, on and on, like maybe if I keep moving I can stop the shadow that's trying to catch me, because inside there's this terrible feeling like parts of me are falling away and will never come back.

Eventually, I realise I'm on the bridleway, high up on the Downs.

I stop, finally. Seems even I can't keep going forever. As soon as I do, I realise how much pain I'm in: my breath burns in my chest, my feet are blistered. My hand throbs and I open it to see I'm holding the library key Mrs H gave me, that I've been gripping it all the way here, so tight it hurts to open my fingers. When I do, there's a white welt running across my palm.

I stare at the blank blue sky. There's a strong wind up here. It feels vicious, blurring my eyes. And that feeling is still building, the pressure getting unbearable, and I know I can't outrun it any more.

With a sudden movement I draw back my arm and throw the key as hard as I can. It bounces and lies glinting in the sun, and maybe it's that or I just can't hold on any more but suddenly I'm screaming. My legs give way and I pound the grass with my fists, as every word and look comes back. I punch my rage and humiliation into the ground, as though they might set off earthquakes. The earth could crack apart and send this whole beautiful, horrible town plunging into the gap, for all I care right now.

Because it's only ever beautiful for some people, not the ones like me.

I remember all the times I thought I could hope for things, how I believed in Annabel and how much we loved each other. How I felt like a giant with her. The memories keep coming and they won't stop, and I'm shaking with it. Then it comes, finally. The thing the running and the anger were trying to hold off.

Pain. So much I don't think I can stand it.

This wail comes out of me. It goes on and on. I feel the sun burning my neck and I suddenly get why people say it beats down on you.

I think about my job at the library, how the little bit I was doing to keep our family afloat has gone. Jack'll never get his school trip now. About the buyout and the bitter taste in my throat, knowing Annabel's dad is behind it all. The fear that no matter how hard we fight, we'll never be big enough to win against him.

I think about Annabel, the gap between us we could never close now.

And I start to cry.

A long time later, I sit up. The day has gone on without me.

I'm so tired. I push myself to my feet, wincing as every muscle in my body screams, and slowly begin to limp home.

It must be late afternoon by the time I get to my house, if the light is anything to go by, but I'm too tired to even get my phone out and check. My face is dry now and everything feels oddly numb, like something is hardening inside me.

I open the front door and take a deep breath before I go in. I don't know how I'm going to bear telling anyone what's happened. I don't even know if I can speak.

'Joni? Is that you?'

Mum's not supposed to be home today. A pulse of fear goes through me.

They're all in the kitchen: Mum, Dad, Jamie and Jack.

'We've been calling,' Jamie says and his face is pinched, angry.

For a second I want to turn and run again because I can't face anything else, not today, but I'm too exhausted. Instead I sit at the table and put my head in my hands.

'Joni? Are you OK? Jack, get the kettle on, love.' Mum's voice seems to come from a distance. I hear Jack's chair scape back. Then Mum says, 'You've already seen?'

I raise my head slowly and she frowns as she takes in my face. Then I look at the thing Jamie's waving under my nose.

It's a newspaper. I recognise the *Guardian* logo and a weird detached part of me is still able to think Jamie must've bought it, because Dad only reads the *Daily Mail*, even though as far as I can tell, the *Mail* basically hates people like us.

Just like Annabel's dad.

I blink and try to focus on the article.

Right next to a huge picture of Douglas Lattimer and a headline that screams *Tory MP Evicts His Own Constituents* is a picture of me at the march.

I scan the first few sentences, then jerk my head up. 'Lattimer has shares in White Light? No wonder he wouldn't help us.' My voice sounds dull.

'There's more, Joni. I'm sorry,' Jamie says.

But I already know what I'm about to read.

The scandal doesn't end there. The *Guardian* can exclusively reveal that White Light Holdings is in fact the public face of a shell company, LCA, owned by Edward Huntington. Huntington, a former hedge fund manager and prominent local resident, prides himself on a reputation for philanthropy. Clearly his charitable works only extend to certain elements of the local population.

I don't read any further. I drop the paper on the table and put my head back in my hands. Mum puts her arms around me. 'I'm sorry, love, I know this must be a shock. I'm sure Annabel didn't know …' She trails off.

'She knows.' I laugh, but it's bitter in my ears.

'You need to see this too.' Jamie pushes something else into my hand. And after everything that's happened today, it really shouldn't feel like a fist to the guts, yet somehow it still does.

It's an eviction notice.

CHAPTER TWENTY-FIVE

We sit at the table for a long time. Mum and Dad want to have A Talk with us all, explain what might happen. Jamie's going on about the campaign.

'It's gone national now. Look at the feeds, and the petition. We can still fight this. We've got people on our side,' he's saying, but Mum and Dad aren't convinced.

'Even so, son, it's not going to be soon enough for us,' Dad says.

He's been quiet throughout and now I see how defeated he is.

'You can't give up now, we're just getting started. I'm telling you –'

But we don't hear what Jamie has to say, because Dad's reached his limit. He slams away from the table and he's shaking with rage. 'It's time to get real, Jamie. They've had it all worked out, right from the beginning. Your campaign's just been prolonging the inevitable. There's no way to win. Not against that scum. There never was, never will be.'

He stomps out the back door, crashing it behind him. It sounds like he's smashing up the garden furniture out there, like the pain of what's happening has overtaken anything his back's giving him. No one speaks for a minute and then Mum says, 'Get the tea going,' to Jamie, and, 'You two go and do some homework,' to me and Jack. She disappears into the garden.

I escape upstairs, because some of Dad's helpless rage has reignited my own.

I need to call Annabel.

My hands are shaking as I get out my phone. There's several missed calls and a string of texts from Kelly. *You're in the papers!* Then, *Oh shit, just read about A's dad. Did you know? Did SHE know? Are you OK?* And, *Joni? Call me.* And finally, *Joni???? Xxxxx.*

Nothing from Annabel.

She answers as I'm on the point of hanging up. 'Joni?' Her voice sounds muted, like she's exhausted too.

'Yeah, it's me.'

There's a silence. I try to keep my voice steady as I say, 'I know you didn't know before last night …'

At the same time Annabel says, 'I wanted to speak to you. I feel terrible …'

We both stop. Then I say, 'You go.'

I can hear Annabel breathing at the other end, almost feel her hesitation as she tries to find the words. 'I'm so sorry. I didn't know his company owned White Light, I swear.' I think she's crying. 'When I tried to tell him about the campaign and ask if he could help, he just started shouting. He'd already seen your picture in the paper. It was like lighting a match the second I mentioned your name. He thinks you only got to know me because of the campaign, that you're some sort of – I don't know, a spy or something. That you never – that you made up your feelings. But I know you didn't.'

There's a hint of uncertainty in her voice that sends white heat through me. 'How can you even think … Jesus, Annabel.'

'He threatened all sorts of things if I didn't … I know I should have stood up to him, but I'm not … I'm not brave like you … And he's my father,' she lets out a sob, but I can't feel for her.

'We got an eviction notice today,' I say.

'What? I – I don't know what to say.'

I'm finding it hard to speak, but I make myself. 'I thought I knew who you were. Who I was. But it turns out I was worrying about the wrong thing. See, I kind of get why your dad was so worried. Wouldn't exactly look great in the papers, me and you together. And maybe someone like him would believe all that crap about me. Screwing people's the way he operates, isn't it? Why shouldn't he think everyone else is doing the same? But what about you? You were worried he'd find out about us way before last night.'

'No, I –'

'Stop lying. All this time I was thinking you were scared of coming out, but it wasn't that at all, was it? No, you were worried I wasn't going to be good enough for your precious daddy. Not good enough for you. Well, I guess you made your choice. But you know what? I've realised something. You're not good enough for me.'

I hear Annabel's intake of breath at the other end, then it's like a storm breaking. 'Why has everything got to be a competition? Everyone's the same! Did you ever consider you might have things I could never have? Like parents who love you for you, unconditionally. Not as some sort of fucking trophy?' She's shouting now, the sound of it shocking me into silence. 'You know, it didn't even cross his mind you might actually like me for *me*,' she says, and her voice is bitter like mine.

But I'm still so angry. 'And how hard did you try to convince him? You're the one who's too scared to do anything that might threaten your oh-so-perfect life that you pretend you hate anyway. You're terrified of even thinking about letting go of your massive bit of the orange, even when –'

'What on earth –' She's more controlled now and posher than I've ever heard her. It feels like a weapon. '– has an orange got to do with anything?'

'Everything. It's got everything do to with it. But you'll never get that because you won't open your eyes.'

I hear her breathing hard down the phone, picture her fighting for composure.

But I only have one thing left to say.

'You remember the talk we had at the stones? About being brave?' My voice is starting to crack, but I plough on. 'Well, I did do the research and I decided what I want to be. I'm going to become a conservationist,' I say, and then my voice gives in completely.

I press the button to end the call without waiting for her reply.

Heartbreak isn't like in songs. This pain is too big for music. I stay in bed for a whole day and then I find I can't keep still. I spend a lot of time on the Downs and in the tree in the garden, trying to find comfort in the branches, the open sky and the birds, but nothing helps. It's like someone's ripped out my insides and had a good stomp about.

A couple of weeks in, I cut my hair, slicing off strands with vicious snips of the scissors. Then I dye the remainder bright purple. Mum gets really pissed off about the dye marks on the bathroom rug, but even she relents when she sees my face. About the only person I can stand to be around is Jack, and now it's the summer holidays and I have nowhere else to be. I spend a lot of time with him on the PlayStation, shooting stuff, which kind of helps.

I go to see Kelly and tell her everything.

She listens right through and then she simply says, 'What a bitch,' and holds me while I cry.

The anger comes back slowly, then all at once, but this time it has a different texture.

It finds me in my dreams, where Annabel's face is so vivid. I feel it in the sharpness of the wind up on the Downs. And it lifts my head up, slows my tears until they dry altogether and in their place is a cold fury that feels strong.

I can't change what's happened with Annabel, can't undo what she said, how stupid I still feel. But there's one thing I can still do and that's the campaign. Every time I picture Annabel's dad's face on those steps, or the way Mrs H simply went along with him because of who he was without even talking to me first, it makes that fury inside harden that bit more until I feel like I've got icicles shooting out of my fingers.

Dad's still in bed most days and Mum is working every single shift she can manage, even though it's not going to do any good. The eviction process is rumbling on, a date set for the end of September.

One day I go through every single bit of information on the campaign that I can find on Jamie's laptop.

I'm waiting at the kitchen table for Jamie when he gets in from work that night, a notebook and his laptop open in front of me.

'How you doing, chick?' he says, then takes in the stuff on the table, the hardness in my eyes. 'Like that is it?'

I nod and he sits next to me, starts to read the list I've made over my shoulder. 'You've been busy.'

'I had to do something.'

Jamie nods slowly, then gives me a long look and I suddenly see it again in his eyes, the thing he backed off from telling me before.

'You know I would never say I told you so,' he begins and I raise an eyebrow at this, because he totally would, but he's still talking. 'There was a reason I said what I did about Annabel. You remember when I was working up at the old place? Well, I didn't just leave for no reason.'

'Figured as much,' I say.

Jamie stares off for a while. 'I really thought I had it made there. Anton was going to teach me everything, and I'd get my own restaurant eventually.'

'I remember.' I could hardly forget; Jamie used to talk about nothing else. The old Jamie. 'So what happened?'

'Mr Campbell. Or his son at least.'

I frown. Mr Campbell was the guy who owned the hotel; Anton was the Head Chef but he didn't actually own the whole place.

'I don't think you said –' Then I do remember suddenly, Jamie mentioning a guy called Tarquin, mainly because we all thought the name was hysterical. 'Didn't there used to be a guy called himself Quinn?'

'That's him. *Tarquin* Campbell.' Jamie narrows his eyes. 'One of the Edrington types, although he'd already left there. Pretty sure he'd have been booted out if it hadn't been for Daddy's money. Anyway. He was a posh twat all right. He'd come swanning in when we were doing service, getting in everyone's way, bragging about how he knew his cuts of meat or some bollocks. And we all had to tolerate him, even if Anton threw him out once for wrecking a plate just before it was due to go out.'

'Sounds like a knobber.'

'Oh, he was more than that. He'd mess with the waitresses as well, try and grab their boobs or arse as they went by, and everyone was too scared to say anything because one girl did and she got the sack. I used to give them the nod when he was coming, so they'd go the other way.'

I raise my eyebrows, but he's not done.

'Anyway, one night after service had finished I was walking out with one of the waitresses, Gemma, and he did his usual trick of grabbing her arse as she went by, and the look on her face … I lost it, shoved him up against the wall and threatened to smack him one if he carried on. After that, I knew I wasn't going to last there long and funnily enough, about a week later at the end of one of my shifts,

Mr Campbell marches in with a coat, shouting he wanted to know whose it was. Well, it was mine, wasn't it and guess what was in the pocket? A nice shiny bag of white powder. He said if I went quietly – without my wages of course – he wouldn't call the police. Didn't want the scandal in his establishment. God, he looked at me like I was a piece of scum when he told me I wasn't going to get a reference and he'd see to it I'd never work in any high-end restaurant again. And that little scrote stood behind him, giving me these looks like he knew someone like him would always win and someone like me would always lose.'

'Jesus Christ, Jamie. I had no idea.'

I do remember him being out of work, how he went everywhere before he got the job at The Olde Inne – for way less cash than he'd been on before.

'Don't tell Dad, OK?'

I shake my head.

'I'm only telling you now because I think it's important you know what people like them are like. They're all the same and you shouldn't ever forget it. And they've got the dice rigged. Anyone who doesn't think it's us against them is deluding themselves.'

The way he says 'us against them' reminds me so much of Deal that it makes me say, 'Then you met Deal.'

Jamie's face brightens. 'Yeah. He taught me a thing or two for sure.'

And suddenly I can see what a big gap Deal filled for Jamie, after he lost Anton and the restaurant. I sling my arm around him and he hugs me back. 'I'm sorry, Jamie.'

'I just wish I could've stayed there, you know? Someone like that Quinn knob gets as many chances as they want, but that was my one shot.'

I stare at him, at the mixture of pain and humiliation on his face, and I know what he's feeling, because that's where I am too.

He blinks a couple of times and then says, 'It's all right. I'm over it now. But it taught me a lesson about people like that. I kind of hoped I was wrong, about you and Annabel. I'm not pleased I was right.'

I put my head on his shoulder. 'God. I can't believe you never said.'

'I was embarrassed as well. The whole thing, it made me feel really small inside.'

'I know.'

'And I swore to myself I wouldn't let anyone make me feel small like that again.'

'I'm glad you told me.'

We sit for a while, my head still on his shoulder, and then he stirs himself and points to the stuff spread out on the table. 'So what's all this then?'

'I guess it's like you said. I don't want to be small either. I don't want to just leave here without a fight. And I've been doing some thinking. Petitions and demos aren't going to do anything. They're like, I don't know, a fly on a horse. Annoying, but doesn't exactly hurt.' I point to the list I've made. 'But some of these things, they might. I don't know if they'll stop the eviction – probably not, but we can at least cause some pain, make it harder for him. That would be worth it on its own.'

Jamie's nodding. 'Show them we're not flies they can squash without bothering to even think about it.'

'Yeah.' I square my shoulders and look at him. 'Why shouldn't we show them we've at least got some bite?'

'Well, then.' He grins at me suddenly. 'I'm in.'

CHAPTER TWENTY-SIX

I don't feel nervous. Instead I'm filled with this coldly buzzing energy as I go through the huge iron gates of Edrington's with Jamie, Deal and Kelly the evening of the *Grease* showcase. Pete's already inside. He wasn't one hundred per cent happy about the idea, but Kelly talked him round, though she's sworn him to secrecy where Ananya's concerned.

We've been working all week on the main event, which is going off on Saturday, so this is kind of a warm-up. We want to send Edward Huntington a sign and where better to do it than on his home turf?

The musical's already started; we didn't want to get there too early and get spotted, so we're going in now. Kelly talks us past the person in the main office and leads us through the grounds towards the theatre, which is in its own separate building. Edrington is something else: all cold stone pillars, red brick and a beautiful central square of grass. It's like stepping into some costume drama, going back hundreds of years to when people had servants and you were either born rich or a peasant, and nothing you could do would change that. Sometimes it feels like nothing's different on that front. I remember suddenly that first evening I saw Annabel, how out of place I felt in the restaurant. The way I thought about that school trip and the servant costume.

But things have changed. They do change. It might not be easy but we don't have to put up and shut up any more.

I wonder whether Annabel and her parents really will be here tonight. His name's on the bursaries so we've assumed he is, but what with how much he's been in the papers this week, he might want to keep a low profile. I'm betting not though; he's styled it out the last few weeks, giving no comment beyond some rubbish about regeneration and local prosperity and multiple mentions of his charity work and the library. I actually think he believes he's in the right.

You see, people like him don't simply refuse to see the rest of us. They can't. As we go under a stone arch and into the theatre, I wonder if maybe I'd be like it too, if I grew up with all this.

It's huge, compared to the tiny Drama studio at our school, with proper seats and a lighting rig and big stage. There's a song just finishing.

We don't stop when we get inside, but keep walking, taking out our signs and holding them above our heads as we go down the central aisle. They've all got one picture on them: Edward Huntington's face and the words *Local Hero?* printed across it. Deal's right in the front, but tonight Jamie wanted to do the talking.

The song finishes with a flourish as we stride up on stage and line up in front of the open-mouthed kids in their leather jackets and jeans. The last notes die away and then there's total silence. I can't see anything except lights, only rows of dark heads, but I know, I can feel, Annabel's there in the audience with her parents.

'What on earth?' I hear someone say and then Jamie starts to speak.

'You don't know us, but we see you. We live here like you, but ours isn't the same town as yours. Our families clean your toilets, cook your food, pick up your rubbish. We keep your lives turning and you don't even notice us unless you have to. And now one of you –' He holds up his sign with Annabel's dad's face, '– wants to make us homeless so he can turn a fast profit. I'm talking about Edward Huntington and his company, LCA, buying up the entire Cherry Tree Estate and evicting the families who've lived here for years.'

Jamie takes a breath to go on, but a tall suited man is on the stage now, catching at his arm, saying, 'You need to leave before I call the police.'

Jamie shakes him off roughly enough that the man takes a step back and I can feel this worried thrill go through the crowd.

One of the lads in costume behind us says, 'Look, I think you should –'

'I think you should shut your mouth,' Deal snaps, and stares him down. I look out into the crowd again, still holding my sign up, and feel like my heart should be going fast, I should be feeling something other than this strange calm, but I can't seem to.

'We'll go when we're ready but first we're here to tell you, *Mr* Huntington, that we're not going quietly, cos you know what? This is our town too, and we have just as much right as you to live here.'

Jamie casts one more look at the rows of shadowy faces staring back at us and then says, with bitterness in his voice, 'Enjoy the rest of your evening.'

He marches out and we follow. Behind us this babble of noise erupts. A moment later, I hear someone yell my name. I turn to see Ananya, hair teased into big curls, leather jacket on, her make-up smudged, running out after us. 'Oi! Joni!' she shouts.

More people are coming out behind her: the man in the suit who I think must be a teacher, some of the parents. And then I see Annabel and her parents. Annabel's face is white, her dad's flushed with anger.

Ananya gets to us first. 'What the hell was that?' she yells.

'We were making a point,' I say.

'Well, thanks very much. I worked on that play all fricking summer and now it's all wrecked because of you. Didn't you stop to think about anyone except yourself?'

I give a short bark of laughter at that, but then Annabel's dad walks up and he's not looking at me, he's looking at Jamie.

'You don't intimidate me in the slightest,' he's saying, but I'm not sure. There's the tiniest flicker of something in his eyes as he says it. Deal spots it too and pushes forward.

'Oh yeah? Well, we will before we're done. Don't you worry.'

I'm getting anxious now. Someone's talking about the police behind me, Deal and Annabel's dad are practically nose to nose. I tug on Jamie's arm.

'Come on. We've done what we wanted.'

Out of the corner of my eye I see Annabel's mum holding on to Annabel's wrist. I'm not going to look at her, I refuse to even meet her eyes, but the next moment I can't help it.

She's just standing there, looking at me, and I can't work out her expression from this distance, only that she's thinking hard. I can't seem to look away. Then Jamie moves his arm to my back and steers me away.

'That's it?' Ananya yells. Then to Kelly, 'Should've known you'd do something like this.'

Kelly stiffens next to me, then says, 'It's not about you.'

'Oh yeah?'

I glance at Ananya and see she's almost ready to cry. For a second I feel bad for her and the others up on the stage who just had their big moment ruined, but then I shut it down, mutter, 'Come on,' to Kelly, and keep going.

Behind me, I think I hear Annabel's voice and it sets off a jolt of pain, but I walk on, head up, following my brother, until the pain is replaced by an almost brutal feeling of triumph.

Outside, we walk faster in case they do call the police, but like Deal says, we had tickets and all we did was stage a 'peaceful protest'. That feeling of triumph is growing as we walk, the initial nervous reaction being replaced by shouts and laughter.

'Did you see his face?'

'You were brilliant, Jamie.'

Then Deal: 'Next time maybe our protest shouldn't be so peaceful.'

And before I can ask him what he means, Kelly starts up a song and we all join in and we're singing together and laughing, high on adrenalin and this feeling like all the rules we got told were for us and not them might be breakable after all.

Even with my crumpled-up heart, it feels good.

CHAPTER TWENTY-SEVEN

We don't stop after the Edrington play. I'm working flat out updating social media, and getting people to sign the petition, which is growing faster now. I can't be bothered with school any more, even though the new year's started. I go in sometimes, to get Mum off my back, but I mainly sit in the common room working on the campaign. I've changed my tune on trolls too. Every time I get an abusive message, I reply with the most cutting things I can think of, which takes hours but gives me a strange sense of satisfaction. Sometimes the abuse gets personal now my face has been in the papers. I get called a bitch dyke so often it almost starts to feel meaningless. Almost. It's like I've wrapped a stone block around myself and every threat just makes it thicker.

We got Pete to film the whole Edrington protest on his phone and I post it online with a link to our website. Jemima picks it up and then she's in the papers too because she's just won some award, and suddenly things are taking off. The petition is getting more signatures every hour and Douglas Lattimer is stopped on his doorstep by journalists. I feel a massive stab of triumph seeing him squirm on the local news as he refuses to answer questions about his involvement, but the story is growing, taking on its own life, a many-headed monster.

Good. Let it swallow up everything.

But the eviction date is getting closer too. Mum and Dad seem to have retreated into two worlds: bed and work, and even though I sit on the side of their bed to update Dad on the campaign, or fill Mum in after her shift, I don't think they believe anything's going to come of it, not really.

Mum does promise she's going to come to the protest on Saturday though.

'I'm glad you're taking a stand, love,' she says, and I can see through the tiredness she's proud.

I wish it was enough.

I start to feel like we're running some sort of race: the campaign versus the eviction date and I've got no idea which one's going to win. But we're pressing on, because that's all we can do. If we keep the pressure up, maybe White Light will decide the money's not worth the bother. Or Annabel's dad will.

Maybe.

Kelly comes over the night before the next protest. We're going to march to the library and post up a new sign over the Huntington one. We sit in the kitchen painting. The sign reads, *Community Library: Knowledge for All*.

'You know, he could just take his money away and shut the whole thing down,' Kelly says as she sweeps blue paint across the C of Community.

I give her a look. She's quiet tonight, less bouncy than usual. 'I guess so.'

'Who'll be the winner then?' she asks, but I shrug.

'That's not what this is about.'

'What is it about then?'

I put my paintbrush down. 'What do you think? Saving the estate, showing Edward Huntington he can't just treat us like crap.'

'Not about showing his daughter that then?'

I grab my brush again and push it down into the blue. After a bit I say, 'This hasn't got anything to do with Annabel.'

Kelly doesn't answer.

'What's up?' I ask when the sign's nearly done.

'Ananya's broken up with Pete.'

I give her a close look. 'That's good, isn't it?'

Kelly sighs. 'No, Joni, it's not. Not really. He never wanted to do that protest at Edrington's anyway, said it wasn't fair to everyone's who's worked so hard –'

'Fair? What's fair about what they're doing to us?'

'Yeah, but it was hardly that lot in the play, was it?'

'May as well have been. You ask me, they're all the same.'

Kelly stares at me, then shakes her head and starts painting again. I follow suit. This isn't a conversation I need to be having. Not now, or ever. Then she says, 'He's mad at me too. And I don't know, maybe he's right. How's it fair to go after a whole group, just because of what one person did? I don't know. It's all got complicated.'

'Seems pretty straightforward from where I'm sitting.' I repeat Jamie's words, Deal's words. 'They're all just as bad.

It's us against them and if we don't stand up for ourselves, no one will. We've got to fight them, no matter what it takes,' I say, but when she doesn't reply I leave it, because deep down I know she's got a point.

It's just not one I'm in the mood to listen to right now.

It's windy the day of the library protest. Autumn seems to be flying towards us, the leaves on the trees crisping, but I don't look out for reds and golds the way I do most years. Another thing I can't seem to see the point in these days. I'm with Dad, now: you can't eat the scenery.

I've got a hoodie on, the keys to the library in my back pocket. It took forever to find them again up on the Downs. I don't know if the locks are the same, but if the keys work we can sort out the Huntington plaque inside. Otherwise we'll just have to do the outside sign. The main thing is to show Edward Huntington up for the sham he is, pretending he gives a crap about the community when all he's really interested in is his name on the side of a building.

And that, we can fix.

'You ready?' Jamie says to me before Deal arrives.

'Think so. What about Mum?'

Jamie shakes his head. 'She said she'd try and join us down there.'

Mum's not long got in from a night shift that overran.

'Right then,' I say as the door goes. I take a quick glance in the mirror and my face stares back at me: older, more fixed. I jerk my chin up at my reflection, then run down the stairs to let Kelly in.

We don't go in Deal's car this time; he's meeting us there. Instead we set off on foot, Jack with us too. As we get to the end of our street, I spot three figures coming towards us: Pete, Ed and Stacey. Kelly runs forward.

'You're here.'

'Hi,' Pete says. He doesn't look like he's totally forgiven us, but he is smiling. Then he looks at me. 'Thought I'd be here for Joni.'

Kelly looks like she's going to say something, then thinks better of it and gives a shrug as if to say, 'That's good enough.'

Seeing the rest of the gang lightens my mood and we're joking as we walk, but even I have to stop when I see the size of the crowd gathered outside the library. The whole car park is full of people milling about, way more than there were at the last march. And this time I'm sure there's even one or two of the Edrington crowd.

I feel it suddenly, this solar flare of triumph. We're winning this. The tide's turning.

We're going to get Edward Huntington.

Well, not 'get' get him.

Perhaps.

Deal and a big group of his mates are handing out signs, starting up songs, getting the crowd going. The atmosphere's like a carnival. It's so packed you can barely move in the car park and people are spilling out on to the pavement.

Kelly grins at me. 'This is brilliant.'

Then a massive car arrives and out comes Jemima. A cheer goes up and the next thing there's paparazzi too, proper paparazzi like you see on the TV and Jemima's got a megaphone and she's yelling some stuff through it while all these photographers take her picture.

'Oh my God, this is going to be everywhere by this afternoon,' Kelly shrieks.

Deal's waving me over. 'You got the keys?' he shouts over the noise. I hand them to him. He tries one in the lock and it turns, then he grabs the sign off Kelly and Pete and opens the door, disappearing inside with a couple of his friends. Next thing, they've gone up on to the roof and I watch as they fix the new sign over the Huntington one.

There's another cheer from the crowd and a sudden burst of camera flashes. I yell too, then Kelly starts everyone off in another round of singing.

It's just like before, but even bigger, more people. There's speeches, singing, chanting, Jemima in front of the cameras. The day stays dry and the sun even comes out as we get towards lunchtime and then a local news crew arrives too.

But even though part of me is buzzing, enjoying the crowd and thinking how this is going to get our message out to even more people, there's also a part of me that wonders.

We've already done this once before, but it didn't stop the eviction notice did it? I stop singing suddenly as it hits me: this is just a fun day out for most of the people here. They're excited to take part, see Jemima, sing a couple of songs, but at the end of it they'll go home and nothing will have changed. Not unless we do something even bigger.

But what?

Before I get the chance to think about it, a police car pulls up, just like last time too.

Except this time, another one follows it. Then another and a couple of vans. And it's not one lone policewoman with a friendly face who gets out, but what looks like a mini army of police officers, some of them wearing body armour, like they're expecting a riot or something.

The crowd falls silent.

'What the hell?' Jamie says from next to me.

He strides towards the policemen and I scurry after him.

'You're all going to have to leave,' a policeman says, his face grim.

'What for? We're protesting peacefully. We've got a right to do that,' Jamie says.

'Nope. This here,' the policeman waves a piece of paper under Jamie's nose, 'says different.' He raises his voice. 'I need everyone here to disperse.'

I look around. The carnival atmosphere has sharpened into something else altogether and for the first time I'm really aware of the crowd as this living thing. A couple of people start to walk away, but lots more are muttering and looking at each other. One woman shouts out in an echo of Jamie, 'What for? We can be here if we want.'

In response, the police fan out and start ushering the crowd, trying to move everyone towards the car park entrance, but plenty of people are still standing there, confused. And I suddenly see: lots of them have never been on this side of things before, being told they've got to get out when they're just trying to do something they think they've got the right to do. And they don't know how to react. Energy's crackling through the crowd now and people aren't moving. Jack's on my other side and I step closer to him as he looks up. 'Why are the police here?' he says.

'I don't know. Guess someone high up doesn't want us out here. But I don't think we should go anywhere.' I'm shouting suddenly. A few people nod.

One of the police starts towards me, then another points out the sign and the open library door. They start to move, but just before they get there, this big group of Deal's friends move forwards too and suddenly there's a face-off on the library steps, more police coming up. Then one of Deal's friends shouts, 'Piss off, you pig!' and that's it: two policemen literally jump on him. I'm not sure if he slips and falls or if they push him down, but his head hits the ground with a smack and this yell goes up from several people. Another two of Deal's friends try and pull the police off, and others are moving forward, then the crowd shifts as one, people going all over the place.

Lots are making to leave, but others are crowding forward, shouting at the police to stop.

Several of Deal's friends have run into the library.

And now shouting is erupting all around. I grab Jack's hand and start pulling him to one side, getting bumped into, and there's this sudden atmosphere of panic rising up on the heat of the crowd as a couple more scuffles break out. I look back to see people running into the library and the police following, while most of the crowd is streaming away now, their faces scared.

Jack's fingers are holding on to mine in a death grip. He's really white, his eyes wide. Then Jamie's pushing his way towards us and I more or less throw Jack at him and shout, 'Take him over there.'

Jamie's got no choice but to do what I say.

I shove through the crowd back towards the library and now my heart's pounding, rushing in my ears, because I can't believe the police just came and broke everything up like that. It had to have been Lattimer and Huntington, getting them to come in so heavy handed, and it strikes me again how unfair this is, like they even get to buy whose side the police are on when it shouldn't be like that at all.

Two lads I don't recognise, from Deal's group I think, are shouting, then the next thing one of them picks up a large stone – I wonder for a second where that came from – pulls his hand back and hurls it at the library window. It shatters, the sound like a gunshot going off in my head. And suddenly all the rage of the last few weeks crashes through me. I want to smash stuff too. I want to tear the whole library down.

I open my mouth and scream, like the day on the Downs when Annabel's dad sacked me, when Annabel refused to stand by me. One of Deal's friends pauses and takes a small step to one side when he gets a look at my face, but the other one grins, this angry light in his eyes like he's enjoying it, and I know how he feels; how much I want to give in to that rage, to become it. He hands another stone to me.

I take it, feeling its weight, not cold now but like it's on fire in my hand. I think of the eviction notice, how Mum's already started packing.

As I pull my arm back, I let out another scream and it feels so good, so powerful, like I could fly up into the air and rain rocks down on everyone.

Then I hurl the stone with all my might, right through the next window.

There's a crescendo of noise in my head and then everything seems to go silent again. There's a police officer coming our way and the two lads scarper to one side, but I'm still standing there, reliving the sound of breaking glass and looking at my hand like I'm not sure it's even mine any more.

Not sure I'm even me any more.

What am I doing?

I look at the jagged glass with a hole in the centre of it. I did that. I remember how the last time I felt like I was flying, it was down to love, not through rage. And it's as though something bursts and drains away inside me and I'm left panting, tears in my eyes, my hand still tingling where I held the rock.. Then the crowd's noise comes back and I hear shouts coming from the library.

The library.

My library.

I run up the steps and through the doors.

And then I have to stop because I'm not sure what I'm seeing is actually real.

CHAPTER TWENTY-EIGHT

Deal's being handcuffed. That's the first thing I see.

And then, red.

So much red everywhere. It's splashed on the walls, over the books, and for one horrifying moment I think it's blood. I move in slow motion to crouch behind the desk. Two more protesters are being marched out by more police officers. I get a sudden urge to run away, to go home and hide. To let Mum cuddle me and tell me everything's going to be all right, even though I was way too old to believe that a long time ago.

But I can't go home. And I can't unsee what's in front of me.

One bookshelf is tipped over and all the books have tumbled into a mess on the floor. Nearly every single bookcase is covered in thick red paint, like several tins have been upended and thrown about. There's broken glass on the floor.

Broken glass from the window I smashed.

My stomach twists suddenly and I have to take long breaths to fight the urge to be sick.

Then I hear a voice spit, 'Get your hands off me – I can walk.'

I peer out from my hiding place and see Deal, his face blood-spattered, shrugging a policeman off violently. The policeman steers him out with one hand on his back.

The place has cleared out now, but I stay where I am. If the police search the place they'll arrest me, which right now is probably what I deserve. But they don't. I stay under the desk for a long time, until I'm sure everyone's gone and then I straighten, my legs protesting, and walk slowly to the middle of the room.

I pick up a book and turn it over. The paint's gloss: there's no way it can be cleaned off. It's seeped into the edges of the pages, like the book's bleeding. I realise with a sudden pain in my chest it's one of the new ones Annabel bought all those weeks ago.

And then I start to cry.

Jamie finds me a little while later, still holding the book.

'Come on, Joni, come home.' He puts one arm around me. 'The police are going to be back to seal this place off soon. It's a crime scene now. Let's not get arrested, on top of everything else today.'

Outside, the car park is empty apart from a carpet of trampled on signs and litter.

'God,' I say. Then I look at Jamie and he seems a bit heartbroken as he looks back. 'That's it, isn't it? No one's going to support us now.'

Jamie gives a kind of helpless shrug.

'Who the hell were all those people?'

'I don't know what Dealo was playing at. I know he's been in touch with other groups, but I don't think even he knew some of the people who rocked up today.'

'Do you?'

'No. I don't know. People who want to break things.'

'Yeah.' I feel so sad suddenly, and tired.

We stare at the wreckage in the car park.

'Come on, let's go,' Jamie says.

Kelly calls as we're on our way back. 'Where are you? You disappeared when it all kicked off. That was intense. What do you reckon … ?' but I'm not really listening. The gang are all back at Kelly's, but I don't fancy going around there and facing them all. From Kelly's voice, it sounds like it's still a game to her, but then she never saw the inside of the library.

There's worse when we get home. Mum and Dad are in the living room with Jack and they're not exactly happy. Jack's got a massive bruise forming on his shoulder where someone knocked into him in the crowd. Jamie told me on the way back how he ran Jack halfway home before Mum screeched up in her car and grabbed him. Then Jamie sprinted back to the library to look for me because in the heat of everything I wasn't exactly answering my phone.

Mum looks so disappointed. 'Jamie, Joni, sit down,' she begins, and her voice is the sort of quiet it only ever gets if you're about to be in for a serious bollocking.

And we get one.

We organised the march. We took Jack. We were responsible.

Jamie tries to defend us. 'We didn't know Dealo had got all those people involved.' But Mum's not having it.

'Your brother was hurt. You could've been arrested. How are you going to get a job, with a criminal record? And it sounds like you don't even know anything about this Mason Deal, if that's even his real name,' she adds.

Jamie's face is closed but I can tell he's thinking hard. I sit there quietly, because the thing they don't know, the thing that seems to be getting bigger and bigger until I'm filled with shame, is that I joined in. I threw that rock.

I enjoyed it. In that moment at least.

And Jack – God, we're lucky he only wound up with a bruised shoulder. He could've been crushed or anything. Everything just got way out of hand.

Dad's chiming in now. 'We know you were trying to do what you felt was right, but all this protesting, it stops now. It's not going to do any good anyway. We're moving soon and we'd all best focus our energies on sorting that out and looking for jobs. You too, Joni.'

I nod, still ashamed, not wanting to look either of them in the eye, because I'm sure Mum will know if I do.

'A fresh start away from here might even turn out for the best,' Dad says, but I'm not sure any of us really believe him.

Especially me. I'm not sure about anything any more.

CHAPTER TWENTY-NINE

For the next two days I don't leave the house except for a fast trip to the corner shop for milk. At the till I ask for a lottery ticket.

Gotta be in it to win it! says a sarcastic voice in my head.

I can't help noticing Mrs Jenkins serves me with pursed lips and doesn't chat like she usually does.

There's endless comments online about what happened with the protest, which range from the mild (rare) to the stuff of nightmares (basically most of it). Eventually, I turn all notifications off, but I can't help looking from time to time. Jamie's hardly home and when he is, he stays in his room. Deal's not been in touch, but we find out the next day that three people have been charged with criminal damage.

Mum's constantly at work and apart from going to his jobcentre appointment, Dad stays in bed. Even Jack's spending more time at Dylan's than with us. He probably wants to make the most of it before we have to move. The eviction date is looming closer and closer like a monster out of those nightmares you have as a kid, when you can't move and it feels like something's on your chest. Or maybe he just wants to escape the tension at home.

It feels like whenever I close my eyes I see the rock leaving my hand, smashing through that window. The broken glass lying on those wrecked books, red paint splashed everywhere. I still can't work out what went wrong. With the protest. With me. And we've lost any chance we had of changing things. Not just so we can stay, but for everyone – God, even for annoying Lorraine next door. Although perhaps less annoying than usual, given I heard her chatting to Mum downstairs and loudly proclaiming it was, 'All the bloody police's fault. Why'd they have to show up like that? It was like they were the ones who wanted trouble.'

This should make me glad, but I'm pretty sure no one else around here shares her views. Even if they do, it's not going to make any difference. The campaign's dead. I'm actually going to really miss Lorraine. And I don't even want to think about what Jack's going to do without his best mate next door.

The papers, if they were ever really on our side, are definitely not now. The *Daily Mail*, the *Sun* and the *Express* all pick up the story. Far as they're concerned we're practically Enemies of the People or something. And Lattimer's stupid face is all over the place as he 'condemns the violence' – like it was that bad.

OK, it was kind of bad. But we never hurt anyone.

Even Jemima doesn't want to be involved any more. Kelly, who is about the only person I'm speaking to, pops round with a massive bag of doughnuts to tell me. I start eating one, my jaw working mechanically on the too-sweet gooeyness.

'I can't get Jemima to reply to my tweets or messages,' she says. 'I reckon her manager or agent or whoever told her to write this.' She shows me one of those statements posted up as a tweet where Jemima basically pulls a Lattimer and is also 'condemning the violence'.

I shrug. 'Doesn't matter anyway.'

Kelly tries for a light-hearted smile, but her eyes can't really make it past worried. 'Well, what's the next step? Where's Deal?'

No one knows. And I can't be arsed to sit around speculating. It's like I said, none of it matters now. The writing was there right from the very start.

We lose.

They win.

It's the way it always is for people like us.

Four days after the library protest, I wake up again with everything aching, like I've been clenching all my muscles in my sleep. There doesn't really seem much point in getting up and I lie there for ages, just staring at the ceiling, wondering how everything has gone so wrong.

It's not until I hear Jamie's raised voice downstairs that I haul myself out of bed.

'Bastards,' he's saying as I go into the kitchen.

What now?

Mum's sitting at the table in her dressing gown.

'What's going on?' I say.

'Fucking bastards,' Jamie says again, and for a horrible second I think he's going to cry. His Adam's apple is working underneath his stubble and his eyes are damp. He gives them a rough swipe with the back of his hand.

'Mum?' I say, and hate the fear in my voice.

Mum says, on a sigh, 'It seems the papers thought they'd run a little story.'

'Haven't they got bored yet? Let me see.' I take the paper out of her hands and scan it. The *Daily Mail*, of course it bloody is.

And then I feel like someone's come up behind me and given me a bear hug that's crushed all the air out of my lungs.

There's a picture of Jamie, taken the other day by the looks of it. He's wearing his old tracksuit bottoms and they've caught him at a really unflattering angle, looking over with a frown on his face that'd make someone who doesn't know him think he's aggressive or something.

'SOCIAL JUSTICE' YOB'S VIOLENT DRUG HISTORY

I grit my teeth at the headline, then scan the handy bullet points they've put underneath.

- Cherry Tree thug Jamie Cooper 'assaulted a co-worker after he was sacked for drug dealing'
- Neighbours say Cooper family 'Have wrecked our estate'
- Dad Derek branded 'a scrounger'

I don't want to carry on reading the rest, but my eyes have already tracked down to the start of the article.

Disturbing details have emerged about the thuggish past of the self-styled 'social justice warrior', Jamie Cooper, two days after he sparked a near-riot in a sleepy market town in middle England. The *Daily Mail* has learned that a year ago, Cooper, 19, was fired from the award-winning Molray's restaurant after he was allegedly caught dealing drugs and assaulting a co-worker. Now a neighbour has branded the family 'troublemakers' and 'scroungers'.

The neighbour, who did not want to be named, added that dad, Derek Cooper, 48, claims disability benefits of nine thousand pounds a year, despite being able to work, saying, 'Everyone knows the Coopers around here. Their eldest has been stirring up trouble for months now. Derek reckons he's out of work because he's got a bad back, but we see him walking about fine, all the time.'

Last week, Jamie and his sister, Joni, were ringleaders in a violent protest outside the town library, shocking local residents. Three people were arrested. The area is home to the world-famous Edrington School, which regularly tops league tables, but it's a world away from the violent, scrounging lifestyle of the Cooper family.

The MP for Wiltshire, Douglas Lattimer, condemned the violence ...

There's a load more, but I've read enough. I rip the article out of the paper and tear it into shreds.

'Who the hell fed them all that crap anyway?' I say, and my unspoken question is whether everyone around here hates us now. I think about Mrs Jenkins at the corner shop yesterday.

'They probably just made it up,' Jamie is saying.

'They haven't even got half of it right! Dad was turned down for disability. And what about Mum's job? Or why we were protesting in the first place? We should sue, that's what we should do.'

'With what money, Joni?' Mum says. And then she suddenly puts her hands up to her face and I see her shoulders start to heave.

Me and Jamie both put our arms around her. 'Come on, Mum, don't cry, it'll be OK,' I say.

'What's your dad going to say when he sees this? Never mind having to live in a B & B – this is going to bloody well finish him off. Those complete, total *bastards*.' Mum's voice rises to a near-shout.

I don't know what's more shocking; Mum crying or swearing. And all I can do is cuddle her and offer to make a cup of tea, when really what I want to do is smash the cup to pieces against the wall. Because smashing stuff went so well for me last time.

I'm so tired of being angry.

'How could they do this?' I say.

'Because they can.'

'But it's not fair!' Jamie's words burn in my mouth.

'What isn't?' It's Dad, standing in the doorway. I look at the shreds of newspaper in front of me, Jamie's picture still visible.

'What's all this?'

'It's nothing.' I grab the pieces of paper and start to squash them up, but Dad looks from one face to another, his own dark, and says, 'I'm not stupid. Tell me what it is.'

Jamie does it in the end. He has to bring his laptop down so we can see it in all its glory, online for everyone we've ever known to read. Dad scans it through without a word, his face getting paler by the second. I think it's the fact that it's the *Daily Mail*, his paper, which somehow hurts him the most.

When he's finished, there's possibly the most excruciating silence of my whole life, which is saying quite a bit considering how things have been recently. He raises his head slowly to look at Jamie. 'I'm only going to ask you this once. Is any of this true?'

'You even got to ask?'

'It's not, Dad, course it's not. Jamie didn't –' I begin.

Jamie stops me with a look. 'It's all right.' He turns to Mum and Dad. 'I'm sorry I didn't tell you at the time. I didn't want to worry you.'

And he sits at the table and tells them the story he told me. When he's done, Mum gets up and kisses him on top of his head. 'You did the right thing. I'm proud of you for sticking up for that girl. Right, Derek?'

'Right.' Dad's voice comes out in a croak, like he's holding back tears. He looks again at the paragraph about him. 'I'm going up The Crown,' he says.

Mum hesitates, then says, 'Do you think you should? What if there's more of those journalists out there?'

Dad stops in his tracks, then gives Mum this awful look. 'I've still got a decent enough right fist.'

'Derek.'

But he's barrelling past her now, intent on getting to the door, limping heavily.

'I'll go with him,' Jamie says. He follows Dad out.

Mum sinks back into a chair.

It seems like our whole family is falling apart.

Then, because things can hardly get worse, or because I've always been the sort to pick off scabs before they're ready, I ask in a small voice, 'Are we definitely going to a B & B?'

Mum takes a sip of tea, her hand shaking so much she slops some down her dressing gown, then says, 'I'm sorry, love. I went to see the Council again the other day and that's the only thing doing. It won't be forever. We've just got to pull together. I don't want you and your brother thinking you have to keep secrets from us. Things might be a bit tough at the moment, but we're still your parents. Let us know if there's something going on.'

I nod fast, ignoring the fact there's no way I'm talking to her about Annabel. 'We will, Mum. It'll be OK, you'll see.' Although I have no idea how. How will Jamie and Dad ever come back from this? How will any of us?

*

A few days later, I realise I can't sit around worrying about it all any more. I consider going to school briefly, but change my mind. I've got to see this B & B for myself. I get on Jamie's bike and cycle the hour-long journey. As I rattle along, I can't help thinking about Annabel's bike, abandoned at the library the day I ran away. Will it always feel so raw?

I stand outside the building for ages until someone buzzes in, and then duck through the door after them. They don't bother to turn around and look at me. There's heaps of post from all the people who have lived here piled in the communal hallway, spilling on to the stained carpet. I go into the shared kitchen, which has two fridge freezers and a grimy cooker, plus a big metal sink with dirty washing-up piled high in it.

When I open the door to one of the toilets I have to back out again fast; the whole thing is covered in crap. Someone's shouting behind a closed door. Another toilet has an out-of-order sign on it.

I spot a harassed-looking woman coming out of one of the doors and I go up to her.

'Excuse me.'

'Yeah?' She looks defeated.

'My family … we're moving here in a couple of weeks and I wondered … Can I have a quick look?'

She gives me a once-over, sizing me up, then sighs and says, 'All right.'

I follow her into a room which has a knackered-looking double bed and a mattress on the floor. There's clothes and boxes everywhere and a tiny TV propped up on the only chest of drawers in the place. To one side is a tiny cupboard with a two-ring electric hob on it. There's barely any floor space not covered with stuff. Two kids are sitting on the mattress, one with a book, the other with an old Nintendo DS. I say hi to them and they both grunt, barely looking up, while I try to keep my face from looking appalled. How the hell will Jack do his homework somewhere like this? And how will we cook? Or dry washing?

'How long have you been here?' I manage to get out.

'Three months,' the woman says, and it sounds like three years. 'I've got to get some milk – some bastard nicked our last bottle.' Her faces softens slightly when she looks at me. 'If there are more of you, you might get one of the bigger ones. They've got two rooms and you get your own fridge.'

I thank her and cycle home slowly, my whole body heavy.

The last days leading up to eviction day are pretty crappy, if I'm looking for an understatement. I put off packing for as long as I can, while I think about how to tell Mum what I saw in the B & B. I persuade her to chuck quite a few things out, but whenever I bring up where we're going she just says, 'Let me worry about that, love.'

The abuse on social media never lets up, especially not since the article about Jamie and Dad, but I don't have the energy for it any more. I just stop checking all the accounts, although I know Kelly's making valiant efforts in the background. Whenever I go out of the house, it feels like everyone is watching, so I keep my head down and don't talk to anyone. Nothing Kelly can say will persuade me to go to the pub or even round to hers.

Then Deal shows up.

I'm sat at – where else? – the kitchen table, staring out at the burnt orange leaves of our tree, when someone knocks softly on the front door. For a long moment, I do nothing, then I push myself up and open it.

Deal looks different. He's still dressed the same, but his cheekbones are more prominent and there's something about his eyes that's starker, although now I see it, I realise shades of it were always there.

'Hi,' I say, and I'm not making my voice too friendly.

'Hi.'

We look at each other for a moment. 'Jamie's not in.'

'I know.' His voice is softer, less confident than it was before. I remember the way he shouted at the policeman in the library. I open the door wider and he follows me to the kitchen.

I brew some tea and he puts the milk back in the fridge before we sit down.

'So …' I say.

Deal takes a sip, then puts his cup down. He seems to be having trouble finding words, which is definitely a first for him. And something about this makes me soften, even if part of me doesn't want to. There's been so much anger recently. The wrong sort.

'Your name's not really Mason, is it?' I say eventually.

'No. It's …' He looks down.

'I don't need to know. And I don't need to know why you were helping us.'

I think I might get it anyway.

'I was estranged from my parents. And angry,' he says. And I know what he means. It suddenly dawns on me that perhaps the whole fairness thing hurts everyone in some way, at least some of the time.

We finish our tea.

'Will we see you about?' I say.

He smiles then, and I see shades of the old Deal. But maybe a wiser Deal, kinder. 'I'm getting my job back at The Olde Inne. And –'

'You've got to speak to Jamie.'

He nods.

'You'd best do it then.' It's Jamie in the doorway. His look isn't one-hundred per cent forgiving, but I'm pretty sure it'll work out.

I leave them to it and go outside to climb the tree.

CHAPTER THIRTY

It's eviction day. We're the first family to go, but I guess we're not going to be the last. Most of my stuff, other than some clothes and my toothbrush, is already shoved in boxes stacked at the end of my bed.

Even though the birds aren't making quite as much of a racket as usual, I'm awake anyway, watching the ceiling go from dark to grey yet again. Jazzy's curled up behind my knees, fast asleep. I'll have to take him over to Kelly's later – she's agreed to look after him until we get somewhere proper to stay. I've got to get cracking, finish packing my stuff. I'll shove my covers into a bin bag in a bit, but for now I lie still, listening to the birdsong. Can you even hear any birds at the B & B?

You've been so stupid.

Same words I wake up with every morning these days. But still. I can't lie here in a puddle of self-pity forever; I might go drowning myself with it. Kelly's mum's voice comes to me, how she says, 'Up and at it, feet on the floor now,' in this super chirpy way, partly, I reckon, to drive Kelly wild. She's got a point though. Even when everything is about as crap as it's going to get, you still have to roll over and get your feet on the floor.

So I do.

Downstairs, Mum's putting sheets of newspaper round some glasses before they go into boxes. Dad's sorting out the shed with Jamie.

'Thought Dave had already helped clear that?' I say. In response, Mum hands me a plate and a sheet of newspaper.

'There's breakfast bars in the cupboard. Save that last bit of milk for some tea before –' Her face goes into a quick spasm and just as fast smoothes out.

Before we go.

I don't hug her. It's not the day for it. Today's the day to be practical, to pack and lug and shift and try and squeeze ourselves into whatever our lives are going to be like now. It's not a day for looking back. Still, I can't help stopping at the kitchen window, to stare at the washing line where there's still pegs dangling off the loose bit you need to hook up before you can use it. And the barbecue on bricks down the end, the patch of blackened earth where we've had bonfires and sparklers every autumn since I can remember. The tree line in the distance I always used to think was out of some fantasy book, that I know as well as my own face.

And our tree with the wonky boards nailed to it, the shape of its branches that I love. I've spent so many hours up in that tree; it's almost like another big brother.

It's just a house. Walls and bricks and trees don't matter. Homes are about the people you love, so we can make a home anywhere.

All the things I've told myself, told Jack. And still there's this wide ache in my chest when I think this is the last time I'll see any of it. I gulp down some water, my back to Mum. She doesn't say anything, just keeps packing everything away methodically. Part of me wants to let the glass smash, to ask why she isn't crying, isn't she sad, won't she miss our home as much as I already do? Because where we're going, it won't be the same, and who knows how long we'll be there or what will happen next. And it's so unfair.

It's never fair.

But I can't crack because it feels like if one of us does, maybe we all will, and if nothing else, us Coopers have to be strong for each other. I rinse out my glass, wipe it dry and wrap it up in newspaper like the rest.

Mum presses a hand on my shoulder. 'How are you? Really? I'm sorry we haven't talked properly, what with work ...' She rubs at her forehead. 'Do you want to?'

'Not much point, is there? Let's just get the packing finished.' I grab another glass but Mum's next to me suddenly, easing it out of my hands.

'I didn't mean the move. I know it's going to be hard on everyone, and a B & B isn't ideal, but we'll make it work. I meant, do you want to talk about Annabel?' she says.

I stare. Mum's not asked before now. I was sort of hoping she hadn't noticed, but of course she has. It's Mum. Even when she's stressed to high heaven and busy as hell, she still sees everything. I wonder how long she's been waiting for me to talk to her about it. All of a sudden, I realise she's been asking in her own way for weeks now; like when she's engineered it so we do the washing-up together, or the times she's popped in with clean washing at night and put it away while I sat on my bed, scowling into nothing, when normally she'd holler up for us to come and fold our own clothes and get them put away while we're at it.

My eyes fill with tears. 'There's no point … it's not – she's not.' I take a breath, then look at Mum. 'She's gone.'

And then Mum's cuddling me, stroking my hair, saying, 'Let it all go, love, have a cry,' which makes me howl even more, but it feels good too, not to keep crying on my own.

Eventually, I pull back and because there's no tissues about Mum gives me a dirty tea towel to wipe the tears and the snot. I've left a big wet patch on her shoulder too.

Then I tell her what happened. Not all of it – I leave out some of the physical stuff, though I think from Mum's face she kind of guesses – but enough.

'So that's that.' I finish up. 'She's gone. She was never there anyway, was she? The person I thought she was. But the thing that kills me is I thought it didn't have to be like that with us, that money and where you go to school and if you get to go on holiday to the Bahamas or wherever wouldn't matter. Except it does.'

'It can't have been easy for her,' Mum says carefully. 'We all want our parents to love us.'

'I think her parents do though. Like, they think they're protecting her in their own way. Whatever. It doesn't matter now.'

'So you haven't spoken to her since?'

I think of how I blocked Annabel's number and her on every social media channel I was on. How I wouldn't open the email she tried to send me.

I shake my head. 'What's the point?'

Mum sighs. 'That's not the first time I've heard you say that. Listen, when you love someone, it's an act of courage. You have to let yourself take chances.'

'You reckon she deserves another chance?'

'Only you can decide that. But I don't think you should close yourself off because you're scared, or angry, or hurt. You know, me and your dad nearly went south a few times, especially after Jamie was born. We were young and it wasn't easy, but we talked about it. Even when we couldn't stand the sight of each other. And we realised, underneath everything, we still had love and it was worth holding on to.'

I think about this. 'What about now?'

'Well.' Mum takes another plate. 'Your dad's hurting at the moment. But we'll get through it, I know that much. You don't have to worry about me and your dad, love, OK?'

I nod. 'But how will I know whether me and ...' I can't say her name out loud. 'Whether there's anything worth holding on to for us?'

Mum looks at me then and gives this smile that makes her tired face beautiful. 'You know when you're in love, Joni. It's like floating on the breeze. You felt like that with Annabel?'

'Yeah, up until my face smacked the ground.'

'But you get back up and you carry the scars for a while and you realise it was still worth it. Nothing's ever meant to be perfect, not even loving someone. But –' She looks at me again. 'It should be real. And I don't know it all, but I do know you seem to have had something with Annabel and I think if nothing else it's worth at least talking to her, getting some "closure". She makes air quotes and twists her face into a smile. 'As they say.'

Oh my God, Mum is so old sometimes.

She holds my eyes for a while and then smiles and hands me another plate. 'Can you finish this one, then check on Jack? I'm going to give your dad and Jamie a hand.'

I don't want to be the one to wake Jack up. I stand outside his door, thinking. I can't decide if Mum's got a point or not. I'll have to think about it some more once we've moved. Another stab of pain, then I tilt my chin up and give myself a mental shake.

I knock on Jack's door and call out in a vague approximation of Mum, 'Up and at it.'

'I'm up.'

He's taking down the posters on his side of the room, peeling them really carefully so they don't tear, rolling the Blu-tack into a little ball as he goes. The sight of it feels like my heart is breaking, especially when he gives me this cheery grin that doesn't quite hide the worry that's too old for him in his eyes.

'Want a hand?'

Jack nods and I start pulling down an Avengers poster, making sure I do it slowly, then I fold it down the crease.

'Joni?'

'Yeah?'

Jack takes down another poster before he replies. 'Do you think I'll have to move school?'

Mum's said she's going to drive us back up here every day, but it's at least thirty minutes on a good day and that's without counting petrol or when she has to be on an early. Or a late. Or most shifts. And the car needs new tyres we can't afford and about a million other things …

I bite my lip. I'm about to say, 'Of course not,' or, 'It'll all be fine,' but I don't want to do that to Jack. He deserves me telling him the truth. 'I don't know. I hope not,' I say. 'But if you do, I promise it'll be all right in the long run.'

'You reckon?' he says, and this time I can see the fear on his face. He's been in this house his whole life, like me. Our lives are here. And now we have to start again somewhere new and strange, all of us in two rooms, without even a proper cooker, and we don't know for how long.

Right now, I would do anything for it not to be happening, for me not to have to see that look on Jack's face and know there's nothing I can do about it.

This time, I lie. 'It's going to OK. We'll get used to it in no time. And then the Council will find us somewhere really nice and we can do it up however you like. You never know, Jamie's been talking about renting a room in a house share. You'll probably get a room to yourself.'

'Really?'

'Yeah! And then you can have Dylan round whenever you like.'

I've kind of got my fingers crossed mentally at this last bit, but Jack seems to cheer up a little so it's worth it even though Mum probably won't thank me.

Jack takes my hand like he used to when he was little and for a second I think it'll all be OK, we'll manage. We always do in the end.

Then a movement outside distracts me. I peer out and see it's Dylan, with a giant wheelie suitcase, getting into a taxi with Lorraine. Jack appears at my side.

'It's the trip today,' he says, then he gives a shrug and turns back to the poster so I can't see his face.

I search for something to say, to tell him I'm sorry, but find nothing. We finish taking down the posters in silence. I'm just going out of his room when there's a knock at the door. I freeze in the doorway without meaning to because no one I know would knock on the door like that.

The bailiffs are here.

'Stay there,' I say to Jack. Part of me is heating up inside, because it's not even twelve and the letter said we had to be out by five. We were supposed to be long gone before any bailiffs arrived. No one wants to get marched out.

I take a deep breath and go downstairs. Mum's coming through from the kitchen and by her face I can see she's thinking the same thing as me.

'Funny sort of five o' clock this is,' she says and she's trying to smile, but she looks nervous as hell. 'I think I'd better get it. Go in the kitchen. I don't want your dad or Jamie going off. Or you,' she adds with a 'stay put' look.

Needless to say, I stay in the kitchen for all of half a second, then follow her to the front door.

Mum stands tall and pauses for a second before she opens it.

In my mind, the bailiffs have grown into a cross between something from a gangster film and a heavyweight boxer, but the bloke standing at the front door looks nothing like that. He's in an expensive-looking suit, hair in one of those swept back styles you see on the Edrington types, and designer glasses.

'You're here early,' Mum says, her voice like steel.

'Sorry?' He's only about twenty-five, his neck and face flushed. He glances at a stack of papers in his hands. 'Mrs Cooper?'

'Yeah, that's me. You lot weren't supposed to be here until five. It says so in the eviction notice.'

'Ah, no, that's not why I'm here.' He fumbles and drops the papers, then stoops to gather them up. I crane my neck around Mum, cursing the fact I'm so short. She shoots me a look, but I'm not budging. When the man stands, his face is redder than ever. He shuffles the papers and clears his throat.

Mum's reached the end of her patience. 'Well, what are you here for? It's not a good day if you're selling something,' she snaps.

'No, no – I'm here to explain about the Trust.'

'What trust? Are you collecting for charity, because like I said, it's not the best time.' Mum starts to close the door.

'Wait.'

She stops.

'The New Horizons Trust. My name's Dominic. I'm here on behalf of LCA to confirm the transfer and go through the paperwork. Didn't you get the letter yesterday?'

'What letter?' She glances at me and I shrug. I guess it could've got lost in the packing. We turn back to stare at his shiny pink face, waiting, and then Mum says in an exaggeratedly slow voice, 'We didn't get any letter. We're being evicted today.'

And now he's shaking his head. 'I'm sorry – you should have received – well, I'm pleased to tell you in that case ...'

He fumbles again with the papers. I can feel Mum tense as a greyhound beside me. My breath's coming loud in my ears.

After an eternity, he finds the right one and holds it out to Mum.

'The eviction notice was lifted this morning.'

CHAPTER THIRTY-ONE

'What?' It bursts out of us both at the same time. Mum's staring at him like he's just sprouted several extra heads.

The man, Dominic, clears his throat again and repeats in a clearer voice, 'I'm authorised to act on behalf of White Light Holdings and LCA. I'm here to inform you the eviction notice on this property has been lifted.'

I stand there, jaw hanging, while Dominic starts going on about a purchase and a charitable trust, trying to process what this means, and now Dominic's saying something about a new tenancy agreement, pointing to a figure. Mum is looking about as shell-shocked as me, but she's smiling a little too, and nodding along.

Suddenly, I can't stand it any more. I need to be sure. 'Is this –' My voice sounds weird; hoarse and faraway. They look at me. I clear my throat and try again. 'Does this mean … ?'

'That we're staying? I need to speak to your dad, but yes, seems that way, for now at least,' Mum says and she sounds a million years younger. Then she hollers over my shoulder, 'Derek!' and to me, 'Go and get your dad. Go on!'

But she's yelled loud enough that Dad's already limping as fast as he can through the house, closely followed by

Jamie. Jack comes down the stairs too and for a bit it's all confusion, with everyone milling about and Mum trying to explain, Dad letting out a long breath through his teeth, and Jack looking at us all until Jamie grabs him and says, 'We're staying put.'

And Jack's face is breaking into a grin like he's riding the biggest roller coaster ever and even Mum and Dad are smiling, then inviting Dominic in for a cup of tea. I pause in the hallway, then I touch the wall, right next to the faded mark where Jack once scribbled his name, like I'm trying to make sure it's still there.

Then I go into the lounge.

Dominic's sat with his legs crossed at the ankle, holding a cup of tea. He has a look I know well – one that says he's in alien territory and he's not sure how to act. Mum and Dad are looking through the paperwork, Jamie at Dad's shoulder.

'Rent's staying the same?' Dad thumbs down the page.

'Yes, and that's guaranteed for twelve months initially,' Dominic says.

'Well, that's something,' Mum says, and she smiles at Dad. His face is serious as he squints at the papers like he's trying to suss out if they're fully legit.

'What's this part?' he says.

Dominic leans forward. 'Ah, that's a standard cease and desist clause. We'll need you to sign to complete the contract.'

'Cease and desist what?' I say. Dad hands over the contract. I scan it, then let out a long breath.

'None of us are allowed to say anything about LCA or White Light?'

Dominic spreads his hands and gives this closed-mouth smile, lips curling up at the corners as if to say, 'Don't shoot the messenger.'

I look from his shiny face to Mum and Dad, exchanging glances. Mum nods.

'You're not signing it?' I say.

'Joni …' Mum begins.

But it's Jamie who speaks next. 'We've got to.' His face is tired as he looks at me. 'For Jack.'

I watch them sign and Dominic gather the papers together. Dad stands to see him out.

As they get to the doorway, a thought comes to me. I remember where I heard Dominic's name before; at Annabel's house, the first time I met her dad. 'Hang on. What made him change his mind? Huntington? You're his assistant, aren't you? I bet you know.'

Dominic hesitates, his neck pinking up again. Then he says, 'It's not really my place to speculate. I'm just carrying out orders.'

'Why don't you try?' Turns out I do a pretty good flinty voice too, when I need to.

'Well, I believe someone gave him rather a large nudge. Between us, I think his daughter might have a touch of the Huntington steel herself.'

I open my mouth, but he's already on his way out.

CHAPTER THIRTY-TWO

I stand on the pedals as hard as I can, wind rushing in my face as I push the bike faster and faster. All today's shocks have coalesced into one thought: I have to see her.

When I get to the library, I'm gasping for air. I step off the bike and let it fall. Out front, the sign we put up has been taken down and replaced by a new Huntington Library one, bigger than before, with a shiny crest on one side.

I go in and stop, just like the last time I was here.

The whole inside has been totally kitted out; plush carpet, shelves, a massive desk with new computers. The windows are mended, the walls freshly painted.

There's no sign of the place it was before, of what happened at the protest.

It's like we were never here.

Then I hear a low laugh, see Annabel coming through from the community hall with Mrs H and a crowd of parents and kids. Looks like I caught the end of toddler group.

They both stop when they see me, Mrs H looking around all flustered. Annabel's gone motionless. I look at her as the parents flow past me, ignoring the ones who say hi. She seems different. Paler, taller. There's an ache in my chest, like I'm in a vice, but I push it to one side.

Mrs H walks up. Her face is hard to read.

'I don't want any trouble,' I say, and then feel myself going red as I remember what the place ended up like last time I was here. 'I just want to talk to Annabel.'

Mrs H purses her lips.

'It's OK.' Annabel's moved forward at last.

Mrs H looks between the two of us and sighs. 'I'll give you ten minutes, but if your father asks –'

'You never saw me,' I say. For a moment, her lips twitch, maybe in apology, and then she bustles off into the kitchen.

I'm still breathing hard, my face all sweaty from the bike ride, like it was the first time me and Annabel stood face to face here. I wonder if she's having the same thought as me. Neither of us speaks for an age.

Finally, I say, 'Dominic came round with the new contract.'

Annabel nods, a question in her eyes.

'Don't worry, we signed it.' I can't help the bitterness that seeps into my voice. She winces. 'I know you talked your dad round. Thank you,' I add, but it's come out wrong, still rough-edged.

Annabel's eyes are sad. 'I'm sorry. It was the only way … a compromise, I suppose. You weren't supposed to know … I …'

'Is it for everyone? Or just us?'

'It's for the whole estate. And you won't need to worry … New Horizons has some major donors. It won't need to sell your houses like the charity did. I know it can't make up for – I'm glad your homes are safe.'

I look properly into her eyes now. 'At a price.'

'I know.'

'How did you persuade him?'

She gives a faint smile at this. 'When you finally get up the courage to shout the truth, people listen.' There's a shadow under her eyes. I wonder how rough the last few weeks have been for her too.

I swallow. 'I know I should be grateful and I am. It's just … it was for nothing, wasn't it? The campaign. There were hundreds of us shouting our heads off for months, but it didn't mean anything. He never listened – not to us.'

Her eyes have filled. 'I know. I'm so sorry. It's not fair.'

And the echoes of Jamie's words, of my words, coming from her, break something in me.

How can we be together when I still feel so small?

My voice is shaking with the effort of holding back tears as I look at her. I reach out to touch her hand, just once.

Then I pull back.

'I'm sorry too,' I say.

The library shifts and blurs before me as I turn and walk away.

EPILOGUE

'She's killing it,' Ananya shouts to me over her cider. She turned eighteen last week, a few days after Christmas. We're celebrating at one of Kelly's gigs. Ananya's sitting on Pete's lap. It still seems weird to see them back together and so loved-up, but at the same time Pete looks the happiest I've ever seen him. Kelly's over it, for the most part.

We've had more than a few joint heartbreak sessions over the past few months, Kelly and me.

Stacey and Ed are sitting close together on my other side. Nothing like being a complete gooseberry between not one but two sets of lovebirds, but I can't really get annoyed. I love all these guys. Just wish I still saw them every day instead of once a week. But I guess it's like Mum says; sometimes you've got to leave stuff behind before you can move forwards.

Kelly finishes a song and we clap like mad, Pete letting out a piercing whistle between his fingers. Kelly blows him and Ananya a kiss. Then she launches into a new song.

I take a sip of my drink and don't look at Ed and Stacey's linked fingers.

'So,' Pete shouts over Kelly – she's going to kill him later – 'did you get any more offers?'

Stacey smiles. 'I got into Warwick.'

There's a general screech at this – Warwick was Stacey's first choice, as she's told us a billion times. I glance at Ed to see how he's taking it, but he just looks proud. Then again he's going to Birmingham which isn't exactly far away. It feels weird, knowing this time next year they'll all have moved to uni. And I'll still be here, doing the second year of my Land and Wildlife Management diploma. After all the stress about moving, I did in the end – at least to college. It's a long bus ride, but I've been pretty lucky. Jamie managed to get me a job waitressing at The Olde Inne which helped. Despite the rent being back to what it was before, we still have plenty of money worries; I guess they'll never really go away. Dad still hasn't found a job, although he is now finally getting a bit of disability, since he saw a consultant who confirmed what we all knew: his back's definitely knackered. The *Mail* backed off in the end, even if the disability benefits part of their story eventually came true. I guess they've moved on to some other poor bastards, but I wouldn't know; Dad won't let a copy cross our threshold.

I try not to worry about it all as much these days. Mum sat us all down for a really long talk about how pulling together as a family didn't mean we should be taking on all Mum and Dad's worries. Dad's been chatting about retraining recently anyway, doing something with computers, which I take as a good sign. He's got right into Jack's PS2. Shame you can't play computer games for a living, because between Dad and Jack and me we'd be quids in.

My phone pings with a notification.

I pull up my blog, see the thumbnail of two skylarks twisting up into the sky.

Edward Huntington's blackmail with the contract may have had the exact opposite effect to the one he intended, because I'm definitely not keeping quiet these days. I'm careful not to mention his companies by name, but I still campaign. It's not just us who almost got totally screwed over. Inequality is everywhere in our town, our country. Our world. And it's not only about houses and jobs. It's the environment, global warming, the way people and the planet are used up and thrown away by those in power. It's all linked. Someone's got to shout about it all. And people are. Once you start looking, people are fighting everywhere.

A few weeks after I started the diploma, I found out about the farmers who've set up special nesting places for the skylarks. And the birds are making a comeback – their numbers creeping up every year. So I blog about that, and I badger Lattimer, still tragically our MP, and the Council to do the small things that will maybe one day add up to something big. I set up a local group and we meet every month, with the emphasis firmly on non-violent protest. So far, we've got more farmers to sign up to the conservation programme and we're planning new conservation areas too. It was on the local news and I was interviewed and everything. My face still looked weird – clearly the faulty camera issue also extends to the TV. I'm planning a campaign to get some affordable, eco-friendly houses built around here too.

I guess this last year has made me realise some stuff. Like growing up doesn't mean you have to get used to life not being fair. And that things can change, if you keep trying.

What with the course and work and the activism, I don't exactly have much time to spare, but I think that's probably a good thing.

Stops me thinking too much.

I still miss it all: the library, the gang, even school.

And Annabel.

There's occasions, doing fieldwork on the Downs, when I look into the sky and remember her hair flying up behind her, or the feel of my lips on hers. How free we felt. For a long time, I wasn't sure I'd ever feel like that again, but recently on the Downs I've noticed that old sense of expanding, fitting just right with the wind and the birds, is starting to come back.

It makes me glad.

Kelly's still singing. I smile at her looking so natural up there. Last week round at hers she told me she's deferring uni.

'I'm going to give the singing a go,' she said. 'I'll pack it in after a year if I don't get anywhere, but I may as well try as not.'

Looking at her smiling on stage, I don't think she's ever going to university.

'I have one more song tonight,' she says and then looks over towards our table. 'I have a helper for this one.'

Pete stands.

I think I know what's coming, and sure enough a moment later they launch into 'True Colors'. I listen to the song and for once I don't let thoughts of college or activism or the million and one things that need doing at home fill my mind.

Instead, I let myself feel.

I feel the gap where Annabel used to fit, remember her laugh.

The way her body felt against mine.

Kelly and Pete finish and the whole place erupts in applause. She takes a bow, then hops off the stage and comes over to where I'm brushing away a tear.

'That was beautiful,' I say, and chuck my arms around her.

'It was for you,' she says in my ear. Then she pulls back. 'Right, Joni Cooper. I've got something to say and you're listening. Sit.'

'OK, OK,' I hold up my hands. 'Should I be scared?'

'You know what? You will be if you don't stop.'

I give her the sort of blank look I know drives her wild.

'I get you wanted to prove something to yourself, but haven't you worked it out yet? You are enough, Joni Cooper. With or without the campaigns – and don't get me wrong, what you're doing is amazing. But you're enough without any of that. You always were.' She gives me another hug and whispers in my ear again. 'I reckon deep down you know it now too. Question is, what are you going to do about it?' She lets go and walks off towards the bar.

I stay at the table for the longest time, thinking.

Then I step outside with my phone.

Two days later, I'm standing on the crest of the Downs, right next to the boulder where Annabel lobbed that disgusting cheese.

I scan the sky, but there's no sign of any birds today. I pull out my phone to check the time. It's ten past. I go back to gazing at the sky, willing a bird to appear.

But none do.

Twenty minutes past now.

I close my eyes and listen for birdsong, There's only the wind and my own breath. I think about the campaign and the skylarks and I wonder whether the little local things we're doing will ever be enough. Maybe it's too late to save them, let alone make the world the sort of place that's kind to everyone.

When I open my eyes, she's running over the ridge, hair flying up behind her. I feel those invisible threads in the space between us, looping together, pulling tight.

I don't know what's going to happen, but I realise now that courage will find you in the choices you make: to keep fighting, especially when there's no guarantees.

I step out to meet her.

And I'm tall enough to brush the sky.

ACKNOWLEDGEMENTS

I am so grateful to all the fantastic people who have helped shape *Skylarks*. I could not have done this without your support. Thank you to:

My agent, Claire Wilson, for your wisdom, patience and words of encouragement, and to Miriam Tobin and everyone at RCW for your hard work. A special mention to the wonderful Rosie Price, for all your support during the publication of *Countless*.

My brilliantly insightful editor, Hannah Sandford, for always pushing me to take that extra step, and to Rebecca, Lizz, Anna, Helen and the whole team at Bloomsbury for being all-round amazing – it is such a privilege working with you. Thank you to Andrea Kearney for the beautiful cover design.

My family, friends and most especially Naomi and William, for once again bearing with me during edits and the odd existential crisis. I love you all. Extra thanks to Lexi for quoting the bits you loved when I needed encouragement the most.

The readers and bloggers in the YA community, for your generosity and thoughtfulness. It's been a pleasure getting to know you over the last year. Thank you for everything you do for the books you love.

Finally, thank you, Mum, for all the times you have been the quiet hero of the story.

ABOUT THE AUTHOR

Karen Gregory has been a confirmed bookhead since early childhood. She wrote her first story about Bantra the mouse aged twelve, then put away the word processor until her first child was born, when she was overtaken by the urge to write. A graduate of Somerville College, Oxford, and a project coordinator by day, she's become adept at writing around the edges. Strong coffee and a healthy disregard for housework help. Karen lives in Wiltshire with her family. *Countless* was her first novel.

READ ON FOR AN EXTRACT FROM KAREN GREGORY'S HEARTBREAKING, LIFE-AFFIRMING DEBUT

CHAPTER 1

The cigarette between my fingers is thin, insubstantial. Like me.

I'm hunched up on a square of frozen grass outside Dewhurst House, waiting. Felicity is always late, which is a joke seeing as I'd catch hell if it were me.

Her car finally rattles round the corner. I take a final drag, watch the lit end flare to my fingertips, then drop it next to the others as Felicity reaches my side.

She pretends not to notice, instead saying, 'What are you doing out here? You'll freeze!' in a fake jolly voice.

We go inside, Felicity's hand on my shoulder blade like I'm about to do a runner. Wouldn't be the first time. Or she might be doing a bone check. We exchange a quick look and I duck my head down.

'Do you want a coffee? You look cold. Black if you must!'

Felicity's rapid sentences are already giving me a headache. Bet she hates our sessions about as much as I do. Which is quite a lot, when it comes down to it. Still, she's lasted longer than most of my key workers – two years and counting – and she's all right really. Better than some.

'So …' Felicity leans forward with a Concerned Look on her face. 'How are things?'

'All right.'

'And how are you getting on at the Yewlings?'

'Fine.' I try not to let the sarcasm into my voice but here it comes – drip, drip, like it's trying to form a stalactite. An image of my teeny flat in the Yewlings, Tower Block of Dreams, flashes into my head. I attempt a tight smile, the skin forming hard bunches on my cheeks. 'Really well actually.'

Felicity's not buying it.

'OK, shall we get it over with?' she says, and waves her hand at the scales.

I stand on them backwards, making my face into a mask like we're in a play, and listen to Felicity's pen scratch numbers down.

'What have you been up to?' she says.

I crane my head round, trying to spot the figure she's written, but she's already shifted the book. I slink back to my seat and pick at a loose thread where the chair fabric is ripped and leaking bits of foam. I must have sat here a million times.

'College?'

I look up at Felicity's expectant face. I've been doing this a lot recently, tuning out.

'Sorry, what was that?' I say.

Felicity holds in a sigh. Barely. 'I was asking if you've been attending college?'

My silence says it all. I do mean to go, but half the time I end up circling town or staring out of the window until it's way past the point where showing up might actually make a difference.

I pull my hoodie down lower and curl my knees up to my chest. I can feel my stomach all wrong where I've pressed my thighs against it. I give the thread another tug and it comes away in my hand.

I take a deep breath. I've put this off for weeks, but I'm going to go crazy for real if I don't ask. 'There's something ...'

'Mmm?' Felicity says.

I start to wind the thread on my finger, count how many times it goes round. 'It's nothing really. I just don't feel ... right. Like, more than normal, I mean. I'm tired all the time. And there's something else.' I take another big breath then speak in a rush. 'My stomach ... it's kind of swollen. I was thinking, could it be ... Have I done something permanent, with Nia?'

'Hedda, we've talked about this. You need to stop referring to your eating disorder by that name,' Felicity says. Which is spectacularly missing the point in my opinion.

'Right, yeah, sorry. But about what I was saying. Could it be ... cancer?'

'I don't think ... Well, we could certainly arrange for a check-up.' Felicity gives me a closer look, frowns, then glances again at her book of doom. 'Is there anything that's concerning you at the moment? College, home, friends?' I'm already shaking my head when she adds, 'Boyfriends?' Though she's more or less smiling at this last one.

I don't smile. Instead, I feel my face go hot. Silence stretches as wide as an ocean.

When I look up, Felicity has this expression on her face like she's just seen Elvis. Slowly, she leans forward, and in a gentle voice I've never heard her use before she says, 'Have you done a pregnancy test?'